Then

a Wind Blew

Then
a Wind Blew

Kay Powell

WEAVER

—PRESS—

Published by Weaver Press, Box A1922, Avondale,
Harare. Zimbabwe. 2021

<www.weaverpresszimbabwe.com>

© Kay Powell, 2021

Typeset by Weaver Press
Cover Design: Lia Brazier

978-1-77922-383-8 (p/b)
978-1-77922-384-5 (ePub)

Kay Powell was born in Zambia and grew up in Rhodesia. In 1968 she went to university in the UK and became a social worker. She returned to Rhodesia for a few years in the 1970s, and her two daughters were born there. After a stint at Faber & Faber in London, she returned to Zimbabwe in 1981, first working for Macmillan, then co-founding Quest, a publisher of non-fiction titles. Emigrating to England in 1988, Kay set up an agency to provide publishing services to international development organisations. In 2008, her book on the use of English in the workplace, *What Not To Write*, was published by Talisman, Singapore, and became a bestseller. *Then a Wind Blew* is Kay's first novel. She lives near Cambridge, UK, with her husband, who is also a novelist.

For Emma and Clare

And for Jim

Prologue

Isakata mine; April 1980

Susan Haig ended her life on the night of 19th April 1980, not long after midnight. She slipped out of the house and walked across the lawn to the swimming pool and went in, wearing her nightie.

"It was the gardenboy who found her," said Hentie Prinsloo.

Susan must have walked through the rose garden first, and picked a rose there, then gone on to the swimming pool, because floating near her body were some petals. Red rose petals.

"Yes, Reg told me," said the District Commissioner's wife. "And about the petals."

There was no-one standing in the rose garden. Or near the pool. The sun-loungers, the parasols, side tables, lilos, they'd been put away somewhere. It all looked a bit forsaken, that part of the Haigs' garden. Hentie wondered whether Reg Haig was right to have chosen the garden for this gathering, with the pool being there and everything. It was hard trying not to look at it, she said.

The DC's wife shook her head. "Oh, I think it's the perfect setting! Susan loved her garden. She didn't have a religious bone in her body and a church funeral service would have been the last thing she'd have wanted."

Susan Haig's body had been cremated at Mandura hospital and the ashes put into a silver urn. The urn was on the small folding table beneath the whitethorn tree at the far end of the garden. Some pods had fallen from the tree onto the table, by the urn. Thelma Warde was standing nearby, talking to Willem Prinsloo, and she brushed them off. Long flat woody pods.

Beyond the whitethorn tree loomed the big dome-like granite kopje that overlooked the European village, the brown and white lichens that covered it catching the late afternoon sun. Nyamhanza, they called it. 'The bald-headed one'.

"How sad," Thelma Warde said, "that she can't see all this."

Willem Prinsloo nodded. "Yah, a good turnout, isn't it?"

"I meant the garden."

She gestured towards the beds of primulas, a canvas now of reds, yellows, purples, and the mass of orange tulips nearby, just come into bloom. The lawn still green when everyone else's was turning brown and the patches of bright scarlet along the verandah wall and down the driveway. The salvias were in flower.

But she agreed that, yes, it was a good turnout.

Around sixty or seventy people. Almost everyone from the village was here, as far as one could tell. Including some people one seldom saw except occasionally at a function at the Club. Even Molly from the store, who hardly set foot in the Club, was here. Molly wasn't her real name. No-one knew what that was. Well, except her husband. But over the years Moleiro's Store, down near the road to Mandura, had morphed into Molly's Store, and everyone called its proprietor Molly. She didn't seem to mind.

People from the farming community around Isakata had come in too. Including Hentie and Willem Prinsloo, of course. They'd become close to Susan and Reg Haig over the past year or so. Not a friendship that anyone would have predicted – Susan had been known to be a bit sniffy about Afrikaners – but grief had created a bond between them.

Willem nodded towards the Haigs' son, Billy, who had appeared on the verandah. He'd flown back from the UK two days earlier, with someone from the mine's Head Office in London. One of the directors.

The verandah was wide, with white pillars. One flight of steps led down to the lawn, the other to the driveway. There was gauze between the pillars and a purple bougainvillea creeper covered an end wall, trailing over the roof. The house itself was much the same as all the other houses in the European village, only larger. A large white-washed bungalow with a red roof, the citrus orchard and vegetable garden at the back, the lawn and flower beds at the front. And the swimming pool.

Billy walked down the steps onto the lawn. Behind him was a young policeman who'd come in from the Government station with the Police Superintendent and his wife. He and Billy had been quite friendly; they used to meet up sometimes at the Club to play billiards.

"That poor boy," Willem said. "When you think of everything that our boys went through in the bloody war – Billy more than most – and now he has to go and face this... Jeez!"

Apparently, Susan hadn't left a note. Which some people found odd. There was usually a note. Others said perhaps she'd thought it unnecessary because Reg would know, there was no need for her to write anything. Reg would know why she couldn't go on, what had pushed her over the edge. But Reg hadn't said anything. Neither had Billy.

Willem lit a cigarette and watched Billy walk across the lawn towards someone he didn't recognise. Black, portly. Standing with the white nun from the mission.

"The Af, with Beth Lytton – who is he?"

"The doctor in charge at Nhika," Thelma said. "Trained in London, at Guys hospital. Like Susan and me. He was there much later, of course. Pleasant enough, albeit a little arrogant."

Sometimes, Thelma and Susan had taken patients from the mine clinic to Nhika, the hospital in the African Reserve north of Isakata, near the Inveraray hills. The more serious cases that the clinic couldn't handle. TB, severe malnutrition, childbirth problems, life-threatening injuries. That sort of thing.

A Land Rover with white crosses painted on its doors came down the driveway and parked. It was one of the vehicles that the Commonwealth Monitoring Force had used during the ceasefire and in the run-up to last month's general election. There were still a few of them around. Two people got out.

"Is that the nephew? That nun's nephew?" Hentie Prinsloo asked.

"Yes," said the DC's wife.

"And the African?"

"No idea."

The Police Superintendent overheard them. "The new Minister for Mines, if I'm not very much mistaken. On our most-wanted list in the war. He had a link with the mission, his sister was one of the nuns there. Weird, isn't it, that he can just pitch up like this, when only a few months ago…"

They watched the Minister pause at the edge of the lawn, look around, then walk towards the verandah. Reg Haig was there. They shook hands.

Hentie remarked that there seemed to be quite a few Africans here. "Of course, you would expect to see the Haigs' cookboy here," she said, looking at the tall solemn figure, in his crisp white uniform, standing near the verandah steps. "And him," she added, pointing to the barman from the Club. "But some of the others? Maybe they are from the mine office. Clerks or something. I expect Reg invited them."

She said she wondered what Susan would have made of it, having quite a lot of Africans at her funeral.

***

"I think Mrs Haig she didn't like Africa very much," Molly said.

Around her, people looked a little surprised. Not at what she'd said, but because she'd spoken at all. Molly seldom spoke. Always civil, she would exchange a few words when you went into her store, but otherwise said very little.

"I'm not so sure," Gil Aitchison said. "It's complicated. You did get the impression sometimes, I grant you, that she would have liked to have gone home, back to England. On the other hand…"

"She told me," Molly said. "She told me she was in Africa because of her husband. Like me. We had to stay here."

4

"But she did love it in the early years, Molly. The '50s, '60s. I never got the impression *then* that she didn't like being in Africa."

Gil Aitchison was among about a dozen people who'd come out from the city. His wife Marion was here too. Isakata had been their home once, when Gil had been the mine manager, before Reg took over a decade ago. This garden had been Marion's garden once.

Gil was dressed more casually than most of the other men here. Open-necked shirt, cravat. Light trousers. When Beth Lytton remarked to him that it was quite refreshing, amidst all the dark colours, he said he'd come dressed as Susan had always known him dressed. Beth thought that a nice gesture.

"Have you spoken to Reg? Since it happened?" he asked her.

"No. But he's sent me a note saying he'd like to come out to the mission next week. I've prayed for him, of course. And Billy. On Friday we'll sing Evensong for them. And for Susan."

"Kind of you," Gil said.

During the war, Reg Haig had visited the mission sometimes to see if all was well out there, a neighbourly gesture. Susan hadn't, though. The first time in years that she'd gone to the mission was last October, when she'd first heard about the abandoned baby there, to check up on it. Beth had got to know Reg from his visits and they got on well together, so people assumed that's why she was here. Not because of Susan. Everyone knew that Susan hadn't had a lot of time for Beth Lytton.

The DC's wife looked across the lawn and remarked that it had been quite a while since she'd seen Beth. She said she ought to go and say hello.

"Too commie for me," Hentie said. "I can see why *she's* here, being friendly with Reg and all that. But I can't see why her *nephew's* here."

"Oh, I can, in a way. He's the one the Haigs asked to dig up more about Colin. You remember? More about what happened at Croggan's Place the day Colin was killed, because the army's account didn't seem to add up? I saw them not long after they met up with him to see what he'd found out. Perhaps they've seen more of him since?"

"Yah. Maybe."

"I remember thinking, when I saw them that time, that Reg seemed rather withdrawn, down – come to think of it, he hasn't really been his old self since – but Susan seemed all right. A bit distracted, perhaps, but all right. So it can't have been *too* bad, whatever it was the nephew told them about Colin. At least, not something that pushed her eventually to… do what she did."

Hentie said that as far as she was concerned it was Billy leaving the country that had been too much for Susan. The last straw. Losing both sons, in effect. She'd picked herself up after Colin's death, coped really well, but then Billy going, it was too much.

"And the marriage, well, you know…"

The DC's wife nodded. She moved closer to Hentie and said quietly, "Has anyone suggested it might have been an accident?"

Hentie looked at her. "You mean the drinking?"

"Yes."

"Willem and me, we wondered that too. I don't know." Hentie sighed. "I suppose we'll never know, really, will we?"

People were beginning to move towards the whitethorn tree. Word had gone around that Reg was going to make a short speech. Some wondered if Billy would say anything. Probably not.

The doctor from Nhika hospital walked slowly across the lawn with Marion Aitchison. As they passed the swimming pool, Marion said, "I'm finding it hard to think of Susan here – so soon after Independence night, those extraordinary scenes in the stadium, the Union Jack coming down, the new flag going up – her here, contemplating one ending, while we were all still celebrating another… It breaks my heart, the aloneness of it."

They stopped a little way back from the crowd of people now gathered near the whitethorn tree.

"I think that she wasn't ready for the changes coming," the doctor said. "That she was frightened. The last time she came to Nhika – I think it was January, to bring a man who had been in a bad accident at the mine – she was angry. I saw fear there, in her anger."

"Angry about what?"

"About rumours that the new Government will stop contraceptive injections for women." He leant closer to Marion, said quietly, "She was shouting: 'A waste of all our hard work at the clinic for you people! Years and years of work, all down the drain!'" He shook his head.

Marion sighed. "She always meant well, though, with her family planning work." She added, in a whisper, "The thing about Susan, you know – about many whites here – was that they've never understood the need to *ask* people what they wanted, as opposed to *telling* them what they wanted."

The doctor looked at Marion over the top of his round wire-rimmed glasses. "But now they must leave those old ways behind." He smiled. "Like a snake sheds its skin. The skin of a snake has many parasites. If the snake does not shed its skin, more parasites come. If you are covered in parasites, you cannot move. You cannot move on."

***

Willem Prinsloo remarked quietly that Reg's hands seemed to be shaking a bit. Thelma Warde nodded.

Reg was standing by the table beneath the whitethorn tree, holding a piece of paper. Billy was there, and Reg was saying something to him. Billy nodded. In the branches above them some orioles were moving about, flashes of yellow looking for caterpillars before the night fell.

"Such a tough few years for him," Thelma whispered. "Not just Colin's death, Billy's illness, the war, keeping the mine going, all that, but lately it was Susan too. He hinted about her being difficult, talked of finding her out at Croggan's Place a few times, alone, in a bit of a state. Tearful at home, distracted. I'd noticed that too, her being distracted. Not her usual self, not coping like she did initially."

"Hentie thinks that Billy going to the UK was too hard for her. That she had no strength left, after Colin, to handle Billy leaving."

"I'm sure there's something in that, yes. But something else seemed to be bothering her. She started …"

Reg Haig was saying something.

"… was her favourite time of day. And this was her favourite place to be at this time of day." He looked around and smiled. "With a G&T in one hand, a cigarette in the other."

Everyone smiled. Billy was looking at the ground. Reg thanked them all for being here. He talked of Susan, their meeting, their marriage, their early days in the country, the births of their sons, the promise of it all, the hope in those years that the growing threats to that promise – black restlessness, white recalcitrance – would be addressed before it was too late.

He glanced at Billy and looked down at the paper in his hand.

"Then a wind blew. A British Prime Minister had warned that it would. A wind of change, across Africa. And as the '60s gave way to the '70s, the wind gathered pace here and the more obstacles it met in its path the harder it blew, until everyone was swept along with it, tossed about. We were all caught up in it, one way or another." He stopped, cleared his throat, went on. "And when at last the wind stopped blowing, just a few months ago, it left behind broken lives, a broken country, so much to mend, to put right. And that's what we'll do, mend things and start anew. Not least in remembrance of all those whose lives were broken irreparably."

He looked up, cast his eyes over the gathering, and said, "Like Susan."

He put the piece of paper down on the table and stood there, quite still. Through the branches of the whitethorn tree you could see the sun going down. The top of Nyamhanza was taking on an orange hue. In the stillness, someone coughed.

Reg put an arm around Billy's shoulders. Billy looked around at everyone and said softly, "Thanks for coming here today. My ma would have … you know…"

He left it there, gave a slight smile. Reg took up the silver urn from the table and said they would go now, the two of them, to the rose garden to scatter Susan's ashes there, and then afterwards they'd be honoured if everyone would join them on the verandah for a drink. A farewell drink to Susan.

Someone near Thelma Warde was weeping. In the silence it was quite audible and Thelma turned. It was Marion Aitchison. Thelma fumbled in her bag to find a tissue for her. Standing next to Marion was the director from the London Head Office.

Willem Prinsloo whispered, "Jeez! It was *hard*, listening to that."

He looked at Thelma. "You OK?"

She nodded.

Marion blew her nose. "All too much," she said.

Everyone watched Reg and Billy walk together towards the rose garden, and when they got there some people stopped watching, turned away to allow them some privacy, and here and there conversations started up again, quietly.

Willem said, "You were saying, Thelma, about something that had been bothering Susan recently?"

"Yes. She'd got a bit wound up about a baby out at the mission. Coloured. Abandoned, apparently. Saying it shouldn't be living with Africans, or be taken to an African doctor – that one I pointed out, at Nhika. She went there to check on it, and from her account it sounded perfectly healthy. I told her more than once to leave things be. She…"

Marion interrupted, turning to the director from Head Office. "'Coloured' is the word used here to describe mixed-race people." She looked at Thelma. "I think we ought to leave all that alone now. Whatever the issue was, with that or anything else, it's gone now. With Susan."

Willem said, "They're coming back."

Reg and Billy Haig were walking back from the rose garden, towards the verandah. Darkness was closing in quickly now and with it came a ruffling breeze and the sound of crickets starting their evening chirping. Someone turned the lights on in the house and people began to move across the lawn and up the steps onto the verandah.

1

Eight months earlier... St Anselm mission,
20 kilometres north of Isakata mine

Up beyond the red house, Beth Lytton pushed open the gate to the chicken run and let the chickens out. She lingered there, watching them scurry off down the slope to the vegetable garden, heads bobbing, and then went about topping up the water troughs, sweeping the henhouse floor. They were her pride and joy, the chickens and the chicken run. She'd built the run with Rejoice, one of the younger nuns, willowy and strong, starting with the henhouse. A mud and straw structure, with twenty nesting baskets in it. Around and above the henhouse they'd put wire mesh to create the run and keep the hawks and hyenas out, which it did, mostly. You couldn't do much about the snakes, though.

Down in the valley a cloud of dust moved along the road towards the mission. As it drew closer, Beth could make out a Land Rover. She looked at her watch. Kim probably. Her nephew. He'd said he'd be here about mid-morning. She closed the gate and set off along the path back to her rondavel.

Past the vegetable garden, past the red house where Baba Alfred Sibanda, the priest at St Anselm, lived with his wife, Amai Grace. Baba the father of the community, Amai the mother. Their children were grown up now, two in Canada, one in England. Their home was called the red house because they'd built it of red bricks. For all the other buildings at the mission – the church, the nuns' living quarters, the kitchen area, the storage huts – they'd used grey bricks.

There were leaflets scattered about near the path. Bright orange. The Government planes had been dropping them again. Beth bent down, picked one up and read its exhortations to "Report those who help the terrorists do their evil work!" and "Tell us about any mad dog terrorist gangs who try to steal your children!" There was a photograph, a scene from that massacre two weeks ago, at that American mission up in the eastern mountains. "This is what communist-trained thugs do to Christian people." She screwed the leaflet up, took it into the rondavel and dropped it into the wastepaper basket.

Beth shared the rondavel with Agnes Nyambe, the oldest nun at St Anselm. The other nuns, fourteen of them currently, lived in the long tin-roofed building next to the kitchen area. Beth had asked to live there when she first came to St Anselm, but Baba had said no. She had a little inheritance and put some of it into the mission's coffers and Baba said for that she must have her own place, with Agnes as her companion. And he'd had the rondavel built, two bedrooms, a shower, a sitting room with French doors leading out onto a small verandah, the stoep. But she and Agnes always ate with the other nuns. That battle Beth had won.

When Kim came, she made tea and they sat out on the stoep. He'd taken to visiting her more often these days and she'd say it was very kind of him, so out of his way, and he'd say not really. He'd say it was en route, more or less, to Mandura. Coming here was just a short deviation. Kim was something in Intelligence, Beth wasn't sure quite what, didn't ask. Whatever it was, it involved going to and from the city to Mandura rather a lot now. Mandura was the nearest town to St Anselm, 40 kilometres east. The city was some 80 kilometres south-west.

Kim had hardly sat down before he said what he'd been saying for months now, every time he visited her.

"You really can't stay out here, Beth."

He said, as he'd said on earlier visits, that she ought to go into the city, that he'd arrange everything, that there were many people who'd take her in, Gil and Marion Aitchison for a start. He could too, though that'd be less comfortable.

"Things are reaching a head," he said. "It could all get very bloody. There's a fair chance that peace talks might get going again next month, but until everyone signs on the dotted line there'll be no let-up in the fighting. An intensification, if anything."

Kim had straight black hair that tended to fall, curtain-like, over one eyebrow and he'd run his fingers through it, to push the curtain back. He was doing that now, pushing his hair off his face, looking at her. Almost pleading.

"Come in. At least temporarily, Beth. It's always been dangerous, you being out here, exposed, but things are going to get far worse. Soon everyone will be letting loose with everything they've got. To be counted among the winners when the war ends."

The other nuns had also been talking of new dangers and discouraging Beth from going anywhere in the Reserve where she wasn't known. Baba had asked the guerrillas, the *vakomana*, to explain to new groups of *vakomana* coming into the area who she was. Not a bad white, not a *mubhunu*.

"I'm sure I'll be perfectly all right, Kim," Beth said. "As long as I'm careful."

He meant well. She was touched by his concern, coming out of his way again to see her, especially as she didn't know him that well; he'd not been in the country long. But she wasn't going anywhere, and she told him so.

"Being careful isn't enough anymore, Beth. It's no longer just a war between a white-led conventional army and a black guerrilla one. What the Government has done – bringing so-called 'moderate' blacks into it, appointing a black Bishop as Prime Minister, thinking that would solve everything – has simply created another dimension to the war."

"You mean the militias?"

"Yes, all armed to the teeth by the different black factions in the

Government – including the Bishop's faction! – and unleashed into the Reserves. Picking their targets at random." He leant forward. "The threat lies in that very randomness, Beth."

He took a cigarette from his packet and lit it. Beth pushed the ashtray towards him.

"Then there's Agnes," he went on. "A target for the police, being the sister of someone in the *vakomana* High Command. They've got a bit trigger-happy in recent months, the police. You could get caught up in it."

"Oh, I'm quite sure it won't come to that. They *have* visited the mission more often recently, and they *have* become less friendly, less inclined to say, 'We're here for your own good. Just checking you're safe'." She smiled at Kim. "But I'm no threat to them, nor them to me. To them, I'm just an eccentric but harmless middle-aged English woman who's 'gone native'."

She sipped her tea. "There were two on the last visit, a black one in uniform, a white one in plain clothes. Terribly pock-marked face. He pointed at Agnes and said, 'Tell the nanny that if her brother Mr Comrade Bigshot Nyambe comes anywhere near here and she doesn't tell us, she's in big trouble. And the same goes for that so-called priest of yours. Tell him.' I replied, of course, that whatever messages he had for Agnes and Baba, he should deliver them himself!"

She laughed. Kim didn't. He took out a newspaper from his briefcase. It was an English one. Kim had access to newspapers sent out from England in the diplomatic bags and would sometimes bring a bundle of back issues to her. Beth had long since given up reading the national paper, the *Daily Gazette*, so heavily censored it was now little more than a propaganda sheet.

"What's worrying me more than the police, Beth – or the militias, or the army, or the terrs…"

"The *vakomana*, Kim, please. Or insurgents. But not 'terrs' or 'terrorists' when you're with me." She didn't like it when he slipped into using the terms common amongst whites.

"Of course. Sorry."

He put the newspaper on the table and opened it at a double-page spread of photographs of bodies lying in a field. "This is what's worrying me, the mission attacks."

The first had happened last January. Not long after that there'd been three more, two of them up here in the north-east. A bit too close for comfort. And now that horrific attack at the American mission in the eastern mountains. One photograph in Kim's newspaper was the same one she'd seen earlier in the leaflet dropped from the Government planes. In the leaflet, the photograph had been black-and-white and small. In the newspaper, it was full colour, covered half a page. A woman in a blue nightdress with bloodstained curlers in her hair, her arm stretched out to a little bundle, you could see the small feet protruding, white socks turned red. Two children in yellow pyjamas, huddled together, one face sporting the imprint of a muddy boot. A man with a battered bloodied head and behind him more bodies. American missionaries and their families strewn about a sports field at dawn.

"They're not murdering missionaries because of their faith, Beth, not even because they might be helping the 'wrong' side. It doesn't seem to matter anymore *what* side they're on." He paused and looked at her, touched her hand. "Missionaries are being murdered simply because they – you – are easy to murder."

***

Beth drew her shawl more tightly around her shoulders and wondered where Agnes had got to. She looked out at the *musasa* trees, silver-stemmed in the moonlight, at the silhouette of the kopje that overlooked St Anselm, at the church and its tower with the upturned bucket that passed for a bell. That had been her idea. Someone had stolen the old bell. It was made of copper and, like anything made of copper these days, like the telephone cables all across the country, it got stolen. They couldn't afford another one, so she'd bought a metal bucket from Molly's Store.

She loved to be out on the stoep at night, her only companions the wind that sang in the long grass and the night calls of distant animals. And the crickets, with their non-stop night-time prrp-prrp-prrp-prrp. If stars made a noise – and she couldn't see why they wouldn't – she imagined they'd sound like crickets, thousands upon thousands of crickets.

"Listen to the stars," she'd say sometimes to visitors sitting on her stoep, looking out into the Mashonaland night.

Mashonaland. She loved that word, the rhythm and romance of it. The land of the Shona people. The land in which she now lived. An ancient land on the high African plateau that had been part of the Kingdom of Mutapa. And then foreigners arrived, the Arabs, then the Portuguese, then the British, who came in 1890 to see if the rumours of gold there were true. They drew new boundaries and made new rules and installed new rulers and changed everything.

An owl called and Beth looked at her watch and wondered again where Agnes was. Evensong had ended late. The last hymn had been one of Agnes's favourites, *Akure Kure Kumusha*. If Agnes liked a hymn, she'd insist on singing it again. Everyone loved Agnes. She was the grandmother to the community and they called her Ambuya. Her exuberance was contagious and all the nuns would join in, and Baba would smile and let her get away with it and Evensong would end late.

Akure Kure Kumusha. 'Far from Home'. The melody, the words, danced quietly now through Beth's head. In those early years after she'd arrived in the country in '48, and had worked as a bookkeeper in the city, she'd felt very far from home. The whites seemed to her so regimented in their ways and views, the blacks so deferential and distant, and she thought she might go home. Then, west of the city, she came across a cooperative where blacks and whites lived and worked together, growing crops, rearing cattle, running a school, and in '59 she went to live there. A decade later, the Government labelled the cooperative as 'unlawful' and its leaders as 'communist sympathisers' and detained, gaoled, deported them. Again, Beth thought she might go home. But by now Africa had got into her soul and the hinges that had held her

15

to England had rusted. When, a few months later, she found St Anselm, found what she didn't know she'd long been looking for, she vowed she'd never move again.

She meant it then and she meant it now. Kim wasn't the only one saying she should go into the city, for her own safety. There was Reg Haig, the Aitchisons, others. She wished they wouldn't. She wished Kim wouldn't.

A figure came shadow-like out of the dark. Agnes. She had a blanket over her shoulders and she was in a fluster.

"Come, Mukoma!" she panted. "Amai Grace, she needs us. Now. Quickly, Mukoma!" There was sweat on her nose and upper lip, even on this chilly August night.

Mukoma. That's how Beth was known here. 'Respected elder'. Baba had started it, not long after her arrival at St Anselm.

"Is it the *vakomana?*" Beth asked.

"*Ehe*, they are there."

Large bosomed, with a chubby velvet-skinned face, Agnes was in her late fifties – she wasn't sure of her exact age, she didn't have a birth certificate, but her brother Isaiah did and it said 1930 and her parents had told her that she was about ten years older than him.

Agnes was generally in a fluster. Yet she always managed to look tidy, her clothes neat, the takkies on her feet white and laced. The nuns all wore the same habit, a brown cotton pinafore dress over a white blouse, a short brown veil with a white rim, and takkies. Beth's takkies were dust-caked brown and the laces had long gone. She felt unkempt next to Agnes, conscious of her disorganised teeth and her sun-dried face, the unruly strands of greying hair escaping from her pony tail, the kirby grips falling from her head and ending up on chairs, behind cushions, on the floor, and Agnes tut-tutting and picking them up and putting them on her bedside table. Dear Agnes.

She said again, "They are there, the *vakomana*. But not for food this time, Mukoma. Come!"

It had happened gradually, the *vakomana* coming to St Anselm for food. In the early years of the war they'd pitch up a few times a month, then more often, now once or twice a week. They went to the red house usually, but some came to the rondavel. Word had got around that Beth was in charge of the mission's chicken run. They'd appear quietly out of the night in groups of five or six, or send a child messenger, a *mujibha*, with a note asking for food – chicken always, and biscuits, eggs, bread. Cigarettes too, beer occasionally. Lately there'd been notes asking for tranquilisers. It would be for the young ones mainly, Baba said. They were finding the fight harrowing, especially the bombing.

Once, a *mujibha* with a note asking for chicken had said, "They like only the breasts, sister."

"They'll take what they're given, young man," she replied, and gave him a bundle of chicken legs and wings wrapped in newspaper.

As the dry season had deepened this year and the land turned brown, the numbers of *vakomana* asking for food swelled. More visits, more notes. The *vakomana* were hungry and getting hungrier.

Kim had never asked Beth outright about her contacts with the *vakomana*, asked if she, if the mission, was feeding them. She thought that his job being what it was, though, he probably knew. Just as he probably knew about Baba's trips to the eastern mountains. Baba had acquired an old blue station wagon and every month or so he'd pack it with bags of mealie meal and drive to the mountains and lay up supplies for the *vakomana* coming across the border from Mozambique. At St Anselm they'd pray for him at Evensong every time he set off.

Agnes walked ahead of Beth along the path up to the red house. The white moon lit their way past the kitchen and across the patch of barren ground, the yard, where Baba would preach sometimes on a Sunday under the big *musasa* tree. No need for a torch.

"Two of the *vakomana*, they are girls," Agnes said. "One is in trouble."

Beth followed Agnes up the flight of steps onto the verandah of the red house. A man took fright at her sudden appearance. He whipped out his arm and grabbed his AK, jumped up, knocking over a small table, and she saw the white of his frightened eyes.

"*Eh, eh, eh,* comrade," Agnes said. "*Aiwa mubhunu.*"

In the moonlight Beth could make out three figures, including the frightened one. They wore jeans, denim jackets, T-shirts. One was a woman, wearing a beret. Their AKs and bandoliers were on their laps or on the floor. The frightened one remained standing, one hand clasping the crescent-shaped magazine of his rifle. The third one, momentarily disturbed, looked at Beth sleepily, leant back in his chair, acknowledged her.

"*Manheru,*" he said. She returned the greeting.

Beth became aware of a fourth figure sitting in a cane chair at the far end of the verandah. The burning tip of a cigarette moved slowly from one side of his mouth to the other. He wore a combat jacket, Warsaw Pact issue. Beth was familiar with that grey-brown pattern. Many **vakomana** wore these jackets now. He sat there, said nothing.

A door opened and Baba came out onto the verandah. He took Beth's hand and said, "Blessings, Mukoma Beth. We are sorry for this, to make you come here in the dark and the cold. But it is a difficult business. Will you go now with Ambuya? Amai is waiting for you."

They walked down the corridor to a bedroom Beth knew well. She'd used it when she'd arrived at St Anselm, before the rondavel had been built. Cement floor, grass mats, thin curtains, a metal bedstead with a thin mattress, a Calor Gas light on the bedside table, wooden chairs. She noticed a pile of clothes on the little corner table. A one-bar electric heater cast an orange hue over the room. Little had changed, except for the radio-alert system on a crate in one corner, a box, a two-way handset.

Grace was leaning over the bed. There was a girl in it. Eighteen, nineteen perhaps. She was wide-eyed and still and Grace was sponging her forehead, her neck. Next to the bed a laundry basket rested on some upturned wooden crates.

Beth saw now why she had been called. The soiled sheets on the floor, the jugs, bowl, flannels and towels, kitchen scales. The pervasive smell of body fluids, blood.

Grace said, "He has come early, Mukoma. He could not wait in there to grow."

She wiped the girl's shoulders, one side, then the other. "About seven months. Seven months and two weeks, maybe. But he is all right. There *is* a problem, but it is not a problem from coming too early." She squeezed the sponge out in the bowl, poured more water over it from a jug, and went back to the girl.

"It is not right, this," she said. "These young girls, fighting, living in those camps in Mozambique. It is better for them to stay here, stay in their villages and make food for the *vakomana*."

It was a view Grace had expressed to Beth before, often. As had Agnes, and some of the other nuns, and some of the older women who came from nearby villages to the church at St Anselm on Sundays. Beth disagreed. Why shouldn't young women take their place alongside the men in this war? It boded well, she said, for the time when the war was over. But Grace would retort, "*Aiwa*, Mukoma, you will see when the war is finished. They will say the men are heroes. But the women? They will say they are unclean, not fit to be wives or mothers. For sure."

She bent over the laundry basket and lifted out a small bundle wrapped in a white crocheted shawl. She pulled the shawl back to expose the whole of the tiny head.

"There, that is the problem," she said.

Beth looked down. "Oh dear," she whispered.

The hair, the skin tone. A mixed-race baby. Coloured. They didn't fare well in this country, Coloureds. The products of a union condemned by whites and blacks, and treated with disdain by both.

Grace put the baby next to the girl. The girl turned her head away. She stayed like that for a minute or so, then sat up and started to get out of the bed. She clutched her stomach.

"Toilet," she said.

Agnes helped her stand and held her elbow and steered her slowly out of the room.

"Such a stubborn one," Grace muttered.

It was fear that showed in the girl's face, Beth thought, not stubbornness.

"We have no name," Grace went on. "Just her *chimurenga* one, her war name. It is Kundiso. The *vakomana* on the verandah told us. But the girl, she has said nothing."

The two-way in the corner crackled and a voice came through. Beth recognised it. Silas Chipere, the doctor at Nhika hospital. Grace picked up the handset and spoke in Shona. At one point, Beth heard Grace say, "Four pounds two ounces" and Silas asking about "abnormalities", to which Grace replied, "*Aiwa*, nothing." Beth didn't understand the rest of the conversation. She'd never learned more than the basics of Shona, a deficiency she'd always meant to rectify, but never seemed to get around to. The community usually spoke English in her presence, or translated for her when necessary.

When Grace put the handset down, she said, "Silas says there was a big attack tonight on a farm near Isakata and the army is everywhere, it is too dangerous to travel. He said we must wrap the baby tight, Mukoma, and the girl must feed him every three hours. Silas will send transport for them when the sun rises."

It was nearly eleven o'clock. The baby's next feed was due in about two hours. Agnes would stay up for that, while Beth slept in the chair by the window, to be on hand. Agnes would wake her at four. Grace went to her bedroom, saying she'd be back at dawn with tea and biscuits, but they were to wake her any time if they needed her.

***

Beth stirred with the call of a nightjar. She opened her eyes a sliver, it was still dark. She closed them again and pulled the blanket tighter. She heard the call again, deep in her head. It took on a more human tone, a voice saying, "You cannot stay here." A baby

20

crying and small white bloodstained socks brushing her arm. Beth opened her eyes. The baby in the basket was crying and Agnes was tapping her arm.

"*Mangwanani,* Mukoma," Agnes said. "It is nearly four o'clock."

Agnes usually rose at about five. She'd go to the mission kitchen and light the fires in the old stove and under the water tank. When they were burning well, she'd return to the rondavel, wake Beth and they'd kneel together then, in the sitting room or out on the stoep if it was warm enough, to greet the day with a psalm. Just as Beth loved her time alone on the stoep at the end of the day, so she loved her morning prayer time with Agnes.

"*Mangwanani,* Ambuya," Beth said

Agnes put a cup of tea on the table next to Beth's chair. She turned the gas light up a little, lifted the tightly wrapped baby from the basket. She shushed him and rocked him and he was quiet again. On the bed, the girl was awake.

Beth unwound herself from the blanket and went over to the bed.

"Kundiso?" she said softly. "Are you all right? Hmm? Ready for feeding? Yes?"

The girl looked at her. She sat up slowly, adjusted the pillow behind her, began unbuttoning the pyjama top. Beth straightened the sheets.

"Did she sleep, Ambuya?"

"*Ehe,* Mukoma, she slept," Agnes said, and put the white bundle into Beth's arms.

How small, how light he was! Agnes said the earlier feed had gone well and she would go now, back to the rondavel. No morning prayers together today.

Beth lowered the baby onto the girl's lap. "What will you call him?"

The girl said nothing. She lifted the baby to her breast, but didn't help him as his mouth searched for her nipple. She stared at the window. When the baby found the nipple he struggled again, trying to close his mouth around it. Beth yearned to help him. At

21

last he latched on and she saw his little body relax as he started sucking.

The girl stayed sitting straight up, disconnected, staring at the window. Then she turned to look at Beth.

"Munetsi," she said quietly.

"Munetsi?"

"Munetsi. It is the name I am giving him."

That was better. That she was talking, acknowledging the baby. Naming him. Beth wanted to keep the talking going, but she must choose her words carefully, say nothing that would alarm the girl.

"I would like to say a prayer, Kundiso," she said. "To greet the day. Would you like that? For you and for Munetsi?"

There was no answer. Beth knelt on the grass mat by the bed and clasped her hands and rested them on the side of the bed. She closed her eyes and began reciting the psalm she'd planned to say with Agnes that morning, Agnes's favourite psalm. "... I will say of the Lord, He is my refuge and my fortress... You shall not be afraid of the terror by night, nor of the arrow that flies by day..."

She opened her eyes. The girl was looking down at her. Her eyes were wet and glistening, her lips quivered.

Beth felt flooded by the pain she saw. Or fear, it might have been fear.

The girl let the baby fall from her breast and sank back on the pillow and stared at the window again. Beth took him and put him back into the laundry basket.

"It will be all right, Kundiso," she said. "The ambulance will come soon, when it's light, from Nhika. Everything will be all right there. It is a big hospital, Nhika. Not far from here. A good place. They help everyone. No politics."

She knew the girl would understand what she was saying. That at Nhika hospital they treated everyone who went there, including people who could be *vakomana*.

Beth took the girl's hand and asked, "The father...?"

Then regretted her question immediately. It would only send the girl back into silence again. But she turned to look at Beth. "He

22

was…" she began, then stopped. She put her hands to her face and rubbed her cheeks, her neck, slowly, slowly, as if smearing them with paint. "*Dema*," she said.

Dema. The word for black. Beth knew it.

The girl spread her fingers out, shaped them like claws, moved them down her cheeks, down her neck, slowly at first, then faster. "I was scratching him," she said in a loud whisper. "I was shouting! There by the *chimini*. I was shouting, scratching his face, his neck! The *dema* was coming off…"

She stopped again, stared at Beth for a moment, then turned away. Beth waited, but it seemed the girl had said all she was going to say.

The baby started crying. Beth stroked his forehead until he was calm again and then sat on the bed and held the girl's hand. Noises came from the verandah. A cough and the scrape of wood on the concrete floor, the clink of glass. Beth felt the girl stiffen, saw her eyes widen. There were more sounds from the verandah, some conversation.

The girl pushed Beth's hand away. "I am hungry," she said.

"Yes, of course. I'll go and see what I can find. Lie down now. I shan't be a minute."

In the kitchen Beth found bread and jam and margarine. She heard footsteps in the corridor. Grace must be up.

The water boiled slowly on the little gas ring. A dove wandered in through the back door and wandered out again. Through the window Beth watched the pink tinge along the horizon seeping into the early morning sky. She took out a packet of biscuits from the cupboard and put it on the tray, with the bread and two mugs of tea, and carried the tray along the corridor and into the bedroom.

The girl wasn't there. Beth put the tray on the bed and walked back down the corridor, to the lavatory. There was no one there. Oh Lord, what on earth…?

She called, "Kundiso!"

She hurried back to the bedroom. She saw, now, that the pile of clothes that had been on the little corner table had gone. All that was left was a small dog-eared yellow notebook. She ran to the sitting room and saw Grace there. "The girl! Kundiso! Oh dear Lord, Amai, where is she?"

She felt flustered, dizzy. Grace took her hand and they went out onto the verandah. There was no-one there. The baby cried and Grace went inside again.

Beth stood at the top of the verandah steps and stared out over the mission and the land beyond it. She shuddered. Nothing. The tip of the new day's sun shimmered above the distant Inveraray hills and, near their base, she could just make out the top of the old smokestack at Croggan's Place. The site of the old tin mine. There were caves in the Inveraray hills. Perhaps that's where they'd stay, the girl and the other *vakomana*. Stay until darkness fell and they could move on again. Oh, this damn war! And that poor girl!

Beth's legs were shaking. She sensed the presence of people on the verandah and looked along it, but there was no-one. Empty chairs. Cigarette butts on the floor, some empty beer cartons. That was all.

Grace came, stood beside her. She had fetched the baby and now cradled him. They stood there together, tired, watching the dawn light creep across the dry veld, rousing it from the night.

The baby was quiet. Beth looked down at him.

"Munetsi. She said that was his name. Munetsi." She touched his forehead. "Oh Lord, Amai, what *are* we going to do?"

The morning air was cold and Grace pulled the shawl a little tighter around the baby. "Munetsi," she said. "It means 'the troublesome one'."

2

Isakata mine; late September 1979

The first thing Susan Haig noticed when she arrived at the African clinic was that the bloody boiler wasn't working. Again. When it worked it gave out a low rumble. But today there was no sound. Nothing. Sometimes a kick did the trick, but you had to be careful to avoid the rusty patches by the pipes. When kicking didn't work, she'd phone the mine office and get the handyman down here. Moleiro, Molly's husband.

She put her handbag and basket on the table and kicked the boiler. It rumbled into life. She might be short and heading for fifty-three, but there was plenty of strength left in her yet.

A girl in starched white came in.

"Good afternoon, Sister Haig."

Susan glanced at her.

"Ah, the new girl."

When Susan had started working here there'd been two African nursing assistants. They were competent enough, and had been here several years. Then two years ago, just after the rains started, they didn't turn up. Either of them. Just when the malaria cases were coming in. Thelma Warde, the senior Sister at the clinic, had called Susan when the assistants disappeared.

"Abducted by terrs and marched off to Mozambique, no doubt."

Susan agreed. "Just awful, these abductions. And now all those schoolchildren being taken too. Reg says that's running into thousands now."

Thelma had quickly hired replacements – not one for waiting, Thelma, terribly efficient, something of the headmistress about her – but then one of the replacements went too, a week or so ago, so she hired another assistant.

Susan took her pistol from her handbag, and her cup and saucer from her basket. Royal Doulton, part of the set she'd brought out from England when they'd emigrated here. She put the gun in the safe.

"I start the trays, Sister?"

"Yes."

The African clinic at Isakata mine was at the far end of the African compound. You had to drive down from the mine office and through the compound to get to it. Not good planning, Susan said to Reg. She never felt comfortable driving alone through the compound.

The clinic building was square and whitewashed, with an asbestos roof. There was a dispensary, where she was now, and a large hall with wooden benches, tables and a blackboard. Off the hall was the examination room where a doctor from Mandura held his weekly surgery. The nurses conducted private examinations there, when necessary, but most of their work was done in the hall. Run-of-the-mill things, minor accidents and ailments, family welfare service, dispensing pills for malaria, diarrhoea and bilharzia. Anything more serious was sent off to Nhika hospital in the African Reserve.

Susan looked at the new girl. Neat, this one, no make-up. Susan liked that. Neatness meant cleanliness. Susan seldom wore make-up, apart from face powder and a touch of red lipstick. Sometimes a little blue eyeshadow when she went to the Club in the evening. She considered herself neatly turned out, permed brown hair always in place, nails short, shoes sensible.

The girl laid out the syringes and needles on the trays, and the alcohol and cotton balls. She put the trays on the top shelf of the trolley, the lollypop tin and metal waste bin underneath. Then she

26

went through to the hall to organise the women and give them their clinic cards.

It had been back in '72 when Thelma asked Susan if she'd help out at the clinic. She needed an extra pair of hands, especially with the family welfare service – vaccinations for babies and children, contraceptive injections for women. Susan had declined at first. She'd done a bit of nursing when they'd first arrived in the country, in 1950, but nothing since Colin's birth a year later.

"You'll soon pick it all up again," Thelma said. "Besides, what are going to do with your time now? Just sit at home thinking about your boys?"

Thelma had a point. Colin had left home, joined the police, and Billy had just started at university. So Susan said yes. She did two and half days a week. That included going once a month, under police escort, to the Government station in the Reserve to run the family welfare service there. The abduction problem had left Nhika hospital short-staffed, unable to cover the whole Reserve, so the DC had asked for Thelma's help. At the mine, the family welfare service was weekly, on Saturday afternoons. That was when the women's husbands – those who weren't on shift work – played soccer or went to the beer hall, so they were out of the way and their wives could come for their Depo-Provera jab without their husbands knowing. That was the beauty of Depo. One injection, once every three months, no trace. No pills, no IUDs.

When Susan started running the service, there'd been a rumour going around that Depo could cause bleeding and liver problems, and she worried whether many women would turn up.

"Stuff and nonsense," said Thelma. "Yes, some might have a tiny bit of vaginal bleeding, but that's a small price to pay for freedom from endless pregnancies!"

Despite the rumour, the women continued to turn up.

The girl came back into the dispensary and said everything was ready. She wheeled the trolley out into the hall. Susan followed her. The chattering stopped and a chorus went up. *"Masikati, Sister!"*

She wished Reg could see her at this moment. She felt respected here, and proud of the important work she was doing. The rate at which these people were breeding *had* to be slowed down, for their own good. What was it someone said the other day? – less than a million Africans in the country in about 1910, now six million. *Six million!*

"Good afternoon," she replied. She always spoke English. The girls would translate when necessary.

They went along the rows with the trolley. The women held up their cards to be ticked and hitched up their skirts to expose their thighs. The girl wiped the skin with a pad and pinched it and Susan shook the syringe and inserted the needle into the pinched skin and pressed the plunger. The girl swabbed the skin, marked the card, and they moved on to the next one, with a 'ting' as each used needle hit the side of the metal waste bin. All down the row. Wiping, pinching, injecting, swabbing. Until the whole hall was done.

"I'd say about forty? A good day, hmm?" Susan said when they reached the last woman.

"Yes, Sister."

There were about a dozen babies and children to vaccinate and when that was done Susan opened the lollipop tin and the children lined up, fidgeting. After they'd all received their lollipops, there was a chorus of *"Tinotenda, Sister!"* Then they and their mothers left and the girl tidied everything up and went home.

Susan made herself some tea and sat at the desk in the dispensary to do the paperwork. She turned the transistor radio on. It had been Colin's radio, the casing was turquoise blue. Reg said why not chuck it, it looked a bit ropey and the tuner needle tended to get stuck, but she said no. It had been a part of Colin.

She could see him now, her son, her brave brave boy, sitting in the garden or on the verandah with his blue radio on his shoulder, pressed close to his ear.

"…so lekker *to have you home, darling, even if only for a short time, take care. And that comes from Marlene and the kids."*

The voice of the presenter, Sheila someone or other.

"Next, we have one for Corporal Dave Eggleston, 2 Commando. The message says: Head down, chin up and God Bless in God's own country. Loads of love..."

The show was popular, 'Family Favourites'. It used to be for anyone to send messages to friends and family, but these days all the messages were for the troops.

Half an hour later, Susan filed away her report and the women's cards, locked the cupboards and cabinet, and retrieved her gun from the safe.

"And before I go," the presenter was saying, *"my usual reminder about Goodies for the Troopies."* A jingle played, one that everyone associated with the roadside Troopie Stops that women ran throughout the country. *"Condensed milk, balaclavas, biltong, cigs – anything you can spare for our boys in the bush – just take them to your nearest Troopie Stop. So, till next week, bye for now, totsiens and God bless!"*

Susan turned the radio off. A little less God, if you please. And why still *totsiens?* We're not Afrikaans here, this is not South Africa. Fat lot of good that country has turned out to be, selling us down the bloody river!

She drove through the African compound, past row upon row of small brick houses with iron roofs, each with a patch of ground front and back, mostly planted with mealies. Thelma Warde had persuaded some of the occupants to plant a few flowers – "to jolly the place up" – but Susan couldn't see the point. "They'll soon revert to planting mealies again," she told Thelma. "They don't appreciate the beauty of flowers, landscapes, things like that."

Reg said it would better to plant a few trees here and there. But Susan couldn't see the point of that either. "They'll just chop them down and use them for firewood, like they've done in the Reserves, where they've turned perfectly good land into scrub," she said.

***

Reg loved his classical music. And because Susan didn't, not much anyway, she preferred musicals, he'd play it when she wasn't at home. He'd open the gramophone and put on an LP and turn the volume up high. She knew this because sometimes she'd come home earlier than expected and he'd be there on the verandah, leaning forward with a smile on his face, looking out across the garden, or with his eyes closed. Conducting.

And so it was today. She heard the music when she got out of the car to unlock the gates, and when she reached the house there he was, on the verandah, arms waving about. Reg was a big man, burnt brown from all these years in the sun, a manly man, and she always thought he looked rather silly waving his arms about like that.

He turned the music down as she came up the steps onto the verandah. The rays of the evening sun were streaming in through the bougainvillea creeper at the far end of it.

"Is that something new?" It sounded a bit churchy, not the type of thing he usually played.

"Yes," he said. "And no."

He lifted the gramophone arm, took up the LP, dusted it, and put it back in its sleeve.

"Well?"

"What, dear?"

"What is it? What are you playing?"

"Not really your cup of tea, dear."

"None of it is, much, you know that. But you could tell me what it is."

He sipped his beer.

"Something Beth mentioned the other day. Tallis. Years since I've listened. Knew I had it somewhere. Dug it out. Sublime. Had forgotten just *how* sublime."

Beth Lytton. The nun at St Anselm. That explained the churchiness. Reg went out to St Anselm sometimes, ostensibly to see if all was well, especially with mission attacks on the increase, but Susan knew it was as much about listening to classical music

30

with Beth as it was about being a good neighbour.

"Good turnout at the clinic?"

"Very," Susan said.

She went down the corridor to change and have a bath, and then came back to the verandah, sat down and took a cigarette from Reg's packet. Philemon appeared with the drinks tray, G&T for her, another lager for Reg. She lit her cigarette, inhaled, and blew out a plume of smoke and a long sigh.

"Why can't she be sensible and go into the city?"

"Who?"

"Beth Lytton. Living out there alone, it's asking for trouble."

Reg picked up the binoculars and fixed them on a hoopoe that had landed at the far end of the garden, near the whitethorn tree.

"A white woman sitting in an African Reserve crawling with terrs. Sticking out like a sore thumb. A stubborn woman, causing people a lot of worry. You, for a start. And the Aitchisons, no doubt."

The hoopoe flew up and Reg followed it with the binoculars. "Beth's not alone," he said. "The Sibandas, the other nuns. Plenty of other people there."

Not the same, Susan thought. Not the same at all. Not people she could rely on, people who'd defend her when the terrs showed up at her door looking for another European missionary to murder. And as for that priest, sitting there in his large house, surrounded by women – the wife, the nuns – fetching and carrying for him, cooking, cleaning. He was an African male, and just because he was a priest didn't mean he was any different from any other African male. Who knew *what* went on?

She went through to the kitchen to check on the supper and to see if Philemon had done the silver. She liked it done once a month. He'd been with them for years now, but he'd still forget sometimes to do the silver. Just as he'd forget to tell her when something basic was running out. Flour, sugar, tea, washing powder, floor polish. You had to think ahead out here, living so far from the shops in Mandura, going there only once a fortnight. Unless you counted

Molly's Store, but that didn't really cater for Europeans.

The silver had been cleaned. The vegetables had been prepared and the stew was on the hob. The table had been laid.

Susan heard the drumbeats on the radio that heralded the 7.45 evening news bulletin and she joined Reg in the sitting room. The newsreader said reports were coming in that the terrs had fired a Sam-7 missile at a Viscount again, up near the Zambezi. It was nearly a year since they'd brought down the first Viscount, shot several of the survivors – some said *after* they'd raped them. Then they brought down the second Viscount. No survivors that time, and on the radio their leader had chortled and said "Yes" when someone from the BBC asked him if his lot had been responsible. In this latest incident, said the newsreader, the Sam-7 had missed the plane by a matter of feet.

Susan shuddered. She lit another cigarette and coughed. Philemon appeared with another G&T.

"Operations Coordinating Committee regrets to announce the death…"

It came at the end of every news bulletin now, the OCC communiqué. You had to listen. Often as not, a name you knew would be read out.

"…of Corporal Garret O'Reilly, aged 21, in follow-up action involving the pursuit of terrorists in the Gweshu District. Two members of 4 Commando were evacuated to hospital. Their condition is said to be stable. Thirty-one terrorists were killed in this action, bringing this month's total to 204 for internal operations. OCC also regrets…"

They both heard the footsteps. Reg switched off the radio. The door opened and Billy came in and sat down on the sofa. Wet hair dripping on his T-shirt. Far too long, his hair, straggling around his neck now.

"All right then, son?"

Billy looked at Reg, nodded, looked away. "Yah," he said.

Susan sighed.

"Beer?" Reg asked.

Billy shook his head. The dogs started barking. There were two of them, Alsatians, you had to have dogs these days, whether or not you liked them. Susan didn't.

Billy stood up and walked out to the verandah and stood there, then turned to look at them, first Reg, then Susan.

"Why do you do that? Hey?"

"Do what?"

"That. Turn the news off when I come in. Why do you always do that? You trying to hide the deaths? Hiding the fact that guys are dying out there, being shot to bits out there in the bloody bush? That everything's f... frigging normal?"

"Billy!"

"Son, just trying..."

"Well, don't!"

"Billy! How dare you talk to your father..."

"Leave it, Susan," Reg said.

Billy turned his back on them again. The dogs had stopped barking and the sound of crickets drifted in from the garden. Susan looked at Reg. Reg was looking at the mantelpiece. Lined with family photographs in silver frames.

In the dining room, Philemon rang the bell, and they went through to supper.

Susan dished out the stew. Silence. To break it, she let the ladle drop loudly onto each plate. She waited till Reg and Billy had helped themselves to vegetables, then put some on her own plate.

After a minute or so, Reg said, "More visitors in November, dear. For a few days. We'll need to put them in the guest house. US Senators." He reached for the salt. "With the new peace talks getting off to a start – albeit a tottering one, they'll probably end in deadlock like all the others have... Anyway, now they've started, the visitors will start coming again, I'm afraid – Brits, Aussies, Americans, the rest of them."

"Doing their so-called 'fact-finding'?"

"Yes. This lot will get the same facts from me as the last lot did, from London. That, despite their ill-conceived economic sanctions, we're selling as much chrome as we ever did, only now it's to the Russians. Who then sell it on to them at inflated prices!" He sighed. "Why in heaven's name can't they see that the only people that sanctions really hurt are the poor?"

Susan rang the bell. Philemon came in, cleared the table, went out and came back with the pudding. He put it in front of Susan.

"Jelly today," she said. "Who'd like custard? Billy?"

He shook his head.

"Ice cream?"

He nodded.

Seven months now. That's how long Billy had been at home. Hardly speaking, except when he had nightmares. And never saying anything about Colin. God, it was wearying.

"I'm so sorry, ma, pa," was all he'd said when the army had released him on compassionate grounds after Colin was killed. When he went back, the army promptly sent him home again, on mental grounds. And ever since, if anyone mentioned Colin's name, he just walked away.

The nights were different. Then the words came tumbling out. He'd have flashbacks and shake with sobs and she'd sit with him. Although more often these days he didn't want that, would tell her to go back to bed. A recurrent flashback was about a child caught in crossfire. "A terr's firing at me, ma, from a kopje and I hit the ground and take aim. Then this kid comes. From nowhere! Twelve, thirteen maybe. Running across the ground in front of me and his head splits open. Like a water melon! His blood, brains, splattered on my face, all over my webbing! Fucking terr, he'd fired, ma!"

Another flashback seemed to have something to do with that day at Croggan's Place. The words that Billy used each time were much the same. "Such screaming, ma! Screaming like a wild thing! We're running there… to the smokestack and there's…" And sometimes *he'd* scream then, and the sobbing would start.

But in the day time, not a word about Croggan's, about Colin, about his death in the firefight there. Nothing.

She watched Billy finishing his pudding, his head down. Perhaps things would improve a bit when Jamie Aitchison came to stay in October?

"Marion called," Susan said. "She said Jamie's leave has been confirmed, so his coming out here next month is definitely on."

Billy nodded. Then he pushed his chair back, and got up. Susan watched him go through to the sitting room and out to the verandah again.

She looked at Reg, said quietly, "When *is* this going to stop? Why can't he cope? *We* have. Shed tears, shared memories, dusted ourselves down, got on with things. Why can't *he*? Why can't he *talk*? Is he hiding something? Guilty about something? Honestly, you'd think he'd pull himself together and be raring to have a go at those bloody savages because of Colin!"

Reg got up and went into the sitting room. Susan followed him.

He poured them both a drink and asked, "Did you tell Marion about the new rendezvous point for the convoy? That it's changed?"

Susan had. The rendezvous point for the convoys from the city to Mandura had moved to barracks just north of the city. And the composition of the convoys had changed too. It used to be just two trucks, one leading, one at the rear, armed with machine guns. But it was all Crocs now. Armoured vehicles with V-shaped sides to deflect mines, Brownings mounted on turrets. Susan thought the turrets looked rather like dustbins. Several Crocs to each convoy. That's the way it had been since last December, since the Wednesday before Christmas Day.

Susan shuddered now at the memory of that Wednesday, scrunched her napkin and put it on the table.

"You all right, dear?"

It had been about six-thirty in the evening when Reg had called her that day.

"There's been an ambush," he'd said. "At the Isakata junction."

Everyone worried about that junction. It was where the convoys turned off from the main road to Mandura and had to slow down. Perfect spot for a terr ambush.

"The lead truck hit a landmine and the terrs opened fire. So far as I know, at least two dead. Several injured – no numbers yet. Would you open up the clinic, Susan, in case it's needed?"

As things turned out, the clinic hadn't been needed. Susan had gone down with Thelma Warde and they'd waited there for further news. An hour later Reg had called them.

"Two Europeans injured, one's lost an arm. Neither of them Isakata people. Two Africans injured, soldiers. Choppers have taken them all out. But four dead, I'm afraid. All European. One in the front truck, killed instantly. Two infantry boys. Heading home to Mandura for Christmas. Shot."

"And the fourth?" Susan had asked.

"It's Hendrick, dear. Hendrick Prinsloo. They're saying he was thrown from his car and crushed under the lead truck that hit the landmine, as it rolled. Badly smashed up. Died instantly, they reckon."

***

The G&T was put in front of Susan before she'd asked for it. Winston knew all their preferences. He added a slice of lemon and then returned to his usual place behind the bar, down at the far end by the window, where he kept a book he would read when things were quiet. As they were now.

Friday night was film night at the Club in Isakata. Tonight, they were showing 'On Her Majesty's Secret Service'. Reg liked the Bond films. If the emptiness of the lounge and the Churchill bar was anything to go by, so did most people. You could see the lounge through the iron lattice work that separated the lounge from the bar. There was no-one there.

Willem Prinsloo came into the bar and sat on a stool near Susan and lit a cigarette. She knew from Hentie that he'd just got back from a call-up. Winston poured him a lager, and then went back to his seat by the window.

"You're not going in?" she asked.

Willem sipped his lager. "No, not this evening. Right now

the last thing I need is an action-packed movie. But Hentie is in there. She likes what's-his-name. Lazenby. For myself, I prefer the Scottish one."

Susan seldom watched the films, but she'd usually wander into the hall before they started, watch the hall being transformed into a cinema, stay till the newsreel ended. She'd done that this evening, watched people bring the plastic chairs up from the cellar, put them out in the hall, about ten rows deep. Then someone unfurled the big white canvas screen – rolled up during the week when the hall was used for Scottish dancing or badminton or the Wednesday evening whist drive – and after that the hall began to fill up. In came the farmers from around Isakata, with their wives and children. In came the policemen from the Government station in the Reserve, and the DC and his wife. And in came people from the village. The men wore jackets and ties. That was mandatory in the Churchill on Friday nights. The women, most of them, wore high heels and a little more make-up than usual. The young children were wearing their best clothes and the teenagers were wearing their current uniform, tight-fitting tops, wide-bottomed jeans. They all found seats and sat down and soon the hall was filled with cigarette smoke and the noise of packets of crisps being opened and sweet wrappers being crunched and the clunking whirring sound of the film projector.

"How was it out there this time, Willem?"

A hefty man, blond, with that short stubby nose typical of Afrikaners. Always in khaki, she couldn't recall seeing him in anything else. The Prinsloos had farmed out at Rosendaal Farm for three generations. Pioneer stock.

"Agh, I don't know, Susan. Not good. Jeez, it can get so frustrating sometimes!"

"Yes?"

"Yah. I mean, I have a lot of sympathy for the Afs in the Reserves, but they are so easily intimidated by the terrs. They don't stand up for themselves. You know, we visit an Af village and the headman says, 'Everything is fine. No problems.' Then we look in a hut and there is someone tortured. This last time... A village near Nhika. An old boy lying in a hut, lips cut off, no treatment, nothing. Just lying there. The terrs had come the night before, got drunk, found out that this old boy had a son in our army. Jeez!"

He sipped his beer. "And then you get the opposite, the cheeky Afs. Like at a road block we put up, other side of Mandura. The terrs hit two farms there, last week. You heard about that?"

Susan nodded.

"Well, we're at the road block," Willem went on, "and there's this old Morris Minor coming towards us. An Af behind the wheel. I say, 'Get out. Open the boot.' He looks at me, says, 'It's not locked.' 'You bloody get out of the car!' I say. So he does. Very slowly, mind you. He opens the boot and there's this suitcase. I ask for his passbook. What does he do? Gives me a bloody British passport and says, 'British subjects don't carry passbooks.' Cheeky bastard! That's the other kind of Af we're up against, Susan. They pick up some 'O' levels at a mission school, go to study in London or something. Think they are smart."

It had all got so complicated, Susan thought. When they'd first come to this country, everything seemed so simple. An African went to school if he was lucky – it *was* always a 'he', the girls didn't go to school, more's the pity – got a job on a farm or mine, or became a cookboy or gardenboy in a town, something like that, and as an employer you looked after them and their family, and they stuck with you and were grateful and polite. They had schools and clinics and jobs. Everything they needed. Next thing you know, there's trouble in the African townships and it turns out they're being brainwashed by Russia and China, all part of this Cold War business, and told they are 'freedom fighters'. Freedom from what, for God's sake?

Another G&T appeared before Susan had noticed she'd finished the first one. She thanked Winston and lit a cigarette. Winston, now there was an African who was never any trouble. Polite, clean, hard-working. Wearing the spotted bow tie he always wore in the bar, she liked that. He'd been there, what, twelve, thirteen years? A long time, anyway. So long that no-one could recall whether he'd acquired his forename before or after he'd been appointed barman at the Churchill.

In the interval, people flooded out of the hall, some to the bar, others to the lounge or out onto the Club terrace overlooking the tennis courts.

"Not watching then?"

The Police Superintendent perched on the stool between Susan and Willem, and gestured to Winston.

"I've seen it," Susan said. "On our trip home in '74. And it was several years old even then. Reg was happy to watch it again tonight, though. But then, he's never minded living in the middle of nowhere where everything's about ten years out of date."

The Superintendent laughed. "I'd rather be ten years out of date and live in paradise than be bang up to date, watch the latest films and be squeezed into some semi in Brentwood with miserable weather and traffic jams and endless bloody strikes."

"You have to look at it like that," Willem said, when the Superintendent had gone off, a lager in each hand. "Despite everything, you can't beat this country for the lifestyle, for bringing up kids." He stubbed his cigarette out. "Talking of kids, how is your Billy?"

Much the same, Susan said, but Jamie Aitchison was coming to stay with them in a couple of weeks and that might buck him up a bit.

"Jamie? Someone was telling me that he was involved in that American mission massacre? Yah?"

She nodded. "In the mopping up, yes. Getting out the few left alive."

"Jeez… Anyway, that will be nice for Billy. Time with his best childhood mate."

She hoped so. Oh God, she hoped so.

Willem wrapped a big hand around his beer glass, stared at it. "Four little boys," he said quietly. "Billy, Jamie, Colin, Hendrick. Good boys. I can see them now. Billy and Jamie. Colin and

Hendrick. Racing around here. In the hall, out on the terrace."

Susan could see them too. "Going off into the bush in their floppy hats... our Colin and your Hendrick. With their catapults and pellet guns and coming back with all manner of things, snakeskins, antlers, birds, caterpillars, skeletons of this and that, showing them off to us excitedly."

Willem smiled. "And then Colin joining a unit where he could still wear a floppy hat!"

Susan laughed. "Yes! I must say, though, that I preferred him in his police uniform, Willem. So smart. But when he got through the selection process for the Scouts, although their uniform amounted to little more than shorts, boots, a T-shirt and a floppy hat, I couldn't have been prouder. And I loved the little details he used to tell us about his training, learning how to survive in the bush, and how to pretend to be terrs – like smoking those strong Russian cigarettes so that your breath smelt like the terrs' breath."

Willem looked down at his glass, tapped the rim softly. "Fine young men they were becoming. Yah... all four of them. Before all this. And now..."

He stopped. Hentie was coming into the bar.

And now there were only two. Because Hendrick had been killed in the convoy ambush at the Isakata junction and, less than two days later, Colin had been killed in the firefight at Croggan's Place. Her brave Colin. Her angry brave Colin. He had every right to be angry about Hendrick's death, but she still wished he hadn't insisted on joining the unit that the Scouts deployed to track down the terrs who'd been responsible for it.

She watched Hentie pull out a bar stool and sit next to Willem, and then she caught Winston's eye and held up her empty glass.

3

Isakata mine; mid-October 1979

Susan pulled up in front of Molly's Store and got out of the car and smoothed her skirt. It was hot, that sticky heat you get just before the rains.

The old boy was there, as usual, squatting under the gum trees with his carved animals spread out in front of him on sheets of newspaper. Chickens scratched at the ground and a thin brown dog sniffed around a euphorbia bush. Some years ago, Susan had said to him, "Why don't you carve other animals?" He always carved the same ones. Hares, giraffes, elephants and frogs. Why not lions? Or rhinos or hippos? You'd get more sales, she said, but he shook his head. What he carved, he replied, was all that anyone needed. The hare was cleverness, the giraffe far-sightedness, the elephant strength and the frog renowned among all the animals for always being able to find water. At least, that's what Susan understood him to say.

His frogs were disproportionately large and had a certain charm, and she'd bought several over the years for friends. And she'd bought a giraffe, a rather dumpy one, for herself. It was in the sitting room, a doorstop.

The old boy squatted there, picking up his animals one by one and dusting them down. The patch of ground between the road and Molly's Store was almost bare and when cars drew up there the dust would rise and swirl about in the air and, each time, he'd

41

have to dust his animals down.

"Good morning, madam." He gave a little salute, as always.

"Morning."

He leaned forward on his haunches and dipped a forefinger into one of the Heinz babyfood jars in which he kept his paints and picked up a giraffe and started to paint it yellow.

Susan walked towards the store. It was a barn-like building, light brown from the dust, shaded a little by the gum trees along one side of it. Molly was standing in the doorway of the main entrance to the store, leaning against the frame. The non-European entrance was round the back. Molly passed her hand across her forehead to wipe away the sweat and took a kirby grip from her pocket and clipped back a strand of her dark hair. There was a small smile. You seldom got much more than that from Molly.

"Awfully hot, isn't it?" Susan said, going up the steps to the store. "The sooner the rains come the better."

A woman came down the steps past Susan, a baby strapped to her back. An old blue station wagon pulled up beneath the gum trees and the woman unstrapped the baby and climbed into the back seat, settled the baby on her lap and closed the door. The car drove away.

Susan watched it disappear. Something about the baby struck her as odd. Or was it the woman?

"You here for convoy?" Molly asked. She was fingering the buttons on her dress. Her fingernails were chipped and scraggy, brown-edged.

"Yes. But while I'm here I may as well get some flour. We're a little short. Who was that?"

"From the mission. Her husband, he's the priest there."

Molly went into the store and stood behind the high wooden counter. There was a poster stuck on the front of the counter, with drawing pins. CARELESS TALK COSTS LIVES, it said in big red letters across drawings of gossiping women and dead soldiers. Susan had put the same poster up in the Club lounge. The Government had been distributing posters recently. Another one read: WOMEN'S LIB

42

IS ONE THING – WOMEN'S LIP IS ANOTHER. Susan wouldn't call herself a women's libber, at least not as far as some of the more extremist stuff was concerned – bra burning, disrupting Miss World contests – but she thought that one a little distasteful and hadn't put it up.

It was cooler in the store, and dim, the small high windows letting in dust-laden streaks of sunlight. Behind Molly, the shelves were stacked with tinned food, rolls of cloth, blankets, overalls, servants' uniforms, paraffin, matches, sacks of mealie meal, flour. There were sweets jars by the cash till that had been there for as long as Susan could remember. Bubble gum, gobstoppers, jelly beans, liquorice strips. Colin and Billy loved coming down to Molly's Store when they were young. On a Saturday morning, when they got their pocket money. Molly was as taciturn then as she was now, but she'd always give them a few more sweets than they had the money for. And a packet of Willards crisps.

Susan bought some flour and went out, stood on the steps. She looked at her watch. A minute to go. They ran like clockwork, the convoys. If they were five minutes late, you started to fear the worst.

She heard the sound of vehicles and the lead Croc came over the brow of the hill. A brownish-green metal monster. The convoy slowed a little and a white Peugeot about five vehicles behind the lead Croc peeled away from it and drove onto the ground in front of the store, kicking up the dust. The convoy picked up pace again, the rear Croc flashed its headlights and the gunner in the turret waved. Susan waved back. The convoy went on down the hill, round the bend at the bottom, and was gone.

The old boy picked up an elephant and started dusting it down.

Jamie Aitchison got out of the Peugeot, said something to the driver, and the car drove off towards the mine. Susan went to him and said how lovely it was to see him and opened the boot of the car. Jamie put his kitbag into it, got into the passenger seat and they headed back up the road into the village. You had to go through the village, past the Club, to get to the manager's house.

The jacaranda trees lining the road to the Club had come into flower. A mass of purple bell-shaped blooms. Quite splendid against greyish-brown granite of Nyamhanza, rising up behind the village.

They drove past a house with a garden full of concrete ornaments of one sort or another. Statuettes. Bird baths. Concrete pelicans around a pond.

"The Glaswegians still here then?" asked Jamie.

"Alas, yes."

A large Glaswegian family had arrived in Isakata in '71. A lot of people from home had pitched up in the country round about then, attracted by the Government's advertisements in British newspapers, part of its drive to boost the numbers of Europeans. Which was understandable, and you got some good sorts, but there were also many that Susan thought frankly the country could do without.

"Mrs still looks like mutton dressed as lamb. And Mr still falls off his bar stool in the Churchill at regular intervals and Winston puts him back on it again."

Jamie laughed. She smiled. Such a companionable boy. She'd always thought so. She was feeling uplifted by his company already. He looked well. Tall, bronzed, like Billy. But his hair was dark now, Billy's was still fair.

They drove down the driveway to the house and Jamie exclaimed, "Hey, you have a pool now! It must be four years since I've been here? Five? Back to my childhood home…"

Susan had planned a braaivleis by the pool on Saturday for Jamie. She'd invited a few people who knew him, like Dickie and Thelma Warde, and Hentie Prinsloo. Willem was away on call-up again.

She expected to see Billy on the verandah, waiting for them. He wasn't there.

"Billy!" she called as they went into the house. No answer.

She had decided to put Jamie in the bedroom that had been his as a child, looking out onto the orchard and vegetable garden at the back. Colin's room was bigger, lighter, but she couldn't face having anyone sleep in it yet, with all his things still there. She hadn't yet found the strength to go through them.

Jamie put his kitbag on the bed and opened it. "Some gifts for you, Mrs H." Jars of Marmite and anchovy paste, a bottle of Scotch, Cadbury's chocolate. "Dad's been travelling again."

"How lovely!" she said.

A book fell onto the bed from the kitbag. It had a green cloth cover, a bit stained, and faded gold lettering on the spine.

"That's for Beth Lytton," Jamie said. "Written in the 1890s, Dad told me."

"It does look rather old. Cover's a little moth-eaten."

"Something to do with Rhodes, the Pioneers, all that."

Susan picked the book up and opened it. Thick off-white paper, ruffled and brown along the edges, giving off a musty floral smell. Near the front, a sheet of tracing paper. She lifted the paper gently and saw a black-and-white photograph of some European men in shirtsleeves and large hats, their arms folded, standing next to a tall tree. It took her a few seconds to realise that hanging from the branches of the tree were the near-naked bodies of three Africans.

She snapped the book shut. She stared at Jamie and felt flushed. She held the book out to him and opened her mouth to say something. Then closed it again.

Jamie looked over her shoulder and smiled. Billy was standing there, in the doorway.

***

Susan thought Dickie Warde was looking rather tired. There were shadows under his eyes these days and he'd lost something of the easy manner he once had.

A good-looking man, in her opinion, strong nose, long dark eyelashes, trimmed moustache. He'd come to the mine in '71, the new accountant, single, and had made a beeline for Thelma. Both were in their early forties, then, and enjoyed the same things. Tennis, birds, reading. In all the time that Thelma had been in Isakata, Susan had never known her show the slightest interest in marrying anyone. Until Dickie Warde turned up.

Like most of the men now, Dickie was doing regular six-week call-ups. Unusually, though, he served in the regiment exclusively for Coloureds and Asians, except for the officers, who were all European.

"It can't be plain sailing for you," Susan said. "They're difficult people, Coloureds, one gathers. Misfits."

She'd had little to do with them, you didn't get Coloureds on the mines much.

Dickie stroked his moustache and nodded. "They can be a volatile lot. Which isn't good when they're stuck out in the bush for weeks on end. They don't like it, they're not rural people. Stuck out there manning radio relay stations, guarding road crews, protecting pylons, patrolling railway lines. They get fidgety. You especially don't want to mess with them when they're off duty and likely to be the worse for drink. Or drugs."

Thelma and Dickie Warde had been the first to arrive for the braaivleis. Thelma was on the verandah, with Reg, and they could hear her laughter drifting across the lawn. She had what you'd call 'a hearty laugh'. Susan smiled. A good sort, Thelma. Nothing much bothered her. Except Dickie being in a Coloured regiment. Susan knew *that* bothered her, especially since his last call-up when one of his men had wandered away from a radio station, was spotted by a helicopter gunship, mistaken for a terr and shot dead. 'Friendly fire'. It happened quite a lot with the Coloured units. No wonder Dickie had lost some of his sparkle.

By sundown, everyone had arrived and they stood about on the lawn or sat by the pool, drinks in hand, chatting. The firewood under the half-drum was burning well and the steaks were piled on plates on the trolley nearby, ready for cooking.

Susan was talking to the DC's wife and Philemon was heading towards them with the drinks tray. So was Hentie Prinsloo. Philemon filled their glasses. Hentie nodded towards the swimming pool.

"It's nice to see Jamie Aitchison again," she said.

Billy and Jamie were sitting on the pool edge, feet in the water, lager in one hand, cigarette in the other. They'd hardly stopped talking since Jamie had arrived, Jamie doing most of the talking, but Susan had picked up Billy's voice occasionally. So, some progress.

"And now he is a doctor and everything," Hentie went on. "Always such a clever boy, hey?"

"A lucky boy too, being in the medical corps," Susan said.

"Not doing any fighting, then," Hentie said. "That must suit his parents. Being a bit commie."

Hentie wasn't one to beat about the bush. A no-nonsense woman. No make-up. Brown hair boyishly short. Tough, sunburned. Bags of courage in that small frame. Always said what she thought. Susan liked that about her, but she thought calling the Aitchisons communists was going a little too far, and said so.

"Well, they're friends with that nun out at the mission, aren't they?" Hentie said. "And she is definitely a bit commie."

"They do all seem to be, these missionaries, don't they?" said the DC's wife. "Apparently some are actually *feeding* the terrs!" She gave a little shiver.

"Feeding them so that they can then go and murder their own people!" Hentie said.

"Like your farmworkers," the DC's wife said.

"Exactly. Like our farmworkers. Our baas-boy, our store-boy, both killed in the last attack. They were piccanins on Rosendaal, those two. Grew up there. They used to play very nicely with our Hendrick." She paused, and smiled at Susan. "*Chikabi*. That's what they used to call Hendrick, didn't they?"

Susan nodded. Colin had called him that too. "My *chikabi* friend," he'd say. *Chikabi*, 'the limping one'.

"If he was with them," Hentie went on, "I always knew that he was fine. Sometimes they went a long way into the bush and if they were out late and, you know, it was getting dark, they came with him right to the back door. Made sure he was OK."

Hendrick's protectors out on the farm. In Isakata, Hendrick's protector was Colin. Quite often, at the Club, Susan had seen him lash out at someone he suspected of bullying Hendrick, making fun of him. He'd punched one of the Glaswegian boys once, quite hard.

It struck Susan now, for the first time, that what had made Colin ask to join the unit deployed to track the terrs after the convoy attack might not have been just anger. It might also have been guilt. Guilt that he'd not been there to protect Hendrick. Of course, he couldn't have been there. He'd have known that. Rationally. But maybe it was guilt, irrational as it was, as much as anger, that had made him look for a way not just to avenge Hendrick's death, but to be forgiven for it, somehow. And perhaps being part of that unit was his way of seeking both revenge and forgiveness.

Perhaps. She would never know.

She lit another cigarette and looked across the garden. Thelma Warde came striding across the lawn, a few strands of her sandy hair escaping from the bun she always wore on the nape of her neck. She asked Hentie for news of Willem, and the conversation changed.

The sun had dipped behind Nyamhanza, but the air was still warm. Not long now before the rains came and things cooled down and they could turn off the sprinklers. Keeping the lawn green in the dry season wasn't easy, but in the nine years that Susan had been in this house it had never gone brown. The greenness was important to her. It was part of keeping the bush at bay. She felt threatened sometimes by the dry brownness of Africa, by its attempts to encroach upon her corner of it. When they'd moved into this house she'd got the gardenboy to replace most of the indigenous plants around the lawn with rhododendrons and azaleas, some poinsettias, bougainvillea, much more colourful, and she'd taught him to grow dahlias, primulas, even tulips. More recently she'd put in the rose garden.

Not everything worked. Lupins didn't, neither did clematis. A few years ago, when Reg was going back to London for meetings at Head Office, she'd asked him to bring a couple of small holly bushes back and she'd planted them near the verandah. They didn't die, but they'd never grown to more than about two feet high and there'd never been any berries. Some things just didn't take in Africa, and you had to leave it at that.

***

Philemon rang the bell. It was Jamie Aitchison's last night in Isakata. He'd been out to St Anselm earlier that day, and later he and Billy had gone for a final drink in the Churchill. Wasn't it interesting, Jamie commented, that Winston was studying accountancy. Susan said she wasn't aware that he was.

They sat down at the table and waited for Billy. Reg asked after Beth Lytton.

"She's well, but worried about the nun she lives with."

"You mean Agnes?"

"Yes. The police have taken her away for interrogation. Second time in two months. Beth says these interrogations are really taking their toll on her."

"I thought this might happen again," Reg said.

Susan looked at him.

"Agnes," he said. "Her surname is Nyambe."

"Nyambe?" Jamie asked. "As in *Isaiah* Nyambe? One of the terr leaders?"

"Her brother," said Reg.

"Bloody hell! I had no idea! No wonder dad's been getting so worried about Beth."

"Nyambe's a local, you know," Reg said. "He worked here at the mine in the late '50s for a while. A rig operator, something like that."

He got up to start carving the meat. Susan had decided that roast beef, with all the trimmings, would be a nice send-off for Jamie.

"The baby keeps Beth's mind off things, though," Jamie said. "Keeps her occupied. And she's still got her beloved chickens!"

He chuckled. "She's a mischievous old hoot, isn't she? She calls the chicken run Cliveden – did you know that? – and among its inhabitants are Christine, Mandy, Valerie, Lord Astor, Stephen... I bet the priest has no idea!"

Reg said he'd never met Beth's chickens.

"What baby?" Susan asked

"Someone abandoned a baby at St Anselm," Reg said. "Coloured. The Sibandas are looking after it. Beth helps out."

"You didn't say anything."

"Didn't think it worth mentioning."

Then Susan remembered. The woman at Molly's Store when she'd picked up Jamie, the one Molly said was the priest's wife, getting into an old blue station wagon, settling a baby on her lap, its arm reaching up to her. A light-skinned arm. That's what had been odd.

"When was it left there?"

"Early August sometime, I think."

"Really? It ought to have been brought to us at the Government station for vaccination by now, but I don't recall seeing it. I'd have noticed. A Coloured baby. Might need to look into that."

Reg asked, "Was Beth pleased with her present, Jamie? Her book?"

Jamie smiled. "Very! Dad found it in one of those Charing Cross Road bookshops he's always on about. Tucked it into his suitcase with your Scotch."

Various delegations were coming and going from the peace talks venue, Lancaster House, in London. Gil was in the Bishop's delegation.

Billy came in and sat down. Susan looked at him. Would he say what had held him up? Billy said nothing. Reg turned back to Jamie.

"Does Gil think Britain's serious this time, about the talks? I do wonder sometimes why he sticks with the Bishop. The cleric is clearly incapable of standing up to the old white diehards. They're still pulling all the strings that matter. Economy. Defence. Law."

"And thank God for that," said Susan.

"Dad goes back a long way with the Bishop. He knows he'll be out of his depth at the talks, wants to help if he can. And anyway, it gives him an excuse to be where he's always wanted to be."

"Where's that?" asked Susan.

"With everyone sitting around a table talking about peace, Mrs H. Representing *all* the people of this country. Not like the talks in the past, one white Government to another."

"And what does he mean by *all* the people? Exactly?"

"Everyone," said Jamie.

"Including the terrs?"

"There's no choice, Susan," Reg said.

"And who, may I ask, do the terrs represent? The old people in the Reserves whose ears and lips they've been cutting off for years? The women they've raped? The children they've dragged off to Mozambique and Zambia in their thousands and turned into killers?"

She looked at Billy. He was toying with the carrots on his plate.

"I still can't believe it's come to this," she said. "Sitting round the table with a bunch of bloody murderers. Anyway, I expect they'll break down shortly, the talks. They always do."

"Not so sure this time, Mrs H," Jamie said. "It's all come down to numbers. There are tens of thousands of terrs now, hundreds coming over the borders every day. But us? We're losing people at the rate of knots. Casualties, desertions, emigration. Calling up the over-60s last year was the last straw for many people. There's hardly anyone left to conscript."

Philemon came in with the pudding. He set it down in the centre of the table, with a large serving spoon next to it, handed Susan four pudding bowls and went out of the room. When he'd closed the door behind him, Jamie said, in a low voice, "Basically, Mrs H, we're running out of men."

Susan looked at Reg. He looked back at her. He didn't contradict Jamie.

She spooned out portions of bread-and-butter pudding into

the four bowls and handed them around. She sat looking at her bowl, picked up her spoon, put it down again. She didn't think she wanted pudding, after all.

"Are we running out of doctors too, Jamie? Medics? Is that why you've started doing casevac work? Like at the American mission?"

"Partly. But also, it was getting hard *not* to be out there in the bush, taking the flak with everyone else."

"Must take my hat off to you, young man," Reg said. "Volunteering for that when you could have just stayed in an urban hospital, doing a few call-ups a year."

"Like Colin," Susan said.

They all looked at her.

"Well, he could have stayed with the police, couldn't he? Been in an urban police station somewhere. Safe. But he didn't. He opted not just to join the army, but the Scouts. The most dangerous regiment of all." She touched her lips with her napkin. "He didn't have to do that."

Billy leant back in his chair. He licked his dessert spoon and started to tap it lightly on the edge of the table. His eyes were fixed on it.

"Jamie's doing what he wants to do," he said. "With casevac. He's chosen to do that."

Susan wanted to stretch out and put her hand on the spoon, to stop the tapping.

"Same with Colin," Billy went on. "That's what he wanted to do. He chose to join the Scouts. He made that choice."

Tap, tap, tap.

"What are you getting at, son?"

The tapping stopped. Billy looked at Reg and said quietly, "You know damn well, pa. You know damn well what I'm talking about."

He glanced at Jamie, pushed his chair back and stood up.

"Turning in," he said, and left the room.

Jamie moved to get up. Susan gestured to him to stay. She knew what Billy was talking about. And she knew Reg knew too.

She'd been expecting this ever since Billy's passing-out parade. He blamed her. He blamed her for everything that had happened to him. It was only a matter of time before he said it. Now he had.

After university Billy hadn't wanted to come back to the country because he'd be conscripted. That was selfish, Susan said. Reg disagreed, said Billy should follow whatever course he wanted to, follow his conscience, but she said he owed it to the country, to the place that had given him the best childhood in the world.

"Everyone else is joining up. All your friends," she'd told him. "I hardly know anyone who has a son who *isn't* in the forces."

She knew that wasn't quite true, but she also knew what was said about people whose sons evaded call-up.

"I don't want us being put into that box," she'd said to Reg. "Especially not you, with your position on the mine, managing men who are all doing their bit in the Bush War. And their sons too."

But Billy continued to produce reasons for not joining up. At one point he even suggested that the war had nothing to do with communism, it was just about Africans wanting the right to vote. She supposed he picked up that sort of rubbish at university.

When Billy's intransigence seemed set, she went a step further. "It's your duty to *us*. To your father and me."

The deaths of people Billy knew began to mount. A school friend was killed in an ambush. Another trod on a landmine. A farmstead near Isakata was set alight and a little girl, Afrikaans, was burnt to death. Finally, three years ago, he'd said OK. He collected his call-up papers, did his training, got into 3 Commando. But when they attended the passing-out parade and Reg shook his hand and Susan went to kiss him, he drew back and looked at her, unsmiling, and said, "It's what *you* wanted, ma."

Susan rang the bell and Philemon came in to clear the table and they went out to the verandah, taking their drinks with them.

"Billy's war is – was – the worst, Mrs H," Jamie said. "Me, I just fly in, tend to the casualties, get them into the choppers, fly out again. For Billy, it was different."

"From the word go he said very little about his war," Reg said. "Didn't want to press him. Colin used to talk about it quite a lot. Pretty harrowing stuff, some of it. But Billy, no, hardly anything."

"It's the firefights, Uncle Reg. The guys in the infantry, especially 3 Commando, they're involved in FireForce contacts week in, week out, now. And they can last hours, these firefights. The kill ratio, it's not good. And friendly fire has become a huge problem."

Susan had never quite worked out why, if she was Mrs H, Reg wasn't Mr H. Or she wasn't Aunt Susan. But there it was.

"Billy's last firefight before the one when Colin… about a week before… it really hit him hard. Six lost in that contact. Two in Billy's stick. Really tough for him."

"Where was that?" Reg asked.

"Down in the south-east. About sixty terrs came over the border. A bit of a turkey shoot – our guys are waiting for them – but a couple of dozen survive, run off through a sugar cane field. FireForce are called in to track them, finish them off. There's a blood trail through the cane, and Billy talks about stumbling over dead terrs, at one point tripping over a foot, hacked off, with the shoe still on."

Susan winced, and pointed to the wine bottle. Reg topped up her glass.

"They head for a big kopje and Billy's stick gets orders to do a sweep up one side. Half way up they spot terrs on the top. All hell breaks loose, the terrs open up with AKs, RPGs, grenades. Our K-cars are there, cannon thudding away. Billy's machine gunner goes down. Another hour or more, scrambling about on the kopje. For that contact they'd blacked up, which doesn't help, makes you sweat more. And they're getting ripped to bits by red spike-thorn. God, they're bloody everywhere, those bushes! Terr bodies tumbling down from the top like rag dolls. Then he sees another one in his stick, a few yards in front of him, slumped over his FN. Copped it."

Jamie paused. "I'm sorry." He sipped his beer. His hand was shaking slightly. "I don't normally talk this much about things out there. We're not meant to. But maybe it's good that you know what Billy was up against. It might explain a bit of why he's... you know, not coping so well."

Reg drained his glass and stood up. "Nothing to apologise for, Jamie. Much appreciated, in fact. More we know, more use we'll be to him." He patted Jamie's shoulder. "You're a good chap. And now I must turn in too, if you'll excuse me."

Susan turned to Jamie. "Don't go just yet. A last brandy, yes?"

Jamie nodded and she rang the bell.

"Philemon went off, Mrs H."

"Did he? When?"

"About ten minutes ago. He came out here to say goodnight."

"I don't remember that," she said. "He's not to go till I say so, he knows that."

Jamie went into the sitting room and came back with the brandy bottle and two glasses.

"When did he go?" she asked.

"Who?"

"Philemon."

"Ten minutes ago."

"Why didn't he say? He just went off?"

"No, he..."

"Useless people, African males." She lit a cigarette. "And they think they can run this country? Can't even run a bloody kitchen."

Jamie swirled the brandy in his glass. "There are good ones and bad ones, Mrs H."

"No, they're all a bloody waste of time." She raised her glass. "Cheers!" After a pause, she said, "Name me one. Name me one single damned African male who's worth tuppence."

"Well, seeing that we were on the subject of Billy..."

"Oh God, not all that again!"

In the garden, fireflies darted about in the searchlight rays. Susan felt vulnerable, sitting out on the verandah so late at night, but it was cooler here and Jamie was with her.

"There's that Scout, in Colin's unit."

"Which Scout?"

"The one who was there when Colin was shot. At Croggan's. Billy hasn't told you?"

"No. What about him? What's he got to do with good Africans?"

"He *is* an African."

"Oh. And?"

"Billy said he was good with Colin, held him, kept him as comfortable as possible while they waited for the casevac chopper. When he cottoned on that Billy was Colin's brother, he tried to keep Billy calm too, all the while talking on the radio to the chopper medic. Billy said he had those scars, those initiation scars some of them have? Furrows down their cheeks? He said that tears were rolling down the furrows when they were getting Colin into the chopper. I'd say he sounds like a good Af."

He paused. "Billy didn't tell you any of this?"

"No," said Susan. "Well, not about this African." She drained her glass and poured another. "We know about Billy being with Colin, of course. That dawn. That Billy's stick had orders to head for one of those African villages that had been feeding the terrs. But then they heard…"

She gazed out into the night, then looked at Jamie.

"Did you say Philemon had…?" She coughed. Then she said, "Did he tell you about the screaming? That dawn?"

"Who?"

"Billy."

Jamie shook his head.

"No? It comes up sometimes when he has nightmares. The screaming. He says he's never heard such screaming. He talks about running to Croggan's, where it seems to be coming from, instead of going to the village…" She stubbed out her cigarette. "That's where he found Colin."

She sank a little lower into the chair and stared out into the night again.

"I went there this afternoon, Mrs H, on my way back from visiting Beth at St Anselm. I wanted to clear my head of those photos in the *Gazette*, do you remember? Photos of terrs' bodies piled up by the smokestack? I wanted to see it how it all was when we used to ride out there in the hols on our bikes, as kids, to play there. Me, Colin, Billy, Hendrick, the others. Clambering about on those crumbling stone walls around the smokestack. Disturbing the lizards."

There was a gecko on the verandah gauze. Susan watched it make its way up slowly towards the ceiling.

Jamie was saying, "We'd climb the smokestack and pretend to be lookouts on the mast of a pirate ship and shout across the clearing. There were piccanins there sometimes, standing in a ragged line at the edge of the clearing. Watching us. I suppose they must have been from one of those villages nearby."

The gecko reached the ceiling. Lizards and ships and piccanins. What *was* Jamie wittering on about? She put her glass to her lips, but misjudged the distance and spilt some of the brandy. "Blast!"

She sat up and wiped at her dress.

"Sorry, Jamie, what were you saying? Where did you go?"

"To Croggan's Place. This afternoon. To pay my respects to Colin."

4

St Anselm mission; late October 1979

B eth loved the sense of expectation at this time of year. Waiting for the rains. Watching the *musasa* leaves turn from red to green and the flowers on the *mufuna* trees open pinkish-white against the deep blue sky. She could see Mr Van Rensburg's farm on the other side of the Inveraray river, its land ploughed ready to nurture the mealie seeds he'd plant in the furrows when the rains came. They'd come tentatively at first. Drops pounding the earth, creating small craters in the soil, and then growing bolder, and after that there'd be a deluge, with lightning and thunderstorms and the ground awash with water and the air filled with "the smell of the drinking earth". Kipling's words, not hers, but so apt she thought, even though he was referring to another continent.

The land would turn green and they'd plant out the vegetable garden – pumpkin, marrow, greens – and sow the mealie seeds and, later, the groundnuts. The *mufuna* flowers would give way to butter-yellow fruits and she and Agnes would go into the bush at dawn to gather them freshly fallen from the trees, walking along the winding paths, kicking up the dust as the sun rose and the birdsong built up around them. An owl first perhaps, then the doves, then the thrushes and bulbuls, until the chorus was so multi-layered you couldn't pick out particular calls anymore. They'd collect the fruits and take them back to the mission to make *mufuna* oil, for cooking.

Agnes. Oh Lord, she missed her! Ten days since the midnight banging on the rondavel door and the two of them sitting there, quite still, on Beth's bed, not knowing who might be outside. *Vakomana?* Militia? Army? Police? Kim's words of warning swimming through her head. It was the police and they took Agnes away to Mandura, for interrogation. Again.

Beth pushed open the gate into the chicken run. A chestnut hen scuttled up to her, looking a bit featherless.

"Ah," she said, "Lord Astor's been at it again."

She took up the hen and examined her. "I'll tell him off, shall I?"

The guilty party was the old black cockerel. Most of the hens – there were about 40 now – he got on with perfectly well, but one or two he'd pick on and peck at. This was one of them.

"And who will you be telling off, Mukoma Beth? It is not me, I hope?"

Beth hadn't noticed Baba approaching.

"Oh, Baba! *Mangwanani!*"

"*Mangwanani*, Mukoma. And blessings."

"No, Baba, it's not you." She pointed to the cockerel. "I'm having problems with the aristocracy again."

Baba chuckled. He was acquainted with Lord Astor, in so far as he'd been in England in '63, for a World Council of Churches meeting, and had read about the Profumo scandal, like everyone else. When fact-finding missions from London visited St Anselm, he took great delight in taking them up to the chicken run and introducing them to some of its inmates.

"Kim – it is today he is coming?" Baba asked.

Beth nodded. Kim had phoned to say he would call in on his way to Mandura. A few weeks ago, he'd offered to try to find out more about Kundiso, who she was, where she might be. Now he was saying that there had been some progress in the search for her.

Baba went on his way down to the church to prepare for Sunday Communion. She saw him bend down and pick up one of the orange leaflets that the Government planes had been dropping again.

59

Down in the yard the nuns were gathering beneath the big *musasa* tree. Beth could hear the soft hum of their chatter and through the mission gates she saw people coming on foot, on bikes, heading for the church. Just a trickle now. So many people had gone, fled the burnt villages and abandoned farms, taken refuge in the towns or left the country altogether to take up arms on the other side of the border in Mozambique.

Beth went down to join the nuns and walked with them in single file. In front of her was Rejoice, swinging her long arms and singing loudly with everyone else, "*Mukristu, usanete!*" 'Christian, do not tire!' They were singing it for Agnes.

At the church door the nuns crossed themselves and genuflected and went down the aisle, swaying and singing, and the people in the congregation rattled their *hoshos* and tapped their tambourines. It seemed to Beth that as the numbers who came to Communion on Sundays dwindled, so the singing and all its accompaniments got louder, as if to fill the space left by those who had gone away.

The pulpit in St Anselm's church was a temporary structure. It had been a temporary structure for twenty years. Baba had built it from tobacco crates, a three-sided arrangement on a little dais, with a stool inside it on which he stood to give him height. He was not a tall man.

When the time came for the sermon, Baba walked to the pulpit and stood on the stool. He was holding an orange leaflet. He put it on the pulpit ledge and looked out across the congregation.

"*Ishe ave nemi mese*," he said. 'The Lord be with you.'

And they answered, "*Nemi*, Baba."

"Today I would like to tell you the story of my father," he began. "When he was a young boy, my father lived on his ancestral land, up there in the eastern mountains, and they had cattle and goats. I too lived there as a young boy. Then one day the Government made a law that said we must leave our land. Our chief was a brave man and he refused. After many weeks of refusing, the police came. It was a Sunday, before the sun had risen. The police brought some trucks and a bulldozer and they crushed the village with the bulldozer and chased the goats off the land and put the cattle in the trucks and took them away. Then they came back and put us in the trucks and drove us to a sandy place and put us down there. But my father did not come with us. He fled into the high mountains. His heart was broken. Sometime later his brother went there to find him and brought him here, where St Anselm is now, and gave him some of his land and my father got better. When I was about twelve years old, my father came to collect us from our sandy place to bring us here, too."

He paused and took a sip of water. Beth wondered where this was going. She hoped towards some pastoral allegory. Or loss, or kindness, or familial ties. Quite often, now, strangers sat among those who came to the church on Sundays. Informers probably. So it wasn't a good idea to sail too close to the political wind with these sermons.

Baba continued. "And then the Government made another law. The year was 1951. The law reduced the size of our land and the number of cattle we could own, and some people were told to move, again, to new lands. My father and mother stayed here, they were the lucky ones that time, but my mother complained that now she did not have enough land to produce food for the family. My father said this law would push the people into politics. For too long the white people had been taking their land. But now it was enough. Now they would try to get it back. 'It is called justice,' my father said to me."

A low murmur of "*Eh, eh, eh*" rippled through the congregation.

Beth saw now where this might be going. She knew what was in this latest orange leaflet, she'd read one this morning, and she could guess what it might have triggered in Baba's head. She wanted him to stop. He was already attracting quite enough attention from the authorities.

Some years ago, noticing that the number of nuns at St Anselm was growing, Mr Van Rensburg had offered Baba a piece of his land, fifty acres. Black people were not allowed to lease white land, so he leased the land to Beth and the arrangement worked well. The nuns grew groundnuts and mealies there and built a hut in which to stay overnight at harvest time. But, recently, as the mission's food needs grew because of the increasing numbers of **vakomana** coming here, wanting food, Baba had started looking for new ways of meeting them.

"I am thinking about taking over as Mr Van Rensburg's lessee," he'd told Beth, "and getting a loan to make that piece of land even more productive. This new Government, with its black Bishop Prime Minister, will now surely ignore the bar against black people leasing white land."

And with some optimism he had begun a correspondence. It lasted several months. The final answer had come back a few days ago. No, black people could still not lease white land.

Baba picked up the orange leaflet from the pulpit ledge and waved it in the air.

"You have all seen the Government planes that come and drop their messages from the sky," he said. "This morning they came again and when I walked here to the church I picked one up. This is what it says, in big letters."

He put on his glasses and began reading: 'TELL YOUR SONS AND DAUGHTERS, YOUR BROTHERS AND SISTERS, TO COME HOME — THEIR LAND AWAITS THEM!'

He took his glasses off and scrunched the leaflet up into a small orange ball and held it aloft in one hand.

"What land is this that is waiting for our brothers and sisters? Rocky land? Barren land? Black land? White land?"

He paused, then said slowly, "The land of our ancestors?"

No-one murmured, no-one moved.

Baba stepped down from the pulpit and walked down the aisle. Beth turned. Everyone turned to see where he was going. He stopped at the end of a row of chairs near the back of the church. There were only two people in the row, two men, one with an Afro hairstyle and a blue T-shirt with 'Dodgers LA' printed on it. The other one had sunglasses perched on his head.

Baba handed the small orange ball of paper to the man with sunglasses and pointed to the door. The man got up, and so did his companion, and they both walked out.

Baba walked slowly back up the aisle and stood on the chancel steps and clasped his hands together. "A special prayer now for our beloved Sister, our beloved Agnes," he said quietly. And everyone bowed their heads as he prayed for her safe return.

Then he made the sign of the blessing and said, "*Ishe ave nemi mese.*" He did not smile. He had not smiled once during the service. Beth couldn't remember that happening before, ever.

"*Nemi,* Baba."

***

It was getting on for eleven when Kim drove through the gates of St Anselm. Beth made tea and put some lemon-cream biscuits on a plate and they sat out on the stoep.

"A gift for you," Kim said, handing over a box wrapped in brown paper. "From the Aitchisons. Jamie told them after his visit here the other week that your Scrabble board seemed to be held together by prayers and sticky tape, so Marion went out and bought a new one for you."

Beth laughed, unwrapped it, and said they must christen it later, before lunch. Just one game?

"Of course!" Kim lit a cigarette. "Still no news of Agnes?"

Beth pushed the ashtray towards him. "No. The last time they put her in a corrugated iron shed, behind the police station. To try to make her talk. No light, no windows. Like an oven, Agnes said. God forbid they've done that again! It's barbaric, Kim. No other word for it."

"Hot-boxing," Kim said. "It's one of their favourite methods now." He reached out and touched her hand. "I'll look into it, Beth, see if there's anything at all that I can do."

She thought that unlikely, but said, "That would be good, Kim. It's getting worse for Baba too, now. The police have been here a lot lately, with bribes and threats, trying to get him to cooperate, failing, getting angry. And he doesn't help himself. His sermon this morning, all politics. It'll do him no good. A dear man, but such a stubborn one! It's *him* you should be telling to come into the city, Kim, not *me*."

Kim chuckled. "When it comes to stubbornness…"

Beth smiled. "Yes, yes. I know."

It was stubbornness that had brought her to Africa in the first place. A refusal to 'find a husband, settle down' until she'd seen a bit of the world. Any bit. An Imperial Airways advertisement in a magazine, depicting the Victoria Falls, had invited her to visit 'the land of the sun' and a year later, when she came into a little inheritance on turning twenty-one, she bought an air ticket. "You'll regret it," her father had said. But she hadn't. Not one bit. Even now, with the war on.

Beth poured the tea and offered Kim a biscuit. "So. Kundiso. What news?"

"Well, two things. Number one. The yellow notebook…"

Ah, she'd hoped that might help. It had been several days after Kundiso's disappearance, that morning in early August, before Beth remembered the yellow notebook. She'd hurried up to the red house, found it where she'd last seen it, on the little corner table in the bedroom, and leafed through it with Grace and Baba. There were notes on a few pages, in pencil, nothing illuminating. On the inside cover, some words that were too smudged to be legible. Taking Kim up on his offer to try to find Kundiso, Beth gave him the notebook on his next visit, in case it could help. He thought it might, and promised to say nothing of how he'd come by it.

"The words on the inside cover appear to be 'Kundiso Maseka'," he said. "At Scouts HQ, they told me Maseka was one of those villages near Croggan's Place. So it's possible it was her home village. Nothing there now. The army burned down all those villages after that firefight last year, when the Haigs' son was killed."

At St Anselm they'd heard the helicopters, seen the smoke, that day. Some gunfire too, but only faintly. They were too far away to hear much of that.

"And number two?"

"Number two is that I also discovered at HQ that one of the Scouts with Haig when he died is currently on operation in Mozambique, not far from a camp called Chizonya. The camp's name appeared on several pages in the notebook. It could mean that she's based there. Anyway, we got a message to the Scout and about a week ago he confirmed he'd got it, and would try to find out if she was there."

"But how will he manage to... oh I see, he's a *black* Scout?"

Kim nodded.

Beth sighed. "I tend to forget that some Scouts are black. I forget it because I can't understand it."

In the Reserves, the Scouts were called *sku'zapo*. Which meant, said Baba, 'Excuse me while I slip my knife between your ribs.' Of all the players in this war, the black *sku'zapo* were the group that Beth found most disturbing. White *sku'zapo* she could understand, of course. And black men joining the army she could understand – good homes, good salaries, good schools, all too tempting. But black men becoming *sku'zapo*? Joining a regiment that by all accounts had become a group of ruthless loud-mouthed killers? Once, the Scouts had been admired by many whites for their bush survival and tracking skills, their discretion, their Intelligence gathering. Now, even some of the white population were calling them 'savages'.

"Who is he? Or can't you say?"

"I can say a bit. His first name is Siya. He arrived in Mandura, at Scouts HQ, two years ago. Had been injured in a contact up in the north-east. He was patched up and hooded, like they all are, and flown to HQ, to its hospital, and that's where..."

"Who is 'they'?"

"Captured terrs. Sorry. Insurgents. Captured insurgents."

"He'd been captured? You mean he was an insurgent?"

"Yes."

She felt a little better, hearing that.

"If the Scouts think injured captives might be useful, they fly them to HQ, give them the best medical care. It's Stockholm Syndrome stuff. You know, making them feel grateful to their captors. As a captive convalesces, they talk to him, try to turn him. They go to his bed. It's usually another turned terr – insurgent – who does that, goes to his bed and talks and talks. Shows him the carrot and the stick. Sometimes it takes days, sometimes weeks."

"What's the carrot?"

"Oh, reminding them of the hardships in the bush, persuading them they can't win without air power, that they'll just go on getting bombed, offering them cash, saying their family will be relocated to a safe place. Free housing, good education. That sort of thing."

"And the stick?"

"Hanging."

Beth sat back. "Yes, it would be," she said quietly.

Masked weavers were flitting about in the tall acacia tree that dominated the brow of the kopje, building their shaggy nests. She watched them for a moment, then turned back to Kim and said, "Thank you for being more open with me, Kim. Being less secretive."

He smiled at her and stubbed his cigarette out.

"Nothing I've said about the Scouts and what they do with captives is particularly secret. Or rather, what they *should* do with captives. Those they have no use for they *should* pass through the usual channels, but they don't now. They dispense – quote unquote – with them. They're obsessed with kill rates. They're abusing Intelligence, or not sending it back to us at CIU, as they should. Hence my having to go to Mandura more often these days. OM's losing patience. Everyone's fed up with the Scouts – CIU, police, army, everyone. OM calls them psychopaths now. They've certainly attracted some unsavoury types into their ranks. From Vietnam. And old Congo mercenaries."

OM was Kim's name for his boss. Old Macavity, always

abbreviated. Macavity wasn't his real name. Kim liked him.

He sipped his tea and added, "Now they're beginning to get in the way of cross-border operations. In Mozambique, Zambia. Taking things into their own hands there."

"I'll pray for this Siya, Kim," Beth said. "We'll all pray for him, at Evensong tonight. I'll ask Baba. And for Kundiso too, of course. That he finds her, and that she's well."

Kundiso, who had become more than a girl who came and went one night early last August. She had a family name now, and a village, and there was a chance they'd find her. Beth felt that Munetsi wasn't alone anymore.

Up in the bell tower someone rang the noon Angelus on the bucket-bell. A Catholic ritual, really, but one that Baba liked and had made part of life at St Anselm. Beth bowed her head, said a short prayer, crossed herself and then cleared the tea away and brought out the Scrabble.

They were nearing the end of the game when she thought of the photo, the one she'd taken of Munetsi when they'd brought him home from Nhika, lying on the blue cushion on the sofa. She went into the sitting room to fetch it.

"Could you get this to him, Kim? To Siya? For him to give Kundiso when he finds her?"

Kim looked doubtful. "I could probably get it to him, Beth, but I can't promise that even if he does find Kundiso, he'll be able to give it to her. He can't afford to raise suspicion. With Kundiso, with anyone there. He'll need to choose his moment to give it to her. And choose the story he'll tell about how he got it."

"I'll pray for that too, then. Pray that Kundiso sees the photo, sees that the baby is well." Beth began taking the photo from its frame. "And he *is* well. As I told Susan Haig last week. She pitched up here, you know, wanting to know about 'the Coloured child'. Why hadn't we taken him to the Government station for vaccination yet? We told her he was under Silas's care, at Nhika. She examined him, nevertheless. And asked a lot of questions. Grace was as calm as anything, but I must say I found it hard to hold my tongue."

She reached over for the Scrabble bag, took the last letters out of it and put 'ebb' down on the board. Kim rearranged the letters on his rack. He ran his fingers through his hair, smiled, and used the 'e' of 'ebb' to make 'hone'.

With a triumphant "Ah ha!" Beth picked up all her last three letters – p x y – and put them on the board, and 'hone' became 'phone'.

Kim said, as she knew he would, "What sort of word is that?"

"A real one."

Kim reached for the dictionary.

"You're challenging?" she asked. "I wouldn't if I were you."

"Just because you got away with 'ai' – I bet that even the average three-toed sloth isn't aware that he's known to science as an 'ai' – don't imagine I'm going to assume you're right about 'pyx'."

He opened the dictionary and studied a page closely, then put the dictionary down and pulled a white handkerchief out of a pocket in his jacket and waved it above his head. Beth clapped, laughing, and Kim said, as he put the game away, that she must remind him to turn down all future Scrabble invitations from her. Beth reminded him that it was he who'd brought the board on which they'd just played.

She relished her Scrabble battles with Kim. Most of the visitors she persuaded to play Scrabble with her were good, but Kim was the best of them all. Two years, now, since he'd left the UK and come here – "to see the bit of Africa where my doughty aunt lives". He'd stayed with the Aitchisons initially, but within a week of his arrival he'd got a job, in the civil service he said, and moved into a house in the city suburbs. It was some time before Beth realised, from something Gil Aitchison said, that 'civil service' was a euphemism for CIU. The Central Intelligence Unit. It had made her uncomfortable.

"He's all right," Gil had said. "Don't worry. He's a good lad. You'll see."

***

Beth walked up the kopje and sat on the bench beneath the tall acacia tree. She'd wait there for Silas Chipere. For a few days now, Munetsi had been a bit chesty and Silas said he'd come over before sunset to see him. Grace insisted that Silas stay the night in the red house, it was too dangerous to drive back to Nhika in the dark.

A coiled brown pod fell from the tree onto Beth's lap and she brushed it off. A breeze came and it stirred the leaves and she looked up and thought about the coming rains and the land turning green and the bush thickening. Which meant that the *vakomana* would be crossing the border in greater numbers now. This was the start of the 'fighting season', the time when they could move about in the Reserves and hold meetings with villagers and attack white farms and set up ambushes knowing that the vegetation would hide them and the crops would feed them and the rain would wash their tracks away.

A car drove through the gate. Beth rose and walked down the path to the red house. When she got there, Silas was getting out of his car and Grace was coming down the verandah steps to greet him, Munetsi asleep on her back.

Beth always thought of Silas as 'the round man'. He was round-faced, round-eyed, round-bodied, with a neat moustache and round wire-rimmed glasses on the end of his nose. He'd trained in London as a surgeon, come back in '74 to work at a hospital down in the south-east of the country and found himself still being called 'boy'. He'd told Beth he came close to returning to England then, but the war was getting worse and when the post of Chief Registrar at Nhika hospital came up in '76, he took it.

"And how is our troublesome one?" he asked, as they went up the steps.

"No trouble at all! Quite splendid," Beth said. "He's doing very well. Apart from the chestiness. A whisker short of eight pounds now."

"Very good. Very good."

And when Beth told Silas the news about Kundiso, he said again, "Very good. Very good."

The Sibandas' sitting room was large and square, with whitewashed walls and a dark red concrete floor, some plastic chairs and an old grey sofa with floral cushions. There were grass mats on the floor and a low wooden yellowish table in the middle of the room with a Wedgewood vase on it, empty. Beth couldn't remember ever seeing flowers in it. In one corner was a cane bookshelf. Above it, a drawing of the church, stuck to the wall with sticky tape worn out by time. In another corner, the radiogram. On a Sunday, if the Sibandas were at home, Beth usually went up to the red house to listen to the 6 o'clock news with them and have supper, and afterwards they'd go down together to Evensong.

Baba got up from the sofa and shook Silas's hand. "Ah, my friend. Welcome!" Grace untied the cloth that held Munetsi on her back and laid him on the sofa.

Munetsi had a hole in his heart. Silas had told them that when he was about three weeks old. "It is not something to worry about now, but when he is bigger it is possible he will need surgery." He'd also said that Munetsi was likely to get chest problems. "That is often the way when they come too early." So whenever there was the slightest worry about Munetsi's health, Grace would phone Silas.

Silas examined Munetsi and pronounced him fit, said there was no need for medicine, and Grace took him back to his cot. A few minutes later she reappeared, carrying a large wooden bowl.

Baba beamed. "You have brought *nzungu*?"

"*Ehe.*"

"Ah, Amai is giving us a great treat!"

Sometimes on Sundays, Grace roasted groundnuts that the nuns had gathered from the land on Mr Van Rensburg's farm. She'd shell them and dip them in ground chillies and garlic and put them in clay pots and roast them on an open fire outside the kitchen door. They were for everyone to take.

Baba said, "Did I ever tell you, Silas, that if it had not been for

70

her *nzungu* I might not have met Grace?" Silas shook his head. "One day, when I was up there in the eastern mountains training to be a priest, there were these *nzungu* on the refectory table. I had never tasted anything so good! I asked who it was who had made them and they told me it was Grace and so I went to the kitchen and there…"

"…and there you met me. And if you go on talking so much, my husband, we will miss the news."

Baba laughed, looked at his watch and turned on the radio. The beat of drums, and then: *"Good evening. Here are the headlines tonight. The talks at Lancaster House in London on… The current moves in Washington to… In Pretoria, Mr Botha has urged delegates at the talks… A visiting American Senator has said that …"*

Baba let out a long sigh. "They think it still matters, what is said and done in America, in South Africa, in the white suburbs of the city."

Beth looked at him. "Some of it does, Baba. At least, in Pretoria and Washington."

"No, Mukoma, it is too late for all that. All that matters now is what is said and done in Zambia and Mozambique. That is all."

"But the pressure from world leaders? And some of the black leaders in our Government, they seem to matter a bit. Some of them seem to have big followings."

"They do not matter," Baba said. "And if they have a following it will melt away like a leopard at dawn when the big boys come back from Mozambique and Zambia."

"And when the big boys come back," Grace said, "they will get the big houses and the big cars. It is the way. And then…"

"Operations Coordinating Committee regrets to announce the deaths of…"

Baba turned the volume up and they sat listening to the nightly litany of casualties. The black deaths announced amounted to dozens of 'terrorists' and many nameless civilians. The white deaths announced included an English journalist, killed up in the

71

area where the second Viscount had been shot down in February. And there'd been another mission attack, down in the south-east.

After a pause, the newsreader said, *"OCC announces the successful completion of an airborne attack on a terrorist camp in northern Mozambique..."*

"What!" Beth felt the blood rush to her head. "I thought they'd stopped bombing the camps? With the peace talks going on, with all the refugees in those camps now, the women and children..."

Baba shook his head. "I am not surprised. The refugees, the peace talks – with this Government they do not matter. I hear that everywhere in the army they are saying now 'hit them fast and hit them hard!'"

"The last kicks of a dying horse," Silas said. "And there will be more, Mukoma, until the horse is dead. Big kicks."

When it was time to go down to the church for Evensong, Silas said he'd like to come too. Grace gave them each a torch and Baba led them down. There was no moon and at first there was no light for miles around, but soon Beth saw a line of torches moving towards the church from the nuns' quarters. When they got to the church, Rejoice was there already, lighting the candles by the door, and they watched the nuns come in. One by one, as they came in, they made the sign of the cross and genuflected and took a red sash from the basket by the door to put over their pinafores. They always wore red sashes at Evensong. Red for the Blood of Christ.

Silas sat on a chair near the back of the church and Beth went to help Baba with his vestments. Some nuns lit the altar candles, others fetched the hassocks from a cupboard and then everyone knelt and waited for Baba to come from the sacristy. When he did, they said the Lord's Prayer and then the nuns' voices rose in harmony and for half an hour in the flickering candlelight they filled the space with chants and psalms and hymns.

Beth would often tell friends that Evensong at St Anselm was the closest thing to Heaven she was ever likely to experience.

When the service was over, the nuns filed up to kneel on the chancel steps and receive the blessing from Baba, and then they walked back down the aisle, greeting Silas as they passed him. Beth followed and sat down on the chair next to him. The paintings on the walls around them came and went in the flickering light. They were the nuns' work, executed over many years, with Baba's encouragement. Crosses, crowns of thorns, angels in heaven and hands in prayer, palm leaves and doves, all colourful and chaotic.

Silence. Then from somewhere above them came a noise, something scuttling about on the beams beneath the thatched roof. Swifts. They'd arrived last week.

Beth sat there, her hands on her lap, trying to savour the silence, but the war intruded upon her thoughts and she turned to Silas and whispered, "Do you *really* think there'll be more? More bombing of the camps?"

"Yes, I'm afraid so, Mukoma."

"Oh dear Lord…"

After Evensong, Beth sat out on the stoep, but she found it hard to quell the anxiety she felt and she went inside and stood in the sitting room, looking about. The cloth-covered book that Jamie Aitchison had brought her was on the side table. She picked it up. A first edition, something she'd long wanted. Bless Gil for finding it! A strange story that prophesied terrible times ahead should Cecil John Rhodes be allowed to pursue his ambition of painting Africa pink from Cape to Cairo.

Beth opened the book. The frontispiece was a photograph, black-and-white. She held it up to the ceiling light to see it more clearly. White men standing around a tree in their shirtsleeves, black men hanging from the branches of the tree.

A sheet of paper fell from the book. Along the top of it Marion had written: '*Dear Beth, I came across this letter and I typed it out. NB the underlined part.*' The letter, like the book, was written by Olive Schreiner and dated 1897. The underlined paragraph read:

> *I believe we are standing at the top of a long down-ward slope. We shall reach the bottom at last, probably amid*

the horrors of a war with our native races, then not the
poor savage or the generous race we might have bound to
ourselves by a little generosity or sympathy, but a fierce,
half-educated, much brutalised race, who will have their
own. I always see that day fifty or sixty years hence.

Beth re-read the paragraph and a chill went through her at its prescience. It had taken only a decade or so longer than Schreiner's 'sixty years hence' to 'reach the bottom' and to find there that the once 'generous race' had grown tired of asking for their land back, had armed themselves and would 'have their own'.

She slipped the letter back into the book, between the frontispiece and title page, and went out to the stoep again. She stood there, holding the book to her chest and gazing out into the Mashonaland night. She thought of the **vakomana** out there, bombed and bloodied. Of that black *skuz'apo* somewhere in Mozambique, 'brutalised'. Of all the white boys, fed a myth, knowing no better.

Oh, but for 'a little generosity'...

She sighed and turned and went back inside, quietly shutting the French doors behind her.

5

Chizonya II camp; late October 1979

There were flies on his face, in his hair, and the wheezing was getting worse. Nyanye Maseka brushed the flies away and dipped the old towel into the bucket of water by the bed and wiped his face and his body. She knew that death would come soon now. He had been convulsing and vomiting, and the muscle twitching had started. All signs of this cruel thing that was happening to so many comrades. They had never seen it before at the hospital. Some said perhaps it was a new type of malaria, but none of the usual treatments worked. They tried chloroquine when they had some, and if there was none they used *mufuna* bark, the traditional way. But it was not malaria. There was no fever. And people could get better from malaria. With this cruel thing, no-one got better.

He was young, this one. Fourteen, fifteen maybe. Sometimes it took only two or three days for these patients to die, but this boy had been suffering for five days now. His eyelids twitched. He gasped for air and when she held his hand it seemed that the life had gone from there. She wanted it to go now from all of him. It would be better.

She heard an engine and stood up and through the window above the boy's bed she saw a truck pull up in the hospital courtyard. A man clambered out of the cab.

"*Zvimbambaira!*" he shouted.

That word always brought people running from throughout

the hospital, out through the entrance and into the courtyard. Nyanye went to the entrance, the wet towel still in her hand. It was not her job today, the boy was her job, and the other patients with this new sickness, but she would go there for a few minutes.

"Where, comrade?" asked the driver.

"That way," Nyanye said, and pointed to the corridor on her left.

She watched them carrying in comrades from the truck. Many, many comrades, crying out, groaning. Blood all over torn bodies, clothes dark and wet, blood dripping onto the concrete floor. The border was not far, about 40 kilometres, and all along it now the settlers were putting *zvimbambaira*. Landmines. Rows and rows of them.

Nyanye saw a tall figure at the far end of the corridor. Tamuka. She remembered that his Company had the duty of dealing with the dead this week. There was a rota. She turned and went back to the ward where the boy lay.

The *zvimbambaira* trucks were always a reminder to her that she was lucky to be here in the hospital, not out there in the bush. She was no good out there. When she first came to Chizonya II, nine months ago, she had to do carrying work, like most of the women here. Carrying guns, bullets, grenades, bazookas, first-aid kits for the combatants. Then a Commander heard that she knew about nursing and sent her to work in the hospital. She had only one year's training in nursing – she'd left the country after that, when the settlers burnt her village down – but it was enough.

Nyanye was different from her sister. Kundiso liked being out there in the bush. She had been angry at first, about doing carrying work. She had not come for that, she said. She spoke out, she was the noisy one, and Nyanye tried to quieten her. It was not good to draw attention that way. But then they started sending more women over the border, for fighting, and they chose Kundiso to be one of them. She came running to the hospital and danced down the ward towards Nyanye, shouting, "See, my sister? It was better to talk!"

"You will have more training?"

"Yes, don't look so worried! One month. We are going to Tanzania, for training in radios and geography, more training in weapons, more orientation about the Struggle... ah, everything, my sister!"

And she had left soon afterwards, in the trucks, and came back wearing a green beret, a smart uniform, strong boots, full of fire and laughter, talking with praise of their Chinese instructors, of all she had learnt. In June, when the winter was coming, she was sent across the border for the first time as a combatant. She came back in August, then went over again in September. The next time would be in late November when her whole battalion – 2.1 Battalion, Tamuka was also in that battalion – would be going over.

Nyanye looked at the boy. She bent down to his chest, to listen. His breathing was thin and there was much saliva coming from his mouth. She washed his face and waited. There was a big convulsion and his eyes opened. She knew what would happen next. The paralysis would start, first in the arms and legs, then in the chest. She sat down, took off one of her gloves and waited. There was nothing to do now. After a few minutes she got up and leaned over him and with her gloved hand she closed his eyes.

There was a tap on her shoulder. She turned around. Tamuka. "I have one more body for you today, my friend," she said.

At midday there were more trucks. Not *zvimbambaira* trucks, or the grey trucks of the Mozambique army, Frelimo, that brought weapons. They were the white trucks that brought gifts from donors. When word went around the hospital that they had arrived at Chitepo Block, the Commissariat, Nyanye hurried there with other women from the hospital, nurses, clerks, cooks, and they saw that the trucks had brought many items for the hospital. Medicines for malaria, dysentery, amputations. Boxes of syringes, cotton wool, gloves. Blankets and bed nets. Disinfectant. Boxes of SMA, powdered milk for the babies.

One of the women started ululating. She danced around some

boxes she had unloaded, and Nyanye and the others knew what she was celebrating. Sanitary pads.

The boxes of pads sent by donors were meant for the hospital, but if the women were not there at the unloading, many boxes ended up in the officers' quarters to be used to bribe the women of Chizonya II into their beds. And that worked, because the women feared being sent to Kusuwa, the camp nearby for pregnant and menstruating women. Many women did not menstruate now, hunger had stopped it, but for the menstruating ones usually there were no pads in the camp and they had to use rags or leaves. Or friends lent them pants, so they would wear three, four pairs of pants. But if they could not hide their menstruation, they were sent to Kusuwa. Some officers were doing the same with food now, using it for bribery, and it was working because of the hunger in the camp.

In the late afternoon, Nyanye and one of the hospital clerks set off for Kusuwa, taking boxes of pads and SMA. From Chizonya II to Kusuwa it was nearly two kilometres along the river. Walking was the only way to go there. Inside Chizonya II there were roads, and from Chizonya II a big road went to Vila Macia, a town about 30 kilometres east, and other roads went a short way to Chizonya I, the camp for stores, and Chizonya III, the education centre. But there was no road to Kusuwa, just the riverside track.

Nyanye would have preferred not to walk today. Her toes were sore from sand lice. They got into clothes, into hair, and at night in the sleeping huts, the *postos,* the women would help each other remove the lice, to try to stop the worms from the lice eggs getting between the toes and eating the skin.

But to see the joy of Yeukai when they got to Kusuwa, how she laughed and clapped her hands when she saw what was in the boxes, it was worth the walk.

"Blessings! *Eh, eh...* Blessings on you, comrades."

A soft ululation rippled through a group of women standing nearby, stirring mealie flour and water in big pots over fires, making sadza.

Yeukai was in charge of Kusuwa and it was tough, that job. She had connections in the High Command and did not have to be at Kusuwa, but she chose to be there, it was her religion. Salvation Army. A good woman, about 45 years old, much respected, with a kind voice and a big laugh. Her name meant 'remember'. She made Nyanye remember her mother, kind, strong.

"You have kept enough boxes at the hospital?" Yeukai asked.

They sat on the steps of the mobile unit that was the clinic. There were only two brick buildings in Kusuwa. One was next to the clinic, with beds for the women who got into difficulties at childbirth. The other was the warehouse. For living, the women built their own grass huts or stayed in the tents that the white trucks brought. There were hundreds of huts and tents now.

"Yes, we have enough there," Nyanye replied. "The white trucks are coming more now. So maybe for some weeks, comrade, you will not have so many menstruating women coming here."

"Good! Good! But the pregnant ones... *Eh, eh*, so many. This week more than twelve have come." She sighed, then said, "It is time to stop this business."

Nyanye looked at her. Yeukai's eyes were red and there was a greyness to her skin. She looked weary.

"This business of no contraception here because it is good for women to bear children for the Struggle. Good to be 'mothers of soldiers', but these mothers, they are just dumped in this place! With nothing. I have to fight for everything, comrade! *Everything!* If I was not here... Some are so thin they have no breastmilk, that is why I ask for SMA. It is not good, all this."

Yeukai could talk this way. And did so from time to time. Nyanye could not show agreement. She might be called a sell-out if she showed agreement with this sort of talk, there was much suspicion in Chizonya II now.

A woman, tall and well-built, came out of the warehouse and walked across the ground in front of them. Yeukai nodded towards her. "There, she is one of them who has come this week. She has been hiding it for a long time. Seven months."

"*Aiwa!* That cannot be!" said Nyanye. There was no pregnancy that she could see.

And then she thought of Kundiso, with her pregnancy that no one had seen. Nyanye was tall, they both were, she and Kundiso, but she was thin, she did not have the strong stocky body that Kundiso had. That this woman in front of them had. Ah, she could see it now! She could see now how it was that Kundiso had hidden her pregnancy.

Nyanye and the clerk walked back to Chizonya II along the track and turned off on the path leading to their *postos*. The sun was setting and their day's work was done. They were quiet as they walked. After visits to Kusuwa it was always like that. 'Kusuwa' meant 'sadness'. It was a place of sadness.

Nyanye was pleased that Kundiso had avoided Kusuwa by taking her pregnancy across the border in July. It was not until she came back from that operation in mid-August that she told Nyanye about the pregnancy. She said she needed help, her stomach still hurt. Nyanye saw from a piece of placenta still in there that the baby would have been about seven months. She wanted to know about the baby, about the father – an officer here? – but Kundiso said only, "I cannot talk about it, my sister. One day, but not yet." And Nyanye had left it there. She did not want to make her sister's pain worse.

At the edge of Chizonya II she saw that the comrades were still busy in the graveyard, sweeping, burying, pushing down bones that wind-blown soil had exposed. The old tractor was there, with its trailer. Nyanye watched a man carry a bag from the trailer to a grave. A woman helped him put the bag and a long stick into the grave and then pushed the soil in with her hands until only the end of the stick showed. Nyanye wondered if it was the young boy, the one she had watched die that morning. In time, someone would draw the stick out, as was the custom, and let his spirit emerge through the long thin hole.

Nyanye looked around the graveyard to see if Tamuka was there. She could not see him. She walked on, back to her *posto*.

A great fire burned in the kitchen area always. Day and night. Sometimes there was nothing cooking and they would stand there and gaze at the fire, and then go into the woodland to scavenge. But today as Nyanye walked to the kitchen area she saw the queue winding back past the big mango tree and knew there was food. She sniffed the air. Then she thought, 'What am I doing, sniffing like this?' and shook her head.

Someone passing said, "What is it that makes you shake your head, comrade?"

Nyanye laughed. "I was seeing myself as a dog, sniffing to discover what the food was today. My eyes are telling me now it is *huriri* beans again. But my nose, it wanted to smell kapenta!" She loved those tiny fish, even with their many bones.

She stood in the queue, holding her tin plate and mug and looking towards the parade ground where two thousand comrades marched. A flowing river of grey and brown. Boots beating the ground and AKs glinting in the morning sun. She felt the beat in the soles of her feet and it lulled her as she stood there.

Two thousand comrades. Until she was fourteen she had never heard the word 'comrade', but now it was everywhere in her life. She remembered clearly the day when she first heard it. A still, bright, sunny day. Her village was quiet and there was a heat haze over the field. By midday it was very hot, and the cattle had moved to rest under trees at the edge of the field, their ears twitching to chase off the flies. In the bush everything was quiet. The trees, the leaves, still. Her mother and Kundiso were at one end of the field, talking, hoeing. Nyanye was at the other end. She stretched and looked up into the sky, shading her eyes with her hand. Two big brown birds flew above her. Eagles. Circling, then going away, coming back, circling, going, coming.

And then they collided. Wings flapping, feathers falling. They screeched and screeched and a big disturbance rose up in the bush. Birds calling and animals scampering and she heard a hundred twigs breaking. The cattle jumped up and ran this way and that in the field.

Her mother was shouting, "It is a sign! Run! Quickly! Come!"

She started running back to the village, and Nyanye and Kundiso ran behind her. A great noise, like the roar of a hundred lions, filled Nyanye's head and she saw two aeroplanes flying towards them, nearly touching the trees. She threw herself to the ground and the dogs in the village crouched low and whined. Dust swirled everywhere and the chickens were squawking.

A man, a stranger, was running towards them. "Comrades in those hills, many of them!" He was gasping for breath. "Those planes, they are going after them!" He carried on running, past them, in the direction of the aeroplanes, and then he was out of her sight. After about a minute there came the sound of great explosions from the other side of the Inveraray hills.

Six years ago. That was the first time Nyanye had heard about the comrades. The *vakomana*.

"You want some food, comrade?"

Nyanye held out her plate and some beans were ladled onto it from the big drum. Someone poured tea into her mug. She walked towards the mango tree and exchanged greetings with Amai Makare, who was sitting on the bench beneath the tree. Nyanye sat near her, on the ground. It rumbled beneath her. The combatants were marching away from the parade ground, singing. Such a fine sight!

"*Udye zvakanaka*, my child." 'Eat well.'

Amai Makare had already eaten and was paging through *The Patriot*, commenting now and again on items she read in it.

Nyanye gathered some beans on her plate and put them into her mouth. She was hungry, but she ate as slowly as her hunger would let her. The hunger was always worse in the mornings because in Chizonya II there were too many hours between rising and breakfast. At 5 o'clock each morning a comrade came into the *posto* shouting, "Go and wash, go and wash!" and then it could be three hours before breakfast. Nyanye could not get used to not eating the first meal of the day when the sun was coming up.

After bathing it was PT. Another hour. Chizonya II was a military camp, everyone had to do PT. Jumping, stretching, climbing. Running through the safety pits that zigzagged around the whole camp. At 7 o'clock it was parade for the combatants, breakfast for the non-combatants, but sometimes before parade Comrade Nikita came to talk and everyone had to be there. He talked a lot, so sometimes there would be no breakfast till 8 o'clock or later. Today he had come. It was expected. Ever since the news that settler planes had bombed a camp in northern Mozambique, there had been great anxiety in Chizonya II. People had thought that, with the peace talks going on in London, the settlers would stop bombing camps, but now they were fearful again, imagining planes in the sky every minute. Comrade Nikita came to tell them to stop being afraid.

"We the Commanders are well prepared," he said, "and the High Command has promised us many anti-aircraft guns to shoot down any settler planes that come here."

Nyanye ate the last beans on her plate and licked her fingers. Amai Makare bent down to show her a photo in the newspaper of two hundred children who had arrived at a nearby camp, still dressed in their school uniforms.

"The *vakomana* are doing a good job," she said, "going to all the schools. Moving among the masses. Telling them about the Party, the Struggle."

Amai Makare was always among the first in the camp to get the Party newspaper when it came. That was as it should be. She had been in the Struggle from the early days, from 1964 when the settlers took her husband away. She walked out of her home to join the uprisings in the townships. Stoning cars, burning buses. And then, in 1968, after they let her husband die in prison, she walked out of the country.

Nyanye liked to sit near Amai Makare at breakfast, to hear what news she had to share, what stories she had to tell. It was a senior Party leader who had given her the name Amai Makare. It was not her real name, but it had stayed. Mother History. In the weekly orientation classes in Chitepo Block, Nyanye learned about many things that had not been in her mind before – socialism and colonialism, liberation heroes, Sororenzou Murenga who fought the settlers in the 1890s and whose spirit, *chi,* they now called on for help in this second war against the settlers, this second *chimurenga* – but she enjoyed, far more, listening to Amai Makare.

"Did the *vakomana* come to your school, comrade?" the veteran asked.

Nyanye nodded. "Many times. And we went to the night-time meetings, the *pungwes*, where they educated us about the Struggle and how to pass on information about the settler forces."

After these gatherings the *vakomana* would disappear, they were nowhere to be seen. Someone said that they were magic and could hide in the sky.

"Our mother was not happy about us going to the *pungwes*. She had heard that the police burnt your granaries down if they thought you were going to *pungwes*. She would ask us, 'Why do you not go out and play under the white moon anymore?'"

Nyanye drank some tea and looked up at the veteran. "But we went to the *pungwes*. The settler forces were coming to the school, putting dead bodies in the yard, many with no legs, arms, ears, some no faces. They were making us look at them and saying that the *vakomana* – the 'terrorists' – had done this. That is why we went to the *pungwes*, to find out if this was true, to learn more. And many children became *mujibhas* to help the *vakomana*, to take them food and information. My sister and Shungu, a cousin in our village, they were *mujibhas*."

She could still hear Kundiso crying out, on the day she ran her first errand as a *mujibha*, "Ah, my sister, I have found where the comrades hide and it is not in the sky!"

Nyanye wished sometimes that she could be like Kundiso, so dedicated to the Struggle ever since those first *pungwes*, so proud to be here now in this place. Nyanye did not feel proud about being here. It was not a good place for women, the forced sex, the

84

beatings, the problems with the pads, pregnancies, childbirth. It was not right. It was not the way of their culture. But she could not say so to Kundiso, to anyone, and sometimes her head hurt with having to keep silent about these things.

Amai Makare asked, "Your mother, she is there still, in your village?"

"There is no village now. They burned it."

"So where is your mother?"

"She has gone, Amai. The last time I saw her, it was December. In the holiday I returned from the college where I was training to be a nurse, and one night some *vakomana* came to the village. They wanted food, medicine. Some were injured. I helped them. There were other *vakomana*, many, hiding down by the river."

Nyanye paused. She did not find it easy talking about that time.

"The next night more *vakomana* came to our village. They said they had lost the other ones, they were looking for them. But these ones were not true *vakomana*."

"Skuz'apo?"

Nyanye nodded.

"At first we were not sure. We were careful to say little, but we sang with them and they drank our beer. For many hours. And then one, he went to relieve himself at the edge of the village. When he came back he was whispering to the others and they were not so friendly anymore, and we started thinking they were *skuz'apo*. Then they left. In the morning we saw that where that one had relieved himself, all the grass there was flat from the *vakomana* sitting there the night before. And many cigarette ends. Such a mistake!"

She paused, she did not want to go on, but Amai Makare was waiting.

"The next morning, when the sun rose, helicopters came and brought the settler forces. There was a big battle by the river. Later, we saw bodies piled up by the *chimini*, at a place they call Croggan's. Many bodies of comrades. Then there was smoke rising from the place where our village was and we went there. They were burning our village."

"Eh, eh, eh," Amai Makare murmured, and rocked gently back and forth.

"Everything burning. Flames going up up up. The hut where we were born, it was burning down. The soldiers were there so we were hiding, watching, waiting to see if we could see our mother. Nothing, Amai. One of my aunts found us there later and said she had seen the horn, my mother's cow horn she used for hearing. But she did not see my mother."

The deep pain that Nyanye had felt that day, as she and Kundiso had willed their mother to appear from the ashes of their village, came back. It seemed as real now, beneath the mango tree, as it had been there in the long grass, watching their village burn and smoulder and die. She bent over and held her stomach.

Then she sat up and said quietly, "She did not come from the ashes, Amai. My mother."

The veteran touched her shoulder. "It is enough, comrade. I understand. Come, the lecture is starting soon, let us go over to Chitepo Block."

***

Someone was playing a *hamwanda*. Nyanye could see him in the darkness, silhouetted by the great fire burning in the kitchen area. The horn spiralled up above his head and its warm smoky notes drifted across the camp. Everywhere, on the parade ground, on the sports field, outside the *postos*, comrades sat in small groups around radio sets. Nyanye and Kundiso sat on the ground outside Nyanye's *posto*. Tamuka was there too, and some others. Tamuka had brought a radio.

The sound of drums beating came from the radios. It was 8 o'clock. Nyanye watched the *hamwanda* player lay his instrument down on the ground. The white moon went behind the clouds and the night turned black. All over Chizonya II the chattering stopped.

"Tonight, and every night at 8 o'clock, the Voice of Freedom

brings you news and comment on our Struggle and the worldwide struggle for freedom. Comrades, your courage, your sacrifices are breaking the chains of slavery. Now defeat awaits the enemy. He cannot escape it! On our part, victory assuredly awaits us!"

More drumbeats, then an announcement that there was a message from the Commander-in-Chief. A familiar voice filled the air. His words were wise, as always, and they listened to each one. At the end he said, "Down with the settlers! Down with the Bishop and the other black puppets! Victory is certain!"

Everyone took up the chant – "Victory is certain!" – and raised their arms high. Kundiso punched the air with her fists.

After leaders' messages on VOF there was always a war situation report. Tonight, there was news of bridges being demolished, trains derailed, military vehicles ambushed, enemy planes shot down and enemy forces killed. "Many settler-owned mines are closing and farms are being deserted. The settler regime has admitted that more than 3,000 settlers have fled from the beleaguered British colony since August."

When the report ended, across the camp there was chattering about what it had said and much cheering. Tamuka started to say something, but Kundiso put a finger to her lips. "Shhh!"

From the radios came the sounds of a guitar, signalling the highlight of the week in Chizonya II. Comrade Redhiyo's 'Chimurenga Request Programme'! Every Sunday night, after the war report, Comrade Redhiyo was there. He would read requests and play chimurenga music and they would sing and applaud. Everyone loved Comrade Redhiyo.

"First we have a letter from Moses in the Bikita area. 'Brothers and sisters who are fighting for our freedom – much love. Please play 'Muka! Muka!' for all fighters in the Struggle.'"

Comrade Redhiyo said, "For sure, my brother!"

Muka! Muka! 'Arise! Arise!' The singer sang to the accompaniment of an mbira.

Kundiso took her mbira from her pocket, and began playing along. She carried her mbira with her always. She had played it well since she was a small girl. Nyanye loved to watch her plucking the metal prongs, and to hear her sing.

"From Simukai we have this message. 'Please say hello to my one true love, Comrade Chido Masimba. And to all comrades far from us. Keep it blazing!'"

Comrade Redhiyo asked, *"Are you all blazing out there, comrades?"*

The camp reverberated with laughter. The white moon came out from behind the clouds and Nyanye saw shadows jumping up and blazing away with imaginary guns. She felt the weariness of the past few days lifting. Two nights of duty at the hospital, little sleep in the day, many more comrades suffering from the new cruel disease. And the *zvimbambaira* trucks rolling into the hospital courtyard every day.

When Comrade Redhiyo's show ended, the radios were turned off and the conversations started up again. Some of those who had listened with Nyanye and Kundiso stood up and said goodnight and left, but Tamuka stayed, sitting there. The *hamwanda* player picked up his instrument and began playing his soft smoky notes again.

Nyanye watched him. After a moment she said, "Our mother's cow horn, Theresa. He reminds me of that, the *hamwanda* man."

It had been there always, beside their mother, the cow horn that as children they had decorated with small red and black *mutete* seeds. When she could not hear well, she would put the horn to her ear to hear what people were saying.

Tamuka looked at Nyanye. "I have noticed, sometimes, you call your sister by her old forename. Theresa."

"Yes, it is hard. I have always known her by that name, so it is not easy to change."

"But it does not seem hard for Kundiso. How is that? She always uses your *chimurenga* name."

"Ah, no!" Nyanye laughed. "Nyanye is not my war name!" Many people thought that and she did not contradict them, and the camp officials had said nothing.

Tamuka was puzzled. "It means 'the second one', yes?" Nyanye nodded. Tamuka went on, "So it is talking about the second *chimurenga?*"

Kundiso smiled at him. "No, my friend, it is talking about twins. I was the first born. My parents, they had a name ready for me. But they were surprised to see a second baby coming and they had no name ready. So they called her Nyanye."

"You are twins? Ah, I did not know! But, Nyanye, why do you not use your *chimurenga* name?"

"Because it has a bad meaning," she replied. "'We shall die.'"

"Tichafa?"

"Yes. I do not want that name. There is enough dying. The name Kundiso, it has a good meaning."

Tamuka said, "And mine, too, is good. 'We have woken up'." He laughed. "And if I do not go to my bed now, comrades, I will not wake up tomorrow!" He picked up his radio and they watched him in the moonlight walking back to his *posto.*

Kundiso took up her mbira and began to play it. Ever since she had come back in August from across the border, Nyanye had sensed a sadness in her. It could be because of the pregnancy, Nyanye thought. Kundiso's body had grown stronger, tougher, as had her determination, but in her face and voice there was a sadness. It was there too in the notes she played.

After a moment, Kundiso put her mbira down. "That old cow horn. I have thought many times, my sister, that if our mother could hear well she would not have perished that day. Maybe she did not hear the soldiers' questions, did not give the right answers, made them angry."

Nyanye said, "Sometimes I think that she did *not* perish. That we will find her. One day."

"No, she has perished," Kundiso said, and picked up her mbira again.

Kundiso still felt great sorrow that she was not in the village that morning when the helicopters came. Nyanye knew that. Long before sunrise, when the sky was still black, Kundiso had gone to the river with their cousin Shungu to take food to the comrades and tell them about the *skuz'apo* visit in the night.

"Do not go, the *skuz'apo* could be watching!" Nyanye had begged her.

But Kundiso seemed to have no fear. "The darkness will hide us. And we will return with the pots full of water. What is suspicious about that, women fetching water from the river in the early morning?"

At sunrise, some *skuz'apo* had come into the village. Nyanye heard them shouting. She was frightened for Kundiso and Shungu, crept away from the village and went quickly along the path to the river. Soon the air was filled with the sound of the helicopters. When she got near the *chimini*, she saw Kundiso coming back from the river. And behind her, Shungu, in her red dress.

In that same moment, Nyanye saw three men near the *chimini*. *Skuz'apo*, she was sure. One of them was wearing the same T-shirt he had worn in their village the night before.

And she saw that they had seen Kundiso and Shungu too. They were running towards Kundiso, pulling her, reaching out for Shungu and the newborn on her back.

Nyanye had let out a cry and a shadow fell over her and a figure brought a gun down on her head. That was all she remembered till she woke up in the long grass many hours later. Kundiso had found her on the path and pulled her away from there. Through the grass they could see the bodies piled near the *chimini*. One was Shungu. In her red dress it was easy to see her.

The day after the battle and the burning of the villages, when it was sunset and all the soldiers had gone, they had looked for Shungu's baby. He was by an old wall, near the *chimini*, and they made a grave for him on the edge of their village. They wept quietly as they knelt by it, their hands sweeping soil and ashes into it to cover the body, fill the grave.

Then Kundiso had stood up, wiped the tears from her cheeks, and looked about her at the ruins of their childhood. She clenched her fists and cried, "No more!" She held out her hand to Nyanye.

"Come, my sister, the time is here now. We must join our brothers and sisters there in Mozambique." Nyanye had no strength to argue, to resist, and that night they started their journey to the border.

The journey had taken many days. They hid in caves in the daytime and in the evening they gathered fruits and ate them, then walked again in the night. They spent much time looking for water. Such thirst! When they crossed the border, some Frelimo soldiers saw them and took them in grey trucks to Chizonya II.

Ah, at first it was hard! So much suspicion. When they arrived they had to queue to be searched and when it was Nyanye's turn they stripped her and checked everywhere on her body, even her vagina in case she was hiding something there to kill comrades! They asked many questions, then they took everything away, her clothes, takkies, watch.

On the floor by the queue a man was lying. His arms were tied behind his back, his underpants were soiled. "He's a sell-out!" said a female Commissar, and told Nyanye to go to the showers and threw old clothes at her to put on afterwards.

That night she cried for a long time. Kundiso sat with her to comfort her, held her hand and said it was necessary, all this checking for sell-outs. It was for their safety.

The next day a Commissar had said to her, "Forget your family. No-one here has a family – your mother is not here, your father is not here, you sister is not here, your brother is not here. The leaders of our Struggle, they are your father and mother. The comrades here, they are your brothers, your sisters. You do not have a home, you do not come from another place. You come from Chizonya. Chizonya is your home. And you have a new forename. A *chimurenga* name. Tichafa. Get used to it. You have no forename except your *chimurenga* one."

But Nyanye did have another forename, and she would keep it as long as she could. And now everyone used it, as if it was her *chimurenga* name.

Nyanye stood up and dusted the soil from her uniform. Kundiso

91

stood up too. Then she said, "Who is that coming?" Through the darkness a figure was walking towards the *posto*. It was Tamuka.

"Ah, you are back again, my friend," Nyanye said

"Yes, I am back." He looked at Kundiso. "It is because there is a man – I have not seen him before – he was there by my *posto* when I got back, and he was asking questions."

"What questions?" asked Nyanye.

Tamuka was still looking at Kundiso. "He was asking about you, comrade."

Kundiso's face was like stone. "How do you know it was me he was talking about?"

"There are many women here called Kundiso, like you. I know that. But this man, he also knew your family name. Maseka."

Nyanye saw that her sister was staring at Tamuka.

Tamuka said, "He is called Siya." He smiled at her. "I am sure there is not a problem, comrade, but it is better for you to know, that is why I came to tell you. I must go back now. *Murare zvakanaka.*" 'Goodnight.'

He started walking away.

"*Urare zvakanaka*, my friend," Nyanye said quietly.

Kundiso did not say anything

6

Isakata mine; early November 1979

The noises came from the verandah. Susan's first instinct was to reach out to the bedside table. Her hand touched the alarm clock, the glass. She reached a little further into the darkness. Bloody hell, where was it? Somewhere a door closed. The sitting room door? She leant over the edge of the bed, touched the floor between the bed and the bedside table. Damn! The sitting room, that's what she'd done, the wretched gun was in her bag and she'd left her bag in the sitting room. She stared at the window. Blackness. Reg's gun, she'd get Reg's gun. From the cupboard. Silence. Why weren't the dogs barking? She'd get Reg's .303 from the cupboard.

She bent her knees, curled up a little. Her head pounded. Maybe she was wrong, maybe it *was* there. She reached out again, fumbling. Her hand hit the glass and it rolled. Oh God! She waited to hear it hit the floor. Nothing. Instead, just a drip-drip-drip. Something tapped the window and in an instant she had rolled off the bed and was crouching on the floor. Think, think. She had to move. She had to get Reg's gun. At least get the gun. Then decide.

She crawled towards the cupboard. She could smell the brandy on the floor. When Reg was away she did that sometimes. Take a tot to bed, to help her sleep. Brandy helped with sleeping. Just a tot. She reached the cupboard. Her eyes had adjusted themselves to the dark and she could see now, see enough. See enough to see the gun, get it down. Heavy bloody thing. They'd said, down at the shooting range – she'd started going there for pistol practice when she began running the family welfare service at the Government station – "Have a go with a rifle, a .303, an FN, whatever you like. Just in case." She had. So she wasn't surprised by the heaviness.

She moved along the corridor, staying close to the wall, almost dislodging a painting, going on down the corridor. One hand on the stock, one on the barrel. The door that led into the sitting room was ajar. It hadn't been. She was sure she'd closed it. They always did, they always closed all the doors in the house before going to bed. The last thing they did, every night. That was the advice and they followed it. Tonight? Had she closed all the doors? She couldn't remember. Come to that, she couldn't even remember going to bed. Stop it. Never mind that now. Think.

She inched a little closer. Touched the door frame and looked through the slit between it and the door. She could see the verandah. It was dark, but the searchlights in the garden cast a yellowish hue over it. She saw that the table, the old teak side-table, was upside down.

Then she saw him, moving across her vision. She saw him, quite clearly, his back to her.

"Bloody idiot!"

Susan smacked the door open with the .303, dropped it on the carpet and stood there in the middle of the room.

He turned. He was naked. He was holding his FN and it was pointing straight at her.

"Ma! Christ! What the fuck…!"

She shouted, "You bloody idiot! What the hell do you think you're doing! Put that bloody gun down! Now!"

He stared at her. Frozen. The gun was still pointing at her.

"Now!"

He blinked. He started shivering. The dogs were barking.

He dropped his arms down, gun pointing to the floor. She watched his fingers loosening their grip on the stock. She watched him move to the table, turn it upright and put the gun on it.

"Christ!" he said again, and slumped into one of the cane chairs.

Dickie Warde said later, after he'd got Billy to his bedroom, sat and talked with him for a while, given him a sedative he'd found in the bathroom, that Billy thought he'd heard someone on the verandah. He was pretty shaken up. He'd had quite a shock, Dickie said, finding himself aiming his gun at her. But he'd be all right.

She'd had to call Dickie. With Billy slumped in the chair, refusing to move, his hair flopping over his eyes, hiding them, telling her to go back to bed. "Go, ma! Leave me!" he'd kept saying. His voice choked. And when she'd tried to touch him he said, "No! Don't, ma! Go back to bed."

Then he'd put his hands over his head and whispered, "This is a fucking nightmare…"

Dickie asked if he'd been drinking. No, Susan said, not as far as she knew. They'd had dinner, the usual silent affair when Reg wasn't around, and Billy had gone to his room shortly afterwards. Susan asked Dickie if he'd come back in the morning, see Billy, check the security fence. He said he would. He checked all the doors, windows, grenade screens, then picked up Billy's FN and left.

When Hentie Prinsloo dropped in the next morning at about eleven, on her way back to Rosendaal Farm, Billy still hadn't emerged from his room. Susan thought it best not to go in. Better that Dickie Warde did, when he got here, if Billy was still in bed then.

"When is Reg back from Mozambique?" Hentie asked, after Susan had told her something of what had happened. They were sitting by the pool. Susan had kept her account brief. She didn't want to go on about it.

"Day after tomorrow," she said. Reg had gone to Beira to oversee a big shipment of chrome going out on the Russian boats. He'd do that from time to time now, be away for three or four days down there.

"It is always worse at night, hey," Hentie said. "Especially when the men are away. That waiting alone, listening... sometimes, you know, I actually wish they would just do it. Attack. The waiting is worse."

She pronounced it 'ekshilly'. She had a high-pitched voice and a strong Afrikaans accent. Susan still found the accent grating, even after all these years. Sentences full of clipped vowels and exclamation marks. On the whole, Susan wasn't terribly keen on Afrikaners. When the children were young and Colin had wanted to spend time out at Rosendaal with Hendrick, or Hentie had dropped Hendrick off for the day to play with Colin, Susan had kept her distance. Been polite, exchanged pleasantries, but didn't have them over to dinner or anything like that. The war had changed things, though. Distances between people had shortened, and she'd got to know and like Hentie and Willem. She'd got even closer to them since last Christmas, of course. Reg still kept his distance a bit, with Hentie mainly. He got on all right with Willem. Susan had recently discovered that they played Bridge, she'd had no idea that Afrikaners played Bridge, and from time to time now she made up a four with them, her and Thelma Warde.

"Have you still got that Beretta?" Hentie asked. Susan nodded. "Well, maybe you should... I mean, it is really neat and everything, but those pistols are so small, you can forget where they are. Maybe you should get an Uzi?"

Hentie wore a gunbelt most of the time now, Uzi attached. To be expected, seeing how often she was alone out on the farm, and how often it had been attacked. Three times now. Hentie had said little about the last attack, the one in early August. Which was typical of her. Most of what Susan knew came from Willem, that the terrs had hit the place with a dozen mortar bombs, set the barns alight, stripped and gutted the farm store. Afterwards the army found that about 500 rounds of small arms fire had been pumped into the farm house. And they found Hentie there with the kids, huddled in the pantry.

The week after it happened Hentie had admitted to Susan that she'd been scared, then quickly added: "But you know what? The next morning you see another beautiful dawn and you walk down to look at the seedbeds or just stand there in the veld watching the cattle graze – and it is then you know it is all worth it. It is all worth fighting for!" After a pause, she said, "And our Hendrick – your Colin – they would want that, want us to go on fighting for it all."

You had to take your hat off to Hentie, to all those women out on the farms. Taking on everything when their husbands were on call-up. Planting, harvesting, dealing with the cattle, with the workforce, mending the fences, manning the radio. And being a mum too, often as not.

"And I'll tell you something else," Hentie was saying, "it is really great for posture, wearing an Uzi on your gunbelt. It makes you hold your tummy in!"

A Land Rover came down the drive. It was Dickie Warde. He came across the lawn to them. He was in camouflage. The uniform, the moustache, he cut rather a dash. He said he was heading for Mandura, for a training day before his next call-up, due to start in late November. He asked after Billy and they decided to leave things be, let him sleep.

"Just picked up something about another mission attack," he said as he sat down. "Catholic. Up by the Zambezi. They're saying…"

He stopped. Philemon had appeared with a fresh pot of tea and an extra cup and saucer. He put it down on the table and stepped back, and stood there. Susan looked up at him.

"What is it, Philemon?"

"Master, madam."

"Billy?"

"Yes, madam. Master Billy."

"What about Billy?"

"He is going to the Club. He said I must tell you."

"To the Club? When? I didn't see him go – when was this?"

"Just now, madam. He is going out the back."

Susan excused herself and went into the house and phoned the

97

Club. Winston answered. Yes, Master Billy had just arrived, he was in the billiards room.

"Sorry about that, Dickie," she said when she got back to the poolside. "I had no idea. A complete waste of time for you."

"Not at all," he said "I wanted to see you, too, to see if you were all right. It sounds as though Billy is. And Thelma said you were to call her this evening, if you're at all worried about him."

"So kind of you both. Thank you."

Stalwarts, the pair of them. Of all the people at Isakata, Susan felt most comfortable with Thelma and Dickie Warde. Same sort of people. Sensible, discrete. Reg thought so too.

"Anyway, where were we? Something about a Catholic mission?"

"Yes. Terrs attacked last night. The first reports say several bodies. Priests. Nuns. But no numbers yet. And apparently the terrs wrote something on the church altar there. 'Down with Christ'. Some such thing."

Hentie sighed. "That's what commies do," she said. "Like I keep saying to Willem, we used to have the happiest Afs in the world, but now the Kremlin has made them into communists. Brainwashed them. Some anyway, not all. Lots of good Afs in the army, loyal. And the poor Afs in the Reserves, they don't want all this commie stuff. But the brainwashed ones, the terrs, if they ever get power they will do what commies do. Ban Christians."

Susan thought it best not to comment. She didn't have a lot of time for religion of any sort, Christian or otherwise.

Dickie asked, "And Rosendaal, Hentie? How are things going out there?"

"So, so," she said. "Some of the workers have returned since the attack, so with the new ones the workforce is OK now." She sipped her tea and looked down the garden. "It's just that you know they will come back, the terrs. So all the time you wait for that." She gave a little smile. "But it's the same for everyone. For all the other farms around here."

"Not quite everyone," Dickie said. They looked at him. "Van

Rensburg. Still no attacks. The only farm in a 20-kilometre radius of Isakata where there's been no trouble, nothing at all."

"Come to think of it, Dickie," Susan said, "there hasn't been, has there?"

There'd been rumours for a year or so that some European farmers had taken to giving the terrs food, or at least to turning a blind eye to their presence, in return for being left alone. Was Van Rensburg one of those?

"I saw him at St Anselm last week, as it happens. I must say, he did seem rather pally with that priest."

Hentie said, "At St Anselm? You were there? I thought you never went there."

"They've acquired a child, that priest and his wife. A Coloured child. Their story is that it was abandoned there. That's Beth Lytton's story, too. Anyway, whatever the case, they hadn't brought it to the Government station for vaccination…"

Dickie nodded. "Oh yes, I remember Thelma saying something about that."

"… and so I decided to go out there, see why not. Beth Lytton seemed rather put out about my visit, said Chipere, the doctor at Nhika hospital, was in charge of the baby. Turns out the baby was prem, spent his first few weeks in the hospital." She paused. "He's quite light, his skin, rather an attractive little thing."

Dickie got up to go. "Now with Billy, Susan, try not to worry. He'll be fine. He was pretty choked up last night. About frightening you. Especially finding himself pointing a gun at you. He…"

"Eish! Billy pointed his gun at you?"

Susan had left out that part of her account to Hentie. Dickie said, no, no, it wasn't like that. It was just a trained soldier's instinctive reaction to an intruder.

"Why on earth would Billy want to point a gun at Susan?" he said. "At his own flesh and blood?"

***

At 7.45 Susan sat down in the sitting room and switched on the radio to hear the evening news. A few minutes later she switched it off. She didn't want to hear any news. She picked up her G&T and went out to the verandah.

Billy wasn't in. He'd gone down to the Club. It was Friday night, film night. She'd rather stay at home. She was tired. She'd told Philemon not to make supper, he could have the night off, she'd make herself scrambled egg later, and she'd stood at the kitchen window and watched him walk along the path past the vegetable garden to his *kia*.

She lit a cigarette and looked out into the darkness. Nothing. A torch beam flashed intermittently down by the gate. One of the guards. But apart from that, nothing. Nothing. For miles and miles, nothing. How had she ended up here? Ended up in this teapot-shaped country thousands of miles from home? Stuck out here on this chrome mine, far from anywhere, in the middle of the bush, in the middle of this Bush War in Africa?

"Nurse, there's a soldier to see you, in the courtyard."

1943. London. Guys hospital. Summer. She'd bounded down the stairs, flushed with excitement. It would be her brother, home from North Africa. How marvellous! She ran out into the courtyard. A figure in army uniform stood near the fountain. Gosh, he'd lost weight!

She called out to him, and he looked up and it was someone else.

Someone she'd never seen before who said he was in the Royal Engineers, had served with her brother in Tunisia, was home on leave and was going back the next day. He'd promised her brother he'd look her up and bring him news of her, they'd be linking up again soon. His name was Reginald Haig.

And it had all led from there. In 1946 he proposed, two years later they were married in St Mary's Church in Hampstead and in January 1950 they set sail from Southampton aboard the Carnarvon Castle. And she thought – then – how fortunate it was that Reg had come to Guys on the day he did, looking for her, and not on the following day, when she was off duty, or she mightn't have been there on a ship to Africa.

Susan sipped her G&T. She mightn't have been there then, on that ship, if he'd come the following day. And she wouldn't be here now, in this godforsaken place.

When Reg had first raised the subject of going to Africa, she'd not ruled it out. Things were rather drab at home, what with London looking like a bombsite, and food rationing, and an economy in tatters, Attlee trying to patch it up by nationalising everything in sight, coalmines, railways, you name it. The colonies did seem to be a much brighter proposition and in time the idea grew on her.

She'd asked Molly once, down at the store, had she wanted to come here? Had she wanted to come to Africa?

"My husband, he was very sure," Molly replied. "To go from Portugal. Me, it was OK. What could I do?"

She did what Susan did, what thousands of women did. Left a war-weary Europe and went where their husbands led them, to the colonies, set up new homes there, raised children there, got on with life there. Took along anything that might soften the edges of their new life – they knew it was not all sunshine and servants. Susan took oil paintings of Cornwall, Surrey, the Heath and the Thames, the Persian rugs her brother had given her from his time in Baghdad in the '30s, and the mahogany Georgian gateleg, a wedding present from an aunt, and a trunk of glassware and crockery, the silver candlesticks.

She left behind her family and her friends and her nascent career. Or to put it another way, she burned her boats.

When she'd put it like that to Thelma Warde recently, Thelma said, "You wouldn't really want to go back to England, though, would you? It's not what it was, you know. It's not what it was in the war, everyone pulling together. Getting on with things. Uncomplaining. That's all gone. Quite, quite gone! Strikes. The young *completely* out of control. Pavements filthy. And everything grey! Oh, so endlessly grey!"

Susan recalled a train journey on her last trip home, in '74, with Reg, going back up to town from a weekend in Kent. She remembered the train trundling through a dull grey evening into London, looking down on row upon row of small dull grey houses, the greyness broken only by the flickering colour television screens you could see through some windows.

That trip was the first time she'd gone back in about six years – and she'd not been back since. Yes, it *was* grey. But it was safe and predictable and it smelt like home. She had nudged Reg, then, tried to make him see how it would be if they went back, Colin wouldn't mind and Billy would probably end up in England anyway, being more of an anglophile than his brother. They'd gone walking on the Heath and spent time down at the cricket club, met friends at old haunts in London, seen others in Kent, Surrey, visited museums and taken in some West End shows. Done civilised things. In a civilised country.

But there was no going back. Reg had long since let go of his home country. He didn't hanker for it, the way she did. He hadn't enjoyed the trip much, apart from going to a few Wigmore Hall concerts.

"I'm tired of family and friends offering political opinions on a country in Africa they know little about. Know little, care less."

She'd agreed, adding, "I wouldn't be surprised if, with some of them, it's simply a case of jealousy. Jealousy about our lifestyle."

Susan stubbed her cigarette out in the ashtray and went through to the sitting room to replenish her G&T. But decided on brandy instead. She poured herself a glass and saw that the brandy bottle was nearly empty. Why hadn't Philemon said so? What was the time? Gone ten. Just this one, then she'd head for bed.

She stood in the middle of the room for a moment, holding her glass. Had Philemon gone? Yes, of course he had, several hours ago. She'd let him go. And she'd forgotten about supper. No point now. She walked back out to the verandah, but too late she saw that the giraffe – the dumpy wooden giraffe she'd bought from the old boy down at Molly's Store, that acted as a door stop – was on its side. She tripped and fell and the glass slipped from her hand and shattered across the verandah floor.

"Christ!"

Susan knelt there, on the floor, tearful, unfocused.

When her head cleared she reached out for the chair, hauled herself up, went into the sitting room, poured herself a whisky and went back to the verandah.

She'd told Reg more than once that the damn thing was wobbly. The giraffe. But he'd done nothing about it. Swanning off to Mozambique all the time. Swanning back again. Spending hours up in the mine office, longer than he needed to. Too 'busy' to attend to things around the house.

And as if that all wasn't enough, there was his bloody obsession with African history. What African history! There hadn't *been* any till the Europeans arrived, first Livingstone, then the Pioneers in 1890, and all they'd found was a collection of half-naked tribes who'd spent most of the preceding centuries trying to kill each other. Reg would regularly go off on digs at weekends – well, he used to, it wasn't safe to do that now – with a couple of other amateur archaeologists and come home with shards and trinkets and hypotheses about long-ago African so-called 'civilisations'. Happy as a sandboy. It suited Reg, this country.

It seemed to suit a lot of European men here. 'A white man's country', people said. In some ways it was, but she found the phrase objectionable. She felt it diminished the role that women had played in building the country, shaping its values, creating a lifestyle that everyone agreed couldn't be bettered. Not to mention changing Africans' lives for the better, too. The women had worked every bit as hard as the men here – it was their country too!

Susan sat there, sipping her whisky, smoking her cigarette. She must remember to throw something onto the smashed glass. Cushions. So that Billy didn't step on it when he came home. Philemon would sweep it up in the morning.

***

103

Susan looked through the kitchen window, watching Philemon pulling up carrots in the vegetable garden, putting some in his basket, moving on to the onion patch, pulling up onions. It would be Irish stew tonight. There was neck of mutton in the fridge.

"And for pudding, pawpaw," she said, when he came in with his basket. "We'll have pawpaw. Any lemons?"

"Yes, madam."

"And remember, *maningi* potatoes. Not like last time when you didn't put enough in. I want lots. Yes?"

"Yes, madam."

"*Maningi, maningi.*"

"Madam."

Susan told Philemon that she'd be out this afternoon, that the Boss was due back about six, but she should be home before then. And not to forget to go down to the Club to get a bottle of brandy from Winston, he'd know which one. The Boss wouldn't like to get home from his travelling and find no brandy, would he?

She went to her bedroom and picked up the photograph on her bedside table. Colin in his chocolate-coloured beret, grinning. Taken at Scouts HQ in Mandura on the day of the ceremony that marked the end of his training. It used to sit on the mantelpiece in the sitting room, next to one of Billy, but last January she'd put it in her room where Billy didn't have to see it. She thought that best, for now.

She wanted to be with Colin. She wanted rid of the disquiet that had overtaken her these past weeks, got in the way of things. She sensed an unravelling inside her, a growing anxiety. She wanted freedom from the anxiety, if only for an afternoon. She would go to Colin. She would go to Croggan's Place.

"Can we go, ma? Please, ma? Please?"

Susan put the photo and her pistol in her bag and went out to the car.

"Is Jamie going?"

"Yes, ma."

She drove through the village and past the mine office and

headed north on the St Anselm road.

"All right then, but be back no later than five. Understood?"

"Yay! Thanks, ma!"

And she'd watch him peddling off down the drive, Billy in tow, trying to keep up with his older brother. "Slow down! Wait for Billy!"

They'd go out to Croggan's every school holiday, at least once, loved it. As long as Jamie Aitchison was with them she knew they'd come to no harm. There was a short cut through the bush from the mine office, a path. Sometimes she'd make a little picnic for them, put it in a rucksack.

After driving a few kilometres along the road to St Anselm, Susan turned down the track through the woodland, driving slowly because of the holes, and seven or eight minutes later she came out into the clearing and parked the car. She walked over to the wall nearest the old smokestack. It was low and crumbling and she'd brought a cushion to put on it. A lizard darted into a crevice. She sat down and put Colin's photo on her lap and lit a cigarette. Through the remains of an archway on the far side of the smokestack she could see the river, shimmering in the afternoon sun, and beyond it the Inveraray hills.

Hot, sunny, still. He was here. Her bush boy. Her brave bush boy with the floppy hat. She sensed him in the stillness.

The dull ache in her chest turned into pain, as if a hand was squeezing her heart. It did that sometimes, held her heart so tight that it hurt. Then it would loosen its grip a little and she'd breathe again and go on.

A large bird was sitting on the top of the smokestack, russet chest puffed out, the eyes big and brown, watching her. A rock kestrel, on her nest.

"Hello," Susan said quietly.

Were the others here? The other soldiers who'd died here that day, apart from Colin. Five of them, in Fireforce. She sensed they were all here.

And Croggan, was he here? No, he couldn't be. He'd be in

northern France, if he was anywhere at all. He'd never come back. Poor old Croggan. One of a stream of Cornish miners who'd sailed for Africa in the 1880s and joined the Witwatersrand goldrush. He'd done moderately well, but then the Boer War had got in the way and he'd bought a prospecting pick and a book on minerals and headed north across the Limpopo. She knew all this because in a glass cabinet up in the mine office there was a display of the minerals found around Isakata, and alongside the display was Croggan's book. *Rudimentary Treatise on Mineralogy; for the Use of Beginners*. More than a hundred years old, with colour plates and dog-eared pages.

As things turned out, Croggan hadn't needed his book on minerals. After four years of prospecting and several bouts of malaria he'd come upon lumps of black crystal on the ground and knew at once what he'd found.

"Ma! Ma!"

"I'm here, Colin. What is it? What on earth's the matter?"

"It's Billy, ma! Look what he's gone and done now!"

The cassiterite episode. When the boys were younger – Colin would have been about 13 – Reg had carried out a little experiment with them in the garden, to show them what happened when you heated cassiterite. That's what Croggan had found. Cassiterite. Billy had asked about the smokestack at Croggan's Place, what it had been for, and Reg got Moleiro to knock up a little charcoal forge, brought it home with some lumps of cassiterite, and put it on a metal table on the lawn. Was that a terribly good idea? Susan had asked. The boys put the charcoal on the forge and the cassiterite in the charcoal. Reg lit the charcoal and the boys took turns to operate the blower. Susan watched from the verandah for a few minutes, and then went inside. Ten minutes later there was Colin, limping into the kitchen with a badly burned foot. Bright red, with flecks of black, and she saw that the blistering had already started.

"Ow! *Eina!*" he cried as she touched it.

Reg came in and said it was nobody's fault. An accident. A piece of charcoal had fallen onto the table, then rolled off it onto

Colin's foot.

"It wasn't an accident – it was Billy! He bumped the table on purpose! I saw!"

After Susan had washed and dressed Colin's burn and settled him onto the sofa, propped up with cushions, Billy came in. "Come and see, ma! Come and see what I made," he said, taking no notice of his brother lying on the sofa. She'd gone out. On the table next to the forge were pieces of white metal. Tin.

When Croggan had found the cassiterite, he'd hurriedly pitched camp and pegged five blocks before word could get out. Each block had several claims. The most promising one he registered as 'Croggan's Place'. He bought a five-stamp mill and a steam engine, built a pump house to house the steam engine and a smokestack to house the boiler. Reg said he must have produced enough tin to keep going, but would always have had water problems, with the Inveraray river often being little more than a trickle in a sandy bed. Then the tin price dropped and Croggan would have been in a quandary as to what to do next. Soon, though, his mind was made up for him. The world went to war and so did he. He joined up in 1915 and was sent to France and didn't come back. After the war, a few people remembered Croggan's Place and came out here to look around and that's when, nearby, they found chromite, an altogether more promising proposition.

Susan heard the sound of an engine and turned. A Land Rover was coming down the track. It pulled up next to her car. Reg got out and walked towards her.

There was a gentle flapping and she saw the kestrel fly up from the smokestack, quiver in mid-air for a moment, her wide wings outstretched, and then swoop upwards and away until she was just a speck in the endless blue.

"I thought you weren't home till... How...? Reg, how did you know I was here?"

He sat down on the wall next to her, dislodging a few stones. "Philemon."

"Philemon? I didn't tell Philemon I was coming here."

"He knows when you come here. He said you always take Colin's photograph. When he was cleaning the bedrooms this afternoon he noticed it had gone."

"Oh."

"He said you've been here a few times."

Servants. There was always this uncomfortable feeling that they knew a lot more about you than they let on. Pretended not to listen, not to notice things.

"Have you?"

"Yes," she said.

"Many?"

"Four? Five? I don't know."

He didn't look at her. He hadn't looked at her since he'd sat down. They both sat there, gazing out, and after a moment he said, "It's not safe, Susan, being here on your own. I know it's not far from Isakata, but it's in the Reserve and you shouldn't be here alone."

She knew that.

"Have you been here? Since?" she asked.

"Yes," he said. "Briefly. Just after. Didn't tell you. Didn't think you were up to it."

Susan looked towards a huddle of kopjes in the distance, near the Inveraray hills. "Do you think, in those kopjes, that's where he was that night? The night before?"

"Yes."

"So the African villages must be there somewhere. Where the terrs were. The ones Colin was watching. With his unit."

The sun was beginning to dip behind the trees and shadows played across the clearing. The kestrel came back and stood on her nest on the smokestack, looking out, something dangling from her beak. Perhaps she'd been here that dawn, when Colin moved down from the kopje and came here, to Croggan's. She'd have flown off hurriedly when the helicopters arrived and all hell broke loose, but perhaps at the end of that day she'd come back again, when it was quieter and the helicopters had gone. After they'd taken Colin away.

"Was she here, do you think? That day?"

"Who?"

Susan pointed up at the kestrel.

Reg put his hand on her knee. "Susan…"

His touch took her over the brink and she crumpled and wept in a way she hadn't done since that Friday before last Christmas when he'd come home in the late afternoon with someone from Scouts HQ, Major someone or other, and told her that Colin was dead. Killed in action.

She felt Reg's arm around her shoulders. An unfamiliar feeling. They sat there, together, until her sobs subsided.

Then he said something about coping with Colin.

"Don't tell *me* about coping with Colin! I *am* coping. Or trying to, on the outside. Coming out here, it's part of my coping. To be with him…"

Susan felt the hand squeezing her heart and the tears coming back and she stopped for a moment. Then she wiped her cheeks and sat up and shook her shoulders, shook Reg's arm off them.

"What I can't cope with is Billy. He pointed his gun…"

"I know. Thelma told me what happened."

"Why is it taking so long? I'm running out of strength, handling him. You're stronger. You can't give me Colin back, but you can spend more time on Billy, with him. Find out why he's behaving the way he is. Get to the bottom of it."

Reg stood up.

"We must be getting back home," he said. "Before the sun goes down."

7

Isakata mine; mid-November 1979

Susan was listening to the American Senator. He had a loud voice and a bullish air and the shirt he wore was far too bright. He stood out, as he intended to, no doubt. He was one of four Americans staying at the guest house. Fact-finding.

The Senator was saying, "Give 'em hell! That's what you should do. Go get 'em and give 'em hell!"

He was talking about what everyone was talking about. The massive airborne raids a few days earlier on terrorist camps in Zambia. Today, on the lunchtime news, they'd played a recording from the cockpit of a bomber in one of the raids. Susan and Reg had listened to it, everyone had. They heard the pilot telling Lusaka Airport Tower to keep all their aircraft on the ground, just for half an hour, thank you very much, we've a job to do, we won't be long. And then other voices in the cockpit. "Jeez man, check out those ******* bombs raining down there! ******* incredible! Christ, look at them scattering like ******* ants everywhere! Did you see how they ran straight into the ******* bombs? Ah, man, just ******* beautiful!"

Lots of bleeping out, of course. You couldn't broadcast expletives.

"Serve them right."

Reg had glanced up at her, then looked away, said nothing. Too bad. She meant it. Serve them bloody well right. Too bad if he thought that was going too far. He probably thought, now, that she hated them.

Did she? She didn't think so. She'd never really **liked** them, as a people, he knew that. She'd said so often enough. She'd never got used to their neediness. She'd never understood them, what made them tick, and sometimes she found their blackness... well, threatening. But she'd always done what she thought was right by them. Dressed their wounds and vaccinated them and helped them plan their families. Wrapped presents for their children at Christmas time. Taught cookboys how to cook and gardenboys how to garden and fed them and their families and instilled into them the rudiments of cleanliness. She tolerated them, she put up with them, even when they drove her up the wall, but she didn't think she hated them.

Lord knows, she had reason enough to hate them. For starting this damn Bush War. For their ingratitude. Their brutality. For what they'd done to Colin, the mess they'd left Billy in. For ruining *everything.*

That afternoon, Susan had put the question to Billy.

"Do you hate them?"

They were by the pool. Billy had gone there after lunch. Susan went down a little later and sat on the sun-lounger. For a while neither of them said anything. Billy was lying face-down on a towel at the pool's edge, one hand dangling in the water.

There'd been a change in him this past fortnight, since the gun incident on the verandah. He was calmer. Too calm? And he wasn't going out of his way to avoid them, there was more conversation. Usually, if she joined him anywhere, at the pool, on the verandah, he'd just get up and go. Go to his room, go out. But this past week it hadn't been like that.

"Who, ma?"

"The terrs."

He traced circles in the water. Then he took his hand from the pool and turned over and lay on his back, hands resting on his chest, eyes closed against the sun.

"No, ma."

"Really?"

"Why should I? They're guys fighting a war, like me. A shit war that shouldn't have happened. And they're having a shit time, like me, like everyone out there. Jeez, I hope those talks in London work, put an end to it all."

"But they're not fighting the war like you, Billy. That's the point. They're mowing down missionaries in cold blood. They're mutilating their own people, killing babies, beating up old men and women, cutting their lips off. You've seen some of that, out there. Don't you hate them for all that?"

Billy opened his eyes, looked at the sky. "We're no better. I know you won't believe that. But we're not. You just hear about all the stuff *they* do. You don't hear about the stuff *we* do."

She reached over for her packet of cigarettes, pulled one out and lit it.

"It can't be as bad as..."

"Bloody hell, ma! Leave it, huh?"

He closed his eyes again. He lay there and said nothing. She saw that his hands were shaking. After a few minutes, he got up and picked up his towel and slung it over his shoulder and went inside the house, to his room. Susan worried, after that, that she had re-awakened the demons, upset him, sent everything crashing back to square one. She worried that he might not come down to the party at the Club this evening, but when she asked later if he was coming, he nodded and she felt relieved.

She could see him now, as she stood on the lawn with the DC, the Prinsloos, a few others, listening to the Senator. He was up on the Club terrace, with some of the other young ones from the village, the farms. He seemed to be engaged in conversation. Reg was inside somewhere, organising something or other. It was 9 November and each year at this time there was a party at the Club to celebrate the day the country had declared Independence. Usually, the party was held on the day itself, 11 November, but this year that day fell on a Sunday, so the consensus had been to hold it this evening.

No coincidence, of course, the choice of 11 November. The declaration of Independence on that day in 1965 had been made during those two minutes when, annually, the mother country fell silent in remembrance of the dead of two World Wars. A neat touch, Susan thought. To remind London of the sacrifices that the people *here* had made in those wars.

Isakata's Independence party was usually quite a big affair. People came from the Government station and from the farms. In the village, some people asked if they *should* have a party this year? There wasn't a lot to be cheerful about. The war getting worse, the talks looking shaky. Again. But others said that would look like defeatism, so the party had gone ahead and was now in full swing. The music from the hall was loud and the chatter of the people on the lawn flowed over and around her. A waiter came with a canapé tray and Susan took a vol-au-vent and directed the waiter towards the Senator, who took one and then another.

As he put them in his mouth he said, again, "Just give 'em hell!"

The DC said he didn't think that was the right way to go about things. Bombing people who had little in the way of reliable anti-aircraft guns. Just a few rusty Russian ones, decades old, in those camps, apparently. Sitting ducks. And why bomb now, with the Lancaster House talks going on?

But Willem Prinsloo backed the Senator. "It is the best time of all! We have to show them there is still plenty of fight left in us! If we show weakness, like we seem to be doing now in London, what do the terrs go and do?"

"Fire missiles at a few more planes, murder a few more missionaries."

Susan flicked her cigarette ash onto the lawn as she spoke.

"Exactly, ma'am," said the Senator.

That was the other topic of the moment, the attack on that Catholic mission up near the Zambezi. The toll had risen. Three dead priests, four dead nuns, all European. Seven people on whom, said the *Gazette*, the killers had expended hundreds of bullets from Russian-made sub-machine guns.

"They ask for trouble, some of these missionaries," Susan said, "but they don't ask to be murdered in cold blood. It's barbaric. And shows once and for all – not that we need any more proof – that what's happened north of the Zambezi will happen here. Unless we stop them. It'll be the same old pattern. Barbarity, independence, corruption, law and order out the window, bankruptcy. All those countries to the north. Congo, Kenya…"

"…Angola, Tanganyika – or whatever they call it now," added Hentie Prinsloo.

"And now even Zambia," Willem said. "Not that long ago quite a civilised country. Now you call the police because your house has been burgled, and they can't come. Why? Because their bikes have been stolen. Jeez. And Mozambique has run out of food and inflation has hit – what is it, Reg? – thirty percent or something?"

Reg had joined them, saying there'd been a problem with the freezer in the bar, but that it was now sorted. He asked the Senator if he was enjoying the party. The Senator said indeed, sir, and how privileged he was to be here amongst such plucky people doing their darndest to stop the spread of communism, while his own Government, which had spent so much blood and money doing the same thing in Vietnam, not only didn't help, it kept putting goddamn spanners in the works.

"I don't know about stopping communism," Reg said, "but stopping the bombing would help. Giving the peace talks a chance. If we impress London and Washington with our commitment to making them work, commitment to making their outcome work, then there's hope. But no-one's going to be impressed by our continued bombing of the camps."

"You seriously think, sir, that anything you do now will impress London? Washington? Save from handing over the whole goddam place to the gooks?"

The Senator sighed and his belly heaved.

Susan had grown a bit tired of this 'ma'am' and 'sir' business. At first it had seemed rather quaint, but now it struck her as patronising. They were all the same, these people who blew in from England and America and wherever. Arrogant. Whatever side they said they supported they all had this 'We know what's good for you' attitude. A few days in Africa and they thought they knew all about it. None of them had ever actually lived in Africa. It was all *very* galling.

The Senator continued. "Look, you people are on your own. Washington's out. Sees no way you white folk can survive, politically. Too few of you, too many of them. God knows, in the southern States we've tried to make Congress see things differently, but the fact is you're expendable. London? They just want to wash their hands of the whole thing. They'll use the finest soap, they always do, the Brits, but the effect will be the same. Abandonment. Not even Pretoria's on your side now. You're a nuisance. Pretoria wants its so-called détente with all those bankrupt countries to the north that you talk about, ma'am, and you – this country, I mean – you're getting in its way. So you may as well just go get 'em. Bomb those Zambia camps. Knock the hell out of 'em! And the ones in Mozambique while you're at it. Nothing to lose. Not a darn thing."

"Except our humanity," Reg said. "Or what's left of it."

***

They were playing 'Chattanooga Choo Choo' in the hall. Someone asked Susan to dance, she said no, her dancing days were over, but thank you anyway. She watched some people get up from their chairs in the lounge and go into the hall. The older crowd, attracted by '40s big band music after an evening that had mostly been '60s pop. But Thelma Warde stayed. 'In the Mood' drifted out from the hall and after that it was the 'Isle of Capri'.

Susan smiled and looked at Thelma. "Takes you back."

"Doesn't it. Marvellous!"

They listened for a minute, and then Thelma said, "Brandy?"

Susan nodded and Thelma went into the bar and came back with two brandies. She handed one to Susan. "You might need this." She sat down on the edge of her chair, leant forward a little, looked at Susan. "I'm afraid I've some news you won't like terribly much. Dickie had a word with Reg this afternoon. I said I wanted to tell you myself. Now's as good a time as any."

"What about?"

"We're thinking of going."

"Going? Where?"

"Leaving."

"The mine?"

"The country."

Susan stared at her. "You can't! Thelma, you can't!"

She took a swig of her brandy. "Why *now*? Just when things might actually turn the corner? With the talks going on? When tomorrow might actually bring…"

"That's just it, Susan. That's what we've all been saying for fifteen, twenty years now. That things will change. Wait until tomorrow. It'll get better. But it simply never does! Nothing changes. Including the conversation. Same old topic, same old stalemate. These talks aren't going anywhere. It's wishful thinking – the same old wishful thinking – to imagine that they will. It's not going to get better, Susan, tomorrow, or any day after that. And we're not getting any younger, Dickie and I."

"Oh hell, Thelma, I never thought for a moment…"

"I'm so terribly sorry, Susan." Thelma leaned over, touched her arm. "Really sorry. I knew it'd be a blow for you. But I can't hang on any longer. And the shine's worn off it all for Dickie, too. When he goes off on his call-up next weekend, that'll be his last one."

Thelma sipped her brandy, looked out towards the terrace. "It was all so lovely once, wasn't it, in the '50s, '60s. Even when Dickie first came, it still had that magic. But that's all gone. Instead, here we are, with a war rampaging in the rural areas and creeping ever closer to the urban ones. We think it's time to go."

"Where? Back to Blighty?"

"Good God, no!"

Down to the Cape, to a seaside town there, she said. Friends from Kenya had gone there, after Mau Mau, and an old school

116

chum of Dickie's had recently moved down there too, from Zambia. Thelma said it sounded ideal. They'd hand in their notices in December, leave in January.

An image came into Susan's head. A map of the continent of Africa. Pink, a lot of it. Then the pink draining slowly from the top, down down, and then draining from the middle, down down. Until there was just a small band of pink left at the bottom. At the very bottom of the continent. And in the pink band were lots of Europeans, clinging onto the southernmost tip of Africa.

"Don't you think that's rather like going from the frying pan into the fire? Reg says that in South Africa it'll all boil down to exactly the same problem we face here. Numbers. And then it could turn very nasty. Much more so than here."

"No, no, I don't see that at all. Not with the Afrikaners. They've been there for centuries. It's their home, they don't have another one. Unlike us. They're not going to let go of one inch of it, certainly not in our lifetime. And South Africa's hooked up to the rest of the world, financially, in a way we've never been. It matters. We don't. Never did."

There were times, these days, when Susan thought that if it weren't for Billy she'd be very tempted just to pack her bags and go home. She couldn't, of course, not without Reg. And he wasn't going anywhere. She'd have to stay put.

She lit a cigarette and saw Dickie Warde coming through the porch and into the lounge. He came over to them, put a hand on Thelma's shoulder.

"He's fine. I went in with him, made sure he went to bed. A pity, he did seem to be OK up to that point. More chatty than usual."

Thelma looked puzzled.

Susan said, "Who's fine? What point?"

"Billy."

"Why shouldn't he be fine?"

"Because... didn't Reg tell you? Billy wasn't feeling well, so I took him home. He's in bed at home, he's fine now. Reg said he'd tell you."

"What's wrong with him? Was he drunk?"

"No, nothing like that. We were just chatting on the lawn…"

She had to get home. She asked Dickie if he'd take her. He said he didn't think it necessary, but all right, if she really wanted to. Susan said it was necessary, she must go back and see Billy for herself.

She looked at Thelma. "Would you tell Reg I've gone home?"

Thelma patted her on the arm, said she was quite sure Billy would be fine in the morning, but yes of course, if Susan insisted. She picked up her glass and strode out to the terrace.

In the hall it had gone quiet and someone started playing a guitar. A few people began singing. More joined in and their words drifted through into the lounge. It was one of those songs they always sung on this occasion.

We will never die
We'll keep them north of the Zambezi
Till that river's running dry

Dickie leant down, took her elbow and helped her up. Susan was glad of that. She was feeling a little woozy.

… fight through thick and thin
And this mighty land will prosper
We will never die

They went through the porch and out to the car park. The moon was high in the sky and bright. Beneath it, Nyamhanza, hunched there, a dark brooding mass.

In the car, Susan said, "You're leaving."

"Ah, Thelma's told you."

"I'm rather shocked, Dickie."

"Yes, we thought you would be, but…"

"I didn't have you two down for joining the chicken run."

"Susan…"

"Sorry, sorry. Out of order. It's your choice. Completely out of order. Billy. What happened? I don't understand. What's wrong with him?"

There was a dead animal in the headlights, on the road, and

118

Dickie drove around it. A duiker.

"I think it'd be better if I got you home and you had a good sleep. Sort it out in the morning."

"No. I might have had one or two, but I can understand perfectly well. I want to know what happened before I see Billy. In case he's still up."

"I'm not really clear what happened, Susan. We were out on the lawn. Me, one of the policemen, a couple of the Americans. And later Billy joined us. One of the Americans is a reporter. He was asking me about call-ups with a Coloured regiment."

Dickie turned into their driveway and pulled up at the gates. He got out of the car and she heard him talking to the guard and the sound of the gates clanking open. Then he got back into the car and drove towards the house.

"Anyway, yes, the Coloureds... the friendly fire problem came up, as it always does when you talk about the Coloured soldiers. The Americans talked about Vietnam and the friendly fire problem there. Billy had joined us by then and I noticed he started shaking, that he wasn't looking too good. He said he felt sick and headed up the steps."

"Sick? Did he vomit?"

Dickie drew up in front of the house and switched off the engine.

"When we got to the lavatory he did. I followed him there. He wasn't drunk. Breath didn't smell at all. But he didn't look good, so I said I'd take him home. He didn't argue. I brought him back, went with him into his room, made sure he went to bed. He was fine when I left. Calm."

"I still don't understand," she said.

"It'll take time, Susan. He's got a lot to work through. It must hurt like hell, being there when his brother was shot. That's a helluva lot to handle."

"He wasn't there."

"Oh? I thought I heard that he..."

"He was there when Colin died, in the helicopter. Not when

Colin was shot. He wasn't there when Colin was shot. He came after that, saw Colin on the ground. He was with him when they put him in the helicopter."

She had a clear image of it all, in her head. That place. Her sons. The helicopter. Taking off. Her sons in it, together.

"Colin didn't make it to the hospital. He died in the helicopter. The report said that. I didn't read the report. Or talk to HQ. I couldn't. But Reg did. And he said they told him that Colin died just after they put him into the helicopter."

She turned to Dickie.

"I sometimes wonder if that's at the heart of it, of why Billy's behaving the way he is. He's still not said anything, you know. About that day. Nothing. But maybe that's what it's all about. His not being there in time to *stop* the shooting. Not being there in time to save Colin."

***

Susan sat on the end of Billy's bed, watched him turning this way, that way, mumbling, whispering. She wanted to lean forward, wake him, hold him as she used to do, stop his nightmare, tell him everything was all right. But she couldn't. She was frightened. He might lash out. She might frighten him. So she sat there waiting for him to calm down.

She'd been woken by shouts of "Stop it!" – "No!" coming from his room and when she'd pushed his door open, he'd shouted "No!" again and then "Holy shit!" She'd gone to his bed and sat there, and after a while the shouting stopped. Now he was mumbling, most of it indistinct, but she could make out some words, phrases.

"… the noise, choppers… Jeez!… fucking screaming… stop it!… holy shit, a baby… red dress … leave her!… can't breathe, can't… Oh shit, no!… no!"

The mumbling stopped, and then the tossing and turning. Soon he lay still, and Susan got up and walked to the door. As she touched the door handle, he called out, "No!… Don't! Je-sus!"

She jumped, turned, stared at him. He was sitting up. She

thought he might be awake, but his eyes were closed. He slumped back. She heard Reg's bedroom door opening and he came into the room. She realised that she was shaking.

She whispered what she'd heard. "Wake him, Reg. I daren't."

Reg nodded and told her to go back to bed, he'd take over from here.

It was well past eight when Susan woke the next morning, and when she asked Philemon why he hadn't brought her the tea tray at seven, he said the Boss had told him not to. And Billy, was he up? Yes, he was with the Boss, on the lawn. She went through to the verandah. They were sitting in the deck chairs beneath the whitethorn tree at the far end of the lawn.

Susan ran a bath and lay there and Billy's words last night swirled about in her head. Was he talking about something he'd seen? If so, what was it – a baby being hurt, a woman being attacked? A woman in a red dress being attacked, and screaming? The noise, choppers – was he talking about a firefight?

They were still sitting on the lawn, Reg and Billy, when she went out to the verandah after she'd bathed and dressed. She lit a cigarette, watched them. A moment or two later, Reg leaned forward and put his head in his hands. Billy stood up. He reached out to his father, put a hand on his shoulder, said something, and walked away towards the driveway. Susan heard the car engine start and watched the car go down the drive. Her car. She got up and walked across the lawn, sat down next to Reg.

"You all right?"

He sat up, nodded slowly, but didn't look at her.

"Did you ask him about what he was saying last night, what it meant?"

He nodded again.

"Well?"

"A rape, Susan. To do with a rape." He paused. "Sadly, all too common in war. When soldiers are angry, or have lost it..."

"Soldiers? You mean terrs."

"I mean soldiers. Our soldiers. Our white soldiers."

"No! Our boys wouldn't do…"

"Our boys would, Susan," he said quietly. "Billy's talking about our boys, our forces. About an African woman being raped." He paused, then added, "And a baby. Killed."

"Christ!"

Reg took a cigarette packet from his pocket, offered her one, lit it for her.

"Did he say what it was that upset him last night? At the Club?" she asked.

"No."

They sat in silence. Then Susan said, "Did he say where he saw it? The rape?" Reg nodded. "Where was it?" Before she'd finished her question, she knew the answer. "Croggan's Place? That day?"

"Yes."

Reg turned, looked at her. "Billy was there, Susan. That's what he's saying. There in the chaos of everything that was happening at Croggan's, Colin being shot, a rape, a baby dying."

"Oh God!"

So Dickie Warde had been right last night, about Billy being there.

"No wonder he's… In the report you read at Scouts HQ, Reg, on Colin's death, was there anything there about rape, a baby being attacked? And you chose not to tell me?"

"Nothing. And Billy's hardly added to it this morning, except to say that it happened. That's all."

"So the HQ report didn't say everything. Didn't tell whole story about what happened that day, exactly…"

In the stillness that followed she began to see Billy's behaviour in a different light. It wasn't because he *hadn't* been there in time to save Colin, but because he *had*, and hadn't be able to stop it, to stop them killing him.

"If they're covering things up, at HQ, I think we ought to find out. How are we meant to get Billy through this if we don't know what really happened. And besides, we've a right to know the truth."

Reg said nothing.

"Where has he gone?" Susan asked.

"Didn't say. Except that he'll be back for supper. Made me promise we'd not talk about any of this when he's back. All right? You won't, will you?"

That wouldn't be easy. But she nodded. Reg stood up.

"Must get to the office. They'll be wondering where I've got to."

Sitting there, after Reg had gone, Susan felt dirty. Dirty from this dirty war that had just got dirtier. Some tears came, and she dabbed her eyes with a tissue and lit another cigarette and tried to rid her head of images she didn't want to see.

It was late morning before she felt calm enough to phone Dickie Warde to say everything was fine and thanks for helping with Billy last night, driving her home. And to wish him luck. He was going off on his six-week call-up tomorrow. Then she put on her gardening gloves and went to her rose garden, for the scent of it, the solace. It helped. It quelled the noises in her head, diluted some of the images there, but one image would not go away. The rape. She moved among the rose bushes and cut some red roses for the vase on the mantelpiece and thought about Billy, seeing his brother shot, a baby killed, a white soldier raping... Oh God, the poor boy! Later, as she arranged the roses in the vase, another thought came into her head. Was there a child from the rape?

When Reg came home that evening, Susan waited until he was settled in his chair on the verandah, and Philemon had brought him a lager, before she asked, "Beth Lytton, has she told you anything much about that baby there, about his mother?"

"No. Why are you asking?"

"Because..."

"You'd know more than me, anyway, after your ill-advised visit there last month. Don't know what you were thinking of."

"It's my job. There was no record of a vaccination. Anyway, I'm asking because I've been doing some sums. He's a prem baby. Born at seven and a half months, Beth told me. That makes the conception date last December. Late last December."

Reg looked at her.

"So the mother could be a local woman, who got caught up in what was going on at Croggan's that day, knew St Anselm, went there when her labour started, left the baby there – because it was Coloured? – then scarpered."

After a moment, Reg said, "Who knows? Perhaps. Anyway, not your concern, or mine… Ah, that'll be Billy."

A car was coming down the drive. Her car. Billy came onto the verandah, greeted them, went to the kitchen and she heard him talking to Philemon. He came back with a lager and sat down. He was looking composed.

"All right, then, son?"

Yes, Billy said, everything was all right. And he was sorry about last night, about all the trouble he'd been these past months, but he'd been doing a lot of thinking and was clear now about what to do, where to go.

"Where to go? What do you mean, son?"

"I need to get away from all this, pa, ma. Go somewhere else to deal with stuff. I won't get better till I do."

Billy told them that he'd got his discharge last month – didn't tell them at the time, didn't want a fuss – but hadn't been sure what to do next. Now he was. He wanted to leave the country, go to the UK, stay there. At least until he felt well again.

Susan wasn't expecting this. Her chest tightened and she bit her lip. She didn't know what to say except, quietly, "Oh God."

At supper, when it became clear that Billy had made up his mind to leave, that there seemed no way of changing it, Susan said she'd go with him to London, help him settle in, stay for a month or two. But he said no. Emphatically. "Let me go, ma."

The conversation turned to his finances, his medication, the possibility of staying with Susan's brother in London, at least initially. He was measured and calm, and so was Reg.

"When do you think you'll go, son?" Reg asked.

Susan reached out, touched Billy's arm. "You'll stay for Christmas? At least?"

Billy shook his head. "No, ma. I think the sooner I can get a flight, the better."

When Susan rang the bell for Philemon to come in and clear the table, Billy said he'd turn in now, if that was OK.

She watched him leave the room, heard him close his bedroom door and looked at Reg.

"I'm beginning to feel that I have very little left," she said quietly.

8

Chizonya II camp; late November, 1979

All across the camp the comrades were cleaning, sweeping, washing, tidying. In the safety pits around the camp they were scrubbing the breather drums, stacking the water containers, arranging the food boxes brought by the white trucks, the ammunition boxes brought by the grey Frelimo trucks. That was how it had been all day. Tidying, preparing, organising. News had come yesterday that important comrades from Maputo, from the Party's High Command, would be visiting Chizonya II tomorrow to tell them about the peace talks in London.

Then, late in the afternoon, there was more news. To celebrate the visit, the food tomorrow would be from the boxes brought by the white trucks. Nyanye heard the news from a kitchen worker she met as she walked from the hospital to her *posto*.

"If only today could be tomorrow!" she exclaimed.

He smiled. "It is to show the visitors that we are eating well, comrade."

She did not care about the reason. For two weeks now it had been just one meal a day. Always the same thing. Dried mealie pips, boiled. With all the newcomers arriving now – every day many hundreds were coming to the camp, mostly refugees – there was not enough food for more than one meal a day. But tomorrow, ah! Her pace quickened and when she got to the *postos* there were many comrades who had gathered there, talking excitedly about the news of the food.

She saw Siya there, standing near Kundiso's *posto*. He was not looking her way. He would come sometimes to Chizonya II and she would see them, him and Kundiso, talking, talking. He was now an instructor at the education centre at Chizonya III. Kundiso went to Chizonya III a lot these days. It was for political orientation, preparing for when 2.1 Battalion went over the border, next week. She attended some of Siya's classes. She said that he had been a spy in the settler forces and that he was teaching combatants about the settlers' propaganda so that they could teach the masses about it, tell the masses not to be deceived by it.

'Siya', it meant 'leave'. It was a popular *chimurenga* name. It was saying to the settlers, 'Leave!', but Nyanye wished he was the one who would leave. Something about him was not right and she feared for her sister.

Nyanye went into her *posto*. She had been given the job of making sure it was ready for inspection tomorrow by the visitors. By the time the sun was going down the job was done. She poured some water from a metal jug into her cupped hand and washed her face, her arms, her feet, and then sat on her bed to rest a little.

At the hospital these days from morning to night there was no break. Malaria and dysentery were everywhere. More comrades were dying from these sicknesses now than from the bullets and the bombs and the *zvimbambaira*.

And the newcomers had brought another new sickness. The one before, that looked like a new type of malaria, had stopped because the comrades going over the border knew, now, not to get jeans from stores in the Reserves – the settlers had been putting poisoned jeans in those stores. With this new sickness, a doctor noticed that many newcomers had followed the same trail through the eastern mountains to get to Mozambique, and he told Comrade Nikita. Messages were sent to comrades in that sector to check what could be happening and soon an answer had come back. All along that trail the settlers had poisoned the wells.

They also brought fear, the newcomers. Comrade Nikita was

warning that there could be many sell-outs hiding among them.

"Be vigilant!" he said. "Find them! The big bombing in Zambia, some of it was because of sell-outs in those camps! Tell us about the comrades who are false comrades, counter-revolutionaries!"

The news on VOF of thousands of comrades killed in Zambia by the settlers' bombs had made everyone fearful again of planes in the sky and many were sleeping in their uniforms now in case they had to flee in the night.

Nyanye wiped her hand across her forehead. She was tired. Tired from work, from fear, from hunger. But the thought of the food tomorrow had lifted her spirits and taken some of her tiredness away. She got up and set off for the sports field.

Kundiso was there already and had built a small fire at the edge of the field. Many fires burned across the field, groups of comrades around them, talking. Tamuka came, bringing some *mufuna* fruits he had gathered from the woodland to share with them. They exchanged news about the day and took turns to guess what the meals tomorrow might be. Sadza, for sure! Nyanye could almost taste it, and said her greatest wish was for kapenta. The white moon came out and Kundiso took her mbira from her pocket and began playing it.

Through the notes of the mbira, Nyanye slowly became aware that the hum of conversations across the field was changing into louder voices. Then there was stirring, comrades getting up, walking about. Nyanye saw a figure coming to the place where they were sitting. When he was near, she saw that it was Siya.

She said, "He is coming, my sister. Your friend, he is coming."

He was sweating. Usually, he was controlled. Too controlled. It was one of the things about him that Nyanye did not trust. But this night he was talking very fast and in the firelight she saw that the sweat was running down in those deep lines on his cheeks.

"The comrades from the High Command, they will not be visiting," he said. He seemed very agitated. "They have just cancelled the visit."

Nyanye's heart sank. If what he was saying was true, the sadza drums would stay empty tomorrow and the food boxes would stay closed and there would be only dried mealie pips again.

"Come," she said to Tamuka, "we will go to Chitepo Block to see if this is true."

As they walked, she felt the pains coming back in her empty stomach and in her swollen legs, and her cracked lips felt sore again. She told Tamuka that the pains were worse than before. Tamuka said hunger was gnawing heavily at him too and he was tempted to undertake *chirenje* if what Siya said was true.

"*Aiwa*, my friend," Nyanye whispered. "It is foolish even to think about it."

When she first came to Chizonya II, *chirenje* was not a bad word. It was about bartering with villagers living nearby, going to their huts with items from the white trucks – clothes, shoes, blankets – and getting food in exchange and bringing it back to the kitchen, for the whole camp. But with so many more people in the camp, and so much hunger, now some comrades were stealing items and going secretly to the villages to barter for food for themselves, and *chirenje* had become a bad word. Comrade Nikita said it was counter-revolutionary and that if you undertook *chirenje* you would be punished with other counter-revolutionaries. The punishment for counter-revolutionary behaviour happened just before morning parade, in front of everyone. Comrades were stripped to their underwear, their hands and feet were tied, and they were beaten with sticks until their pants were soiled and everyone could see that. If there was no soiling, those who did the beating were themselves beaten. One of the *chirenje* cases Nyanye had tended that morning in the hospital had died. The beating had been too much.

At Chitepo Block a clerk said that there had been a telephone call from Maputo. The caller said that the visitors had flown to Vila Macia, but when they were nearly there the plane had turned back. It had gone back to Maputo.

Another clerk said, "No, I do not think that is right, comrade. I heard that the plane did not leave Maputo in the first place."

Nyanye went to the hospital to find out how the cancellation would change her duties tomorrow, and then she walked back to the sports field. Siya was still there, crouching by her sister, talking. He stood up when she came. She told them what she had learned, and that Tamuka had gone to find his Commander and would bring Kundiso news about tomorrow's changed agenda for 2.1 Battalion. Siya said he must go, there was much to do, he would see them in the morning.

When he had gone, Nyanye sat down by the fire, in the place where she had been before.

"Why is it that he came all the way from Chizonya III to tell you about the visit? We would all have heard soon, it would have spread quickly among the comrades. And the morning? Why did he say he would see you in the morning tomorrow?"

"He is not going back to Chizonya III tonight," Kundiso said. "He is staying here."

"Oh? Where?"

"In the officers' quarters."

Kundiso took a dry twig from the pile next to Nyanye and started drawing a circle in the soil. "You have many questions, my sister."

"Yes," Nyanye said. She looked at the circle. "And there are more."

"I know."

More about that day when their village burned down and they could not see their mother and the settler forces killed their cousin Shungu. There were many things Nyanye still did not know about what happened that day, in those hours when she was unconscious – from seeing the *skuz'apo* there by the *chimini* at Croggan's and a gun coming down on her head, to waking up later in the long grass – because Kundiso had still not spoken about them.

Kundiso drew a V shape next to the circle. Like a flying bird.

"I *will* answer your questions, my sister," she said. "But another day."

She drew a second circle, inside the first one. And a second V.

130

Like two birds circling. Then, quickly, she swept her fingers back and forth across her soil picture until it was gone, and she dusted her hands on her uniform and picked up her mbira.

She began singing a song everyone knew well. *Wakazvinzwa Here?* 'Have You Heard?' It was not a song Nyanye wanted to hear. It was about death.

After Kundiso had sung the chorus, she stopped.

"Sing with me, my sister?"

They liked you to sing in Chizonya II, it was encouraged. At parade, doing duties, when you were running, when you relaxed. It was good for the Struggle, they said. And Nyanye could see that, it could be uplifting, it could take away the sadness.

But not this song, with death crawling through it. Death crawled everywhere now, over everything, into every place. Death filled her days. Death was winning this war.

"*Aiwa,* I cannot," Nyanye said. "I am hungry and tired and I do not want to sing about death."

"Now is a *good* time to sing this song, my sister. When the suffering seems greatest. It will help us bear that suffering. It will remind us we are fighting to end suffering, that if we are steadfast there will be victory. We have suffered much, you, me, our comrades, the masses. I have risked much. I fight with the *vakomana.* I go to bases. I shoot with AKs. I set traps. I sabotage bridges. I throw grenades. I am different now. My head, it is liberated by what I have done, by the things I have learned. But our land, we still have to liberate that. The gun will lead us there. And the song. The gun and the song."

A group of comrades had moved closer to them, attracted by the music. Nyanye saw that Tamuka was there too. She had not noticed that he had come back.

When Kundiso finished talking, they said, "*Pamberi ne chimurenga!*" One of them added, "Down with all *vabhunu!*"

Another comrade, a tall one, said, "There at home in the Reserves and here in Chizonya II, we are all making great sacrifices for freedom. It is never given on a silver platter."

"For sure, my friend," Kundiso said. "But the end is coming, no more Struggle, no more colonialism. Freedom is coming. Tomorrow."

The tall one said, *"Ehe,* you are right. Comrade, it is late, but it would help us with the dangers we face and with our empty stomachs if you would sing that song once more. To remind us what we are fighting for."

Kundiso smiled and took up her mbira and sang the chorus again.

Wakazvinzwa here kuti mvura haichanaya?
Have you heard that the rain no longer falls?
Wakazvinzwa here kuti amai vakashaya?
Have you heard that mother is dead?
Wakazvinzwa here kuti mombe dzakaenda?
Have you heard that the cattle went away?
Wakazvinzwa here kuti baba vakashaya?
Have you heard that father is dead?
Wakazvinzwa here kuti minda yakapera?
Have you heard that the fields have gone?
Wakazvinzwa here kuti bhudi vakashaya?
Have you heard that brother is dead?
Ahhh, vanoona pfumvu vari paruzevha!
Ahhh, they are suffering in the Reserves!

There was silence.

Then someone said, *"Tinotenda,* comrade." And everyone clapped softly and they drifted off into the night.

When they had gone Tamuka said that, with the cancelled visit, it had been decided that the duties for 2.1 Battalion tomorrow would be the same as they had been yesterday. And parade would be at 7 o'clock. The normal time. Tomorrow would be a normal day.

***

Someone shook a branch of the big mango tree and rainwater cascaded down onto the comrades beneath it. They danced about,

132

laughing, soaked, mimicking outrage, and their laughter rippled back along the queue. Nyanye caught it and turned to watch it flow down the line behind her, reaching comrades who could not know the reason for it, but joined in nevertheless.

Everyone was in good spirits today. At dawn, word had gone around that even with no visitors coming there would be two meals today, morning and evening. Nyanye was queueing now with the non-combatants for the first meal. In an hour, after parade, the combatants would queue. There would be no delay today with messages from Comrade Nikita because he was not in the camp. After the telephone call from Maputo about the visitors not coming, some problems had started with the radios, and then the telephones had stopped working, and Comrade Nikita had gone before dawn with another Commander to Vila Macia, to get through to Maputo.

The queue went from the kitchen past the mango tree and on up the slope to the parade ground. Halfway up the slope it turned west and on it went alongside the parade ground, then along the track that led to the hospital. You could not see the end of it. Many hundreds were waiting with their tin plates, tin mugs. Woodsmoke drifted over them.

It had rained heavily in the night and the river had risen, it was running fast now. Rain drops fell from leaves and branches and from the edges of roofs on buildings and huts all across Chizonya II. Near the mango tree some children were jumping in the puddles and their mothers smiled, watching them. They had come with Yeukai from Kusuwa, and Nyanye saw that all the women carried big pots. Yeukai was making sure that Kusuwa was not forgotten!

Nyanye stood on the slope where the queue turned west. The ground beneath her vibrated with the step of the marching combatants, parade had just started. Nearly three thousand there, drawn up in two columns on the parade ground.

The queue began to move. Nyanye could smell the sadza now. It warmed her heart, the smell of sadza and woodsmoke, mixed. There was no smell so good as that one. She gripped her plate and some comrades behind her clapped. Kundiso would have cheered, clapped, if she had been here, or danced, but she was not, she was marching on the parade ground. News came from the front of the queue that in the kitchen there were drums of okra relish, and chicken, and all down the line the women took to ululating.

Nyanye heard the sound of vehicles coming and looked east towards the sun, towards the entrance gate. The sun was still low, just above the trees, but bright. She held her hand up against the glare. Trucks? They came nearer and soon she saw that, yes, they were trucks, grey Frelimo trucks. There seemed to be many.

Others had spotted them and someone near Nyanye said, "Do they not know there are no visitors coming from Maputo today?"

Maybe it was a weapons delivery. Nyanye watched the trucks coming towards the gate. When the first one came through it, slowly, everyone in the queue turned to look because there was shouting coming from it. A second truck came through, then a third, and against the low bright sun Nyanye saw the silhouettes of the Frelimo soldiers in the backs of them. Dancing, waving AKs in the air.

Nyanye saw comrades coming from Chitepo Block, one was walking fast, he had a yellow T-shirt on.

The first truck drove up onto the parade ground, into the gap between the two columns. The combatants broke rank, moved back, as the truck inched through. The second truck came after the first one. You could hear now what the soldiers were shouting.

"Viva Frelimo!"

"Freedom! *Rusununguko!*"

"Victory is here!"

On the edge of the parade ground the man in the yellow T-shirt was walking one way, then the other. It was Siya. He stopped pacing and she looked where he looked and she saw Kundiso. The first truck carried on moving through the two columns, and the second truck, but Siya was not looking there, his eyes were on Kundiso.

In the third and fourth trucks, the soldiers jumped up and

down and waved. They were laughing, holding their AKs high.

"The *vabhunu* have surrendered!"

You could not mistake their excitement.

More trucks came, and now the combatants were surging towards the trucks from every side crying "Viva Frelimo! *Rusununguko!*" and those who were already near the trucks pressed closer and reached up to shake the soldiers' hands, calling out, laughing.

The food queue broke and everyone ran onto the parade ground, rejoicing, ululating, banging their tin mugs against their tin plates, and from every corner of the camp Nyanye saw people streaming towards the trucks. Her heart was pumping! It was finished, this war! Ah, if she could be with Kundiso now, how they would hold each other and shout with joy! She moved up to the top of the slope, but she could not see her sister. She would find her through Siya, she could still just see his yellow T-shirt.

She saw some men running from the entrance gate, four men, running towards the parade ground. They were shouting, but you could not hear their words above the noise of the swirling multitude as everyone tried to get close to the trucks to hear more news.

The first truck had reached the west end of the parade ground and stopped, the other trucks behind it, in a line. Nine trucks down the middle of the parade ground, all around them cheering shouting comrades, children climbing onto the trucks, women ululating, everyone overjoyed about the news that the soldiers had brought.

There was a shout, *"Nzeve! Nzeve!"*

It came from the men running from the gate. A woman next to Nyanye said, "What is this they are shouting about ears?"

Behind the men, Nyanye saw more trucks drawing up at the gate. She turned to look for Siya on the parade ground, but could not see him.

The men were near. You could hear their words now.

"Vabhunu! In the trucks!"

People around her grew quiet.

"Some are *vabhunu! Vakapenda dema!*"

Painted black.

Across the ground, the camp, a sudden silence.

Someone somewhere blew a whistle.

Nyanye thought she heard a cry, "Kundiso!" She thought she saw Siya running into the crowd, a flash of yellow. She thought she saw that, behind the ears of a soldier in the nearest truck, the skin was white.

She heard, "Fire!"

And the soldiers in the backs of the nine trucks with their weapons on automatic began emptying their magazines into the surrounding throng of people, wide-eyed, open-mouthed, aghast.

Nyanye started running. Everyone was running.

Nyanye was running bent down past people falling, over people already fallen. She felt wetness on her face, someone's blood, splashes from a head splitting in front of her. She was running through smoke-filled dust-laden air sliced by screams and the crack-crack-crack of gunshot. She was drowning in the noise of the gunfire rattling out from the trucks, spitting out from the machine guns and the rifles and the cannons. Drowning in the noise of explosions and screaming. Her eardrums hurt and she was crying and the tears blurred her sight.

The gunfire went on and on, the bullets cascaded down. There was no let-up. She was running to get to the river, running with others who were running to the river, screaming.

Then it was as if she was running through silence. Running slowly through silent flashes of light, in front of her a great invisible scythe swinging silently this way and that, cutting people down like stalks in a mealie field and each stalk falling, one after the other. Wave after wave of stalks falling.

She stumbled and the noise came back, louder than before. Gunfire thudded through her head, screams sliced the air, and she fell.

She lay there. Her heartbeat pounded in her ears and bullets hissed past her, above her. In a pause in the gunfire she heard screams coming from the river, screams for help – *"Batsirai! Batsirai!"* – and she remembered that the river was running fast today. The guns started again.

The smell of burnt earth and bad eggs, that smell from gunfire, it was getting into her nose, into her mouth. She raised her head. Bodies. Lying everywhere, bodies. Still, twisted, heaped, some crawling. Near the base of a torn tree trunk, a heap of bodies. The tree trunk. She knew this place. Every day, on the path from the *postos* to the hospital, she passed this tree near the safety pits. There was a hollow on one side of it.

A body was there on the edge of the hollow, a fallen branch on it, a leg ripped and blood flowing like water from a broken pipe. She moved on her belly to the hollow, into it, into the blood from the body. She pressed her hands in the blood, rubbed it on her hair, face, neck, arms, rolled one way then the other for the blood to get onto her clothes. She put her head on the edge of the hollow and pulled the body so that it covered her head, her shoulders, and she could lie with her head to one side, on her arm, and breathe and see out from beneath the body.

She lay there, looking out over the carpet of bodies. Some comrades were crawling. She moved her head down slightly. She could see a corner of the hospital, that part where they tended the *zvimbambaira* cases.

The gunfire stopped.

Groans and cries came from all sides. Wailing, howls like the howls of wounded animals, moans, terrible sounds that filled the air and cut into her heart. Sounds of deep pain and slow dying.

There were calls for help, calls for Jesus, for rescue. Pleas for water.

"Batsirai…! Jesu, chengetedza ini…! Mvura…!"

Nearby someone was praying. *"Baba vedu…"*

Nyanye felt the sun's rays on the arm that was not beneath her, it was hot. She lay still, she felt numb. The cries of the wounded washed over her and she felt darkness swimming through her head.

137

Shots woke her. Then voices, near enough for her to hear the words. It was soldiers talking. *Vabhunu* soldiers.

"....shit, like fucking skittles!"

She could see their boots. Between the bodies, on them. Kicking them.

"Still alive?"

"Yah."

Shots.

The soldiers were moving among the dead and the injured, finishing their terrible business. She wanted to cover her ears, but she could do nothing.

"Another one here, fucking oxygen-waster."

Shots.

"Christ! When I saw all those fucking gooks... You reckon two thousand?"

"Easy. HQ had reckoned eight hundred, one thousand max, but two fucking thousand! Maybe two and a half!"

"All in one place! Jeez, just there for the slotting... Talk about Christmas coming early!"

"You think many could of gapped it?"

"Some. A third, maybe? But a lot of them'll be running around with oil leaks anyway. Won't last long."

One of them was bending down, white hands taking something from a body. Boots kicking a head. Boots kicking bodies, turning them over.

"Shit, a piccanin."

"Croaked?"

"Yah. But just in case..."

Shots.

Some soldiers were very close. Nyanye could see blood on their boots and smell their cigarettes. She could hear their breathing.

"You know, after a while, in the truck, I stopped firing."

"Yah?"

"It was too fucking easy. I just sat there, watched. Hundreds of eyes, mouths wide open. Fucking terrified. And you know what

138

I thought? I thought, 'This is how people look who die without God.'"

Further away, near the path from the *postos* to the river, she saw soldiers firing at a woodpile. From behind it a figure stood up. She could see the figure and the soldiers, up to their shoulders, not their heads. Logs fell off the pile and there was a shout, "Surrender!" The arms of the figure did not move. "Put your fucking arms up!" Still the arms did not move. Shots. The figure crumpled down behind the woodpile.

Nyanye heard the noise of engines. Two trucks were coming down the slope from the parade ground. Side by side. Moving down, bumping down the slope. Over the bodies on the slope. She closed her eyes and retched. When she looked up again the trucks were near, wheels bumping towards her, then turning, turning towards the hospital, moving out of her sight.

Vabhunu voices, again. They were coming from behind her.

"Landmines till bloody kingdom come... Jeez!"

"Fucking armoury down here!"

"Grenades, AKs, RPGs, mortars... Holy shit! Check all these Tokarevs..."

The safety pits, they must be there. Going through them. Going through the boxes there.

"Sarge, check this. Rice, biscuits, corned beef, jam... hey, even tins of fucking mackerel! From Holland! What are the fucking Dutch people...?"

"Cut it, arsehole! Leave the bloody food. Just weapons, ammo. Come on, move it! The trucks'll be here. Sooner they're loaded, sooner we can get the fuck out of here."

"Sarge."

Nyanye heard trucks coming.

"Sis, man! It's starting to stink round here."

"Yah."

She lay there, listening. Listening to them talking, loading the trucks. Their voices, the truck engines, becoming quieter. The groans, the cries became quieter too. She could hear flies buzzing.

139

She closed her eyes.

She drifted in and out of sleep, it was hot. She heard voices now and again, distant, sometimes nearer. She was sweating, she felt weak, she longed for water, she could not feel her legs. Was there a bullet there? She did not know. She slept.

When Nyanye woke she was choking, smoke everywhere, flames crackling. She smelt burning, heard things falling, collapsing. Wood, grass burning. And flesh. The corner of the hospital that she could see, it was on fire. The soldiers were burning everything. She must not sleep. In the Reserves, when the soldiers burnt the villages it usually meant that their business was done. They went. Maybe these ones, they would go soon now. She blinked and blinked, tried to keep her eyes open. Then a sound came that made her heart beat fast. The sound of the air being whipped. Whip-whip-whip. Helicopters.

Take the soldiers away. Please. *Baba vedu...*

She saw boots coming towards her. They passed her head. One pair of boots. She heard breathing. After a moment the boots came into view again, and stopped.

She saw hands on a zip, zipping up trousers. Black hands. They stopped halfway up. She felt the body on her being moved, and then he was crouching down, staring at her. She stared back. She blinked. You can shoot me. It is enough. Shoot me. Kundiso, Tamuka, they were on the parade ground, they cannot be living now. Shoot me too. It is better. The words did not come out, she could not find her voice, she could not make her lips move. She stared and he stared back.

The noise of the helicopters was getting louder.

Someone shouted, "Hey, get a fucking move on! It's uplift in two!"

The black soldier stared at her. Then slowly he rose. She heard the sound of the zip again and she watched his boots, walking away.

***

Great swarms of green flies moved from one body to the other. Some came into her mouth. The smell of death, of faeces and rotting meat, was making her eyes sting. There were some cries still, and moaning, and she could hear the croaking hiss of vultures – they had come already? – but mostly there was silence. A few people walked among the bodies, stopping sometimes, crouching down. One came close to where she sat, in the hollow. Water bottles were hanging around his neck. She called. It came out as a whisper, but he heard her. He slipped the strap of a bottle over his head and knelt down and gave it to her.

"Slowly, comrade," he said. "Drink slowly."

He stood up and went on, moving among the bodies in this place that was like Hell. Nyanye drank some of the water. She would go to the river for more. The smoke from the gunpowder, it made her so thirsty. She got up to walk, but her legs were shaking and the stinging in her eyes, the dried blood on her eyelashes, they made it difficult to see. She cupped her hand and poured some water into it from the bottle, to bathe her eyes. She tore a strip from her shirt and tied it over her nose and mouth, to keep out the smell, and started picking her way through the bodies. Scorched, bullet-riddled, ripped apart, contorted. Cold now, and stiffening, but there were some that were still warm to the touch. She walked in drying blood and slipped on the shell casings that were everywhere and the broken ones cut into her feet. Somewhere she had lost her takkies. A comrade stared at her with dead eyes and she bent down to take the water bottle lying next to his body.

She came to the woodpile where the soldiers had been shouting. In her head she could hear it still, that shouting. Two children were lying across a fallen log and over them was another body, bloodied. She knew before she turned the body over that it was Yeukai. All the water left in the bottle she poured onto Yeukai's face and wiped the blood from it with her shirt. There were no marks there, on the face, it was still a good face. Later she would come back to bury the body, appease the spirits.

141

She touched Yeukai's eyelids, closed her eyes. *Yeukai*. 'Remember.'

At the river Nyanye went in up to her waist, even though there were bodies there, drifting. She put her head beneath the water, for coolness and to wash the blood away. The river was calm now. The bodies it had tossed out in its rage this morning, when the soldiers came, were scattered on the banks, in the bushes, but there were pools in the sand where the water was clean and she drank from them and filled the water bottles. She sat down, her feet in a pool to soothe them. Seeing the bodies around her, but not seeing them. She was empty. There were no words in her head.

Further downstream other comrades were sitting, standing, walking about. The air was still and hot and there were flies.

"Amai?"

She turned around. A girl was sitting there by a tree stump. She had not noticed her before. Young, eleven, twelve. She had a big hole in her small chest.

"Amai, do you think I will live?"

Nyanye went over to her. She gave her water and tore another piece from her shirt and tied it around the girl's stomach, to keep the intestines in.

"E kosi, sisi," she said. *"E kosi."*

'Of course, sister.'

With the water bottles full again, and heavy around her neck, Nyanye went back through the smouldering woodland, over the pits, up the slope and onto the parade ground. She stumbled, slipped, because there was so little room to walk here between the bodies. She searched everywhere, but she could not find them, Kundiso and Tamuka. Others were walking about on the parade ground, looking, turning bodies over, covering their faces against the foul smell.

Nyanye looked over to the *postos*, and went there. Most of the *postos* were blackened ruins now, collapsed. On the ground among the burnt bodies were things that fire could not destroy. Tin buckets, mugs, bowls. A sewing machine. The old tractor stood nearby, burnt out, blackened like everything else, like the woodland behind it. She picked up a jug, it was one of those for keeping water in the *postos*. She would take it, so that when she found Kundiso she would have enough water for washing her body. There was a bullet hole in the jug, half way up. Half a jug of water was still good.

Someone called softly, "…*sisi*… *sisi*…"

He was sitting by the tractor, leaning against a wheel rim. Nyanye went to him and pulled the cloth down from her nose and mouth and knelt by him.

"Sorry, *sisi*," he was saying. "Sorry, *sisi*… Sorry, *sisi*…" Over and over.

She held a bottle to his lips and he leaned forward a little. She felt his pulse. When he had finished drinking he said again, "Sorry, *sisi*."

He was not wearing the yellow T-shirt, it was tied over his thigh, soaking up the blood, there was no leg there. All over his chest the skin was raw pink, blistered, his shoulders and neck also, and his hair was grey with ash. She saw tears there, in his eyes.

"The visitors, *sisi*… not coming. Turning… back. The telephones, radio… not working. I knew it was trouble, *sisi*. That trouble… was coming. But…"

Nyanye tilted his head back and poured some water on his face and wiped it with her hands, feeling the sharp ridges of the markings that ran down his cheeks.

"Trouble… I thought it was bombing… coming. I did not think… Sorry, *sisi*."

She touched his hand. "It is all right, Siya. Do not talk, it is better. Tell me only about Kundiso, where she is. You know?"

He looked at her.

"Kundiso," she said. "She was with you? She is near?"

He coughed and his head dropped back against the wheel rim and she held the bottle to his lips again. He took a little more water.

"To keep her safe. That is what I wanted... all I wanted... these days."

He paused. His breathing was coming, going. "The river. We were trying..." He closed his eyes. "Sorry for you, *sisi*."

Nyanye waited.

He whispered, "Sorry for Kundiso... sorry for the baby."

What was he saying? She leaned closer.

"Siya?"

He did not respond.

"Siya?"

Kundiso was near. Nyanye felt it. She would come back here to Siya, but the sun was getting low in the sky, she must find her sister. She drank some water to take away the death taste in her mouth and pulled the cloth up again over her mouth and nose, and walked on the path that led past the graveyard to the river. Her feet bled and were sore. She took a shirt from a body and tore it into pieces and tied them around her feet. The bodies here, there were not so many and they were not burnt. The flames had not reached this part.

A woman was sitting by a grave. She looked up. An old face, there was no life in her eyes. When she saw the water bottles around Nyanye's neck, she pointed to a bush next to the path, a little further on.

"That one," she said, "before, she was talking."

Beneath the bush Nyanye saw Kundiso. Lying there, her head resting on a big stone, her trousers in shreds. Nyanye sank down to the ground and held her. Tears came. She thanked Jesus and stroked her sister's face and called out to their mother that she had found her daughter, that she was alive! Against the stone she made a pillow of soil and gently propped Kundiso up against it.

She gave her water. "Slowly," she said. "A little."

But Kundiso drank it all. She closed her eyes, then opened them again and looked at Nyanye.

"Ah... it is true." Her voice was a whisper, scratchy. "You are here."

The blood was all around her legs, bones were sticking out. Nyanye could see that Kundiso had dragged herself to this place. There were marks on the ground from her legs dragging, and blood and bits of bone. It was good that she was here, under the bush, and had not suffered too much from the sun. Nyanye felt her pulse, her forehead. She poured water over her legs. She loosened her clothes and told her she needed to fetch more water to clean her wounds. Kundiso nodded.

When Nyanye came back from the river, the old woman from the graveyard was there. She had taken a branch from the bush and was waving it over Kundiso, back and forth, cooling her, keeping the flies away.

"*Ndatenda*, Amai," Nyanye said.

She wet the cloth she'd used to cover her nose and started cleaning Kundiso's legs. They did not move under her touch. She wiped her face and body and talked about going to find iodine, bandages, something for the pain, in the hospital, some of it was still standing, and about carrying her to a vehicle, getting her to Vila Macia. There would be a vehicle somewhere in Chizonya II that was not burnt.

When Nyanye had used all the water, the old woman said she would go to fetch more and then stay here so that Nyanye could go for the medicines. She stood up and held a piece of paper out to Nyanye. "It was falling from her pocket," she said, and picked up the jug and the bottles and went off down the path.

The paper was wrinkled and damp and there were blood stains on it. Nyanye turned it over, and back again. It was a photo of a baby. Lying on a blue cushion.

Kundiso was watching her. "Siya," she whispered. "He brought it."

'Sorry for the baby.' Siya's voice.

"He was there... he told me."

Nyanye crouched down and held her hand.

"Where?"

Kundiso started coughing. Her breathing was shallow and

145

her breath carried the acid smell of hunger. "He came there... to Croggan's. When Shungu was screaming. I did not see him... but he was there."

She closed her eyes. Her face was still, everything was still. Nyanye could hear no sounds from anywhere. Silence. It seemed that it was just the two of them here in this place, and the sinking sun.

Kundiso opened her eyes again.

"Such screaming, my sister..." she said softly. "The *sku'zapo* by Shungu... he was pulling the baby, breaking his necklace... the beads falling on the ground."

The necklace, Nyanye remembered it. Blue glass beads and white cowrie shells. Kundiso had made it for the baby, for his naming ceremony. And she remembered, too, seeing the *sku'zapo* reaching for Shungu's baby. But after that, nothing.

"The helicopters... soldiers coming. The *sku'zapo*... his gun, the bayonet out... it went down. Soldiers coming. A man shouting 'Don't shoot! Don't shoot!' It was Siya... ... the bayonet, it stopped Shungu screaming."

Nyanye reached out for Kundiso's hand, held it tight.

"Siya shouting, shouting 'Don't shoot!'... he saw one by me, white... with *dema*... violating me." She paused, her mouth quivered. "But bullets came. He... fell from me... I... ran away. You... were there... on the path."

Her breathing was faster now, shallower.

Nyanye looked at her sister's face, her poor shattered legs. All this suffering, this trouble that her sister had carried. Alone. She brushed the flies away and whispered, over and over, "So sorry. Sorry for you. Sorry, sorry, my sister." She felt ashamed. All this time, not knowing. Not knowing that this war, this greedy war that had already taken so much from them, had taken this too from her sister. This war, it left nothing. Just blood and bits of bone.

She leant down and held the photo close to Kundiso's face. "It is a boy?"

Kundiso nodded.

"He's from that day? At Croggan's? He did not die, the baby?"

Kundiso whispered, "Munetsi. His name." She turned her head to one side. "I left him…" She closed her eyes.

The woman came back and set down the jug and the water bottles on the ground. Nyanye looked up and thanked her.

She turned back to Kundiso, gripped her hand. "Where?"

When there no answer, she asked, "Is he safe, my sister? Munetsi, he is safe?"

She felt Kundiso's hand squeezing hers.

The woman said, "She is tired, comrade. Let her sleep now. Your questions, you can ask them tomorrow."

9

The city; early December 1979

From the verandah of Redington House you could see the city centre, a huddle of skyscrapers standing high above the Mashonaland plain. The tallest one was crowned by a huge white ball.

"I've always thought that rather vulgar."

"What, dear?"

"The pearl."

The sun had gone down and Marion was in the kitchen, preparing supper. Gil was getting the drinks. Susan said she could do with a whisky, and Reg asked for one too. It hadn't been an easy day, getting Billy to the airport, seeing him off.

Not that tomorrow was likely to be any easier. Kim Dowling was coming up to the house in the afternoon and Susan worried now that she might find what he had to tell them too upsetting, that she'd regret asking to meet him. But what was done was done.

Billy hadn't said another word about what he'd seen at Croggan's Place. Nothing. And Reg had been adamant that Susan shouldn't try getting more out of him. Just as he'd been adamant that she shouldn't involve Beth Lytton in any of it. But she couldn't leave things as they were, it ate away at her, the not knowing. Not knowing exactly what happened that day that Colin died.

"Can you get back to Scouts HQ, see if they could add anything to their report on Colin?" she'd asked Reg.

He did, but they said they had nothing to add, no-one had reported anything about a woman being raped, a baby killed.

"We're being lied to, Reg, and I can't live with that."

She said she still thought it worth talking to Beth Lytton, but Reg came up with another option. He called Gil, told him a little of what had happened with Billy and wondered if Kim Dowling might be able to throw more light on things. They'd heard about Dowling from the Aitchisons, about his job, knew that he was related to Beth and visited St Anselm quite a lot.

"He'll know whatever Beth knows, I should think," Reg told Susan. "Possibly a lot more."

Gil had rung back to say that Dowling would see what he could do, and they'd arranged to have the meeting here, at Redington, the day after they'd seen Billy off at the airport.

Susan smoked her cigarette and gazed at the pearl on the skyscraper and hoped that Dowling would have some answers.

Redington House stood on a hill to the north of the city. It was a long, low, L-shaped building with ochre walls, a brown roof and a wide verandah with elaborate cast-iron columns – from Glasgow, Gil said, dating from 1899 – along both arms of the 'L'. From one end of the verandah a path led to the teaching and student accommodation blocks, and from the other end you went down a long flight of steps to the driveway.

At night the pearl on the skyscraper was lit and looked like a full moon slung low in the dark sky, casting a bluish-white light over the city centre. On beyond the centre you could see the suburbs with their neat criss-crossing rows of bright street lights, then a darkish strip, and after that the industrial sites. To the south-east you could make out the silhouettes of the big oil storage tanks. And then on again to the African townships that jutted out from the city's southern edge and were bathed in a dim brownish-yellow hue, like a dirty petticoat sticking out from beneath a well-tailored skirt.

Beyond that, the bush. And the Bush War.

"It'll be good to see Jamie again," Susan said. He was expected

149

later that evening. He had a few days leave.

Gil came along the verandah, carrying a drinks tray. He'd put on a cravat. He'd always done that, put on a cravat after sundown. When he'd been manager at Isakata, there he'd be in the Churchill in the early evening, most evenings, wearing a cravat. Paisley always. Susan thought it added to his rather professorial look.

He handed them their whiskies, sat down, raised his glass, said "Cheers!" and apologised for not being around much since their arrival. He'd just got back from another session at the Lancaster House talks in London, and there'd been a host of people to brief on what was going on there behind the scenes.

"No need. No need at all," Reg replied. "Marion explained. Completely understand."

Marion had also said that it was all taking its toll on Gil, this coming and going. On top of all the unpleasantness they'd had to put up with over the past few years.

Susan knew that they *had* put up with a lot of unpleasantness. They'd long ruffled feathers, politically, and she thought a lot of their thinking misguided, difficult to swallow, especially when it came to Africans being capable of governing and all that, but she'd always admired the way they stuck to their guns in the face of the unpleasantness. Opening Redington's doors to all races might have brought them some trust from Africans – whatever *that* was worth – but it had also brought opprobrium from Europeans. Some of it quite vicious. Nasty phone calls, threatening letters, people calling them traitors, that sort of thing. Marion said that, in one letter, someone had written: "If any of my sons in the army are killed, your family are also going to die." Another had threatened to "take your husband's head off".

Dreadful stuff, Susan thought. They didn't deserve it. But they hadn't flinched. Gil had carried on making speeches, writing letters, parading outside the Parliament building, drawing attention to 'human rights and human wrongs', as he put it. And to himself.

"But it's eased up now, that sort of thing," Marion said, "with Gil being rather indispensable as a go-between and some white

Ministers telling the newspapers that he's not such a bad chap after all." She smiled, playfully. "We've even had a few dinner invitations from their wives!"

Such a gentle forgiving person. Despite her politics. Susan had seldom met anyone kinder, more patient. Greying now, but still pretty, diminutive, the neat features, the soft grey wide-set eyes.

Reg asked, "Am I right in thinking you had visitors rather late last night?" They'd heard comings and goings, cars, voices, after they'd gone to bed.

Gil looked at them from beneath his shaggy eyebrows, his mop of grey hair. "You are," he said. "Late-night visits have been the norm for some time, as you might have gathered from Marion." He packed some tobacco into his pipe. "Poor lass, it can't be easy for her – not least, keeping the drinks cabinet stocked! Bourbon for the Yanks. Scotch for the Brits. Either for our lot. They all expect a drink or two, you know."

Susan wondered how many of the foreign visitors thought to bring a bottle or two, to compensate for the sanctions their countries had seen fit to impose.

"And vodka for the Russians?" Reg ventured.

Gil laughed. "The Bishop is teetotal, of course. He was our visitor last night." Gil lit his pipe and took a few deep puffs. "Our visitor who comes in through the back door. This senior cleric. This man who managed, almost single-handedly, to scupper Britain's efforts to end this stalemate. This man who a decade later is our Prime Minister. He comes in through the back door! Not the *front* door... the **back** door! Nothing at all to do with not wanting to be seen. Just habit, he says. Feels more comfortable that way."

"No wonder he's not holding up too well at the talks!" Reg said. "What do you think, Gil, are the talks getting anywhere? Or heading for a brick wall again? Not sounding too hopeful."

Susan heard Thelma Warde's voice. Nothing changes. Including the conversation. Same old topic. The same old topic for fifteen years. Twenty. It never changes.

Gil ran his fingers through his hair. "Lord knows. You do sense, though, that the backers of both sides are running out of patience and, having got their protégés to the talks, kept them there for two months now, they're not going to let them walk away without a settlement. Or, at the very least, a ceasefire. Is that just wishful thinking? Perhaps. Though ceasefire or no ceasefire, Reg, I think there's still going to be a lot of blood spilled, people jockeying for power, taking revenge. It could get very rough indeed."

Headlights. A car was coming up the drive. Susan hoped it was Jamie, to change the topic of conversation. To cheer them up. He would do that. He always did.

"I must say, though, that I do feel uplifted by some of the black delegates I've met at Lancaster House," Gil went on. "Assured, confident. And many a darn sight better educated than their white counterparts, who look very second-rate by comparison. Which they are, most of them, hardly a brain between them, incapable even now of seeing blacks as little more than 'noises off', their minds as little more than containers to be emptied and refilled…"

He paused, then murmured, "They did not take the tide at the flood. Too pig-headed even to see it coming in."

Reg said quietly, "And so we've spent all these years 'bound in shallows and in miseries'."

Gil sighed. "Indeed."

When Jamie came up the verandah steps and walked over to them, Susan saw that he looked tired. To be expected, he'd probably had a long journey. He hugged and shook hands and his voice brought Marion running from the kitchen, tearful. He'd dump his kit in his room, he said, have a quick shower, be with them for supper.

Such an easy boy, she thought. Easy with them, easy with his parents. How proud they must be. How lucky.

When they sat down to supper a door slammed somewhere and Jamie jumped. He looked around the table and sighed deeply, said they had no idea how good it felt, being here. But it was flat, the way he said it. Poor tired Jamie.

He opened his napkin and spread it on his lap.

"So. Billy. Really sorry I couldn't get here last night, to see him before he left, but they refused to change my leave arrangements. Plane went off on time?"

It had. She'd stood with Reg on the balcony at the airport and watched Billy walk across the tarmac to the plane and waved to him as he climbed up the steps, shielding her eyes against the bright noon sun. On the top step he'd turned and lingered a little, looked at them. Then he'd given a little wave, there was no smile, and was gone.

"I think he did the right thing," Jamie said. "Leaving. Not just for himself, but also because of morale. Rock bottom now. Everyone's nerves are raw, naked. Lots of guys going AWOL." He paused, sipped some wine. "And now we have the top brass squabbling amongst themselves, rumours of traitors in our midst, foul-ups becoming the order of the day. And the peace talks spluttering…"

The phone rang at the other end of the dining room and Gil answered it. Susan saw a smile spread across his face and when he put the receiver down, he said, "The audacity of it!"

"Of what, dad?"

"Soames. Lord Soames. It'll be announced tomorrow. They've appointed him Governor and no-one's yet signed on the dotted line! There's still a war on and he's about to get on a plane in London and fly out here and take charge. Well, well, well."

"That's jumping the gun a bit!" Reg said. "Mind you, quite an inspired choice. I'd say Soames stands as good a chance as anyone of making things work. Tory, aristocrat, avuncular, the Churchill connection – that'll all go down very well with the parties that matter, white *and* black."

"And he does have a reputation for getting on with difficult people, doesn't he?" Marion said.

Gil nodded. "I think this points to it all being pretty well sewn up, behind the scenes. They wouldn't send Soames out otherwise. Well, well, well." He raised his glass. "Let's hope it's just a matter of time now. And a few signatures."

So that was that. They were heading for 'unqualified black

majority rule'. Susan gripped her napkin and felt tears coming. This was what the Brits had always wanted. And now that they were, to all intents and purposes, in charge of the country – or would be as soon as Soames arrived – this was what they'd make bloody sure they got. Whatever it took and whoever won any election. Even if, God forbid, it was the terrs.

This wasn't what Colin had died for, she thought. Or any other troopie. Or the Viscount victims. Or Hendrick Prinsloo. Or poor Dickie Warde, blown to bits by a landmine two weeks ago. God, that had knocked the wind out of her! Thelma had been her usual stoical self at the funeral, but it wasn't hard to see how broken she was. Too broken to pursue the plans she and Dickie had made to emigrate. Awful.

Susan sat there, holding her napkin, keeping her tears at bay, listening to them talking about the talks, speculating about Soames, forecasting this and that. She said nothing in case she said too much. After a while she stopped listening to them and started thinking about tomorrow, the meeting with Dowling.

***

"I can't help feeling he was holding something back."

Reg said nothing, just gazed across the city.

"Or at least, when *I* was in the room he was."

"Look, dear, I think he was being as open as he could be."

Whatever else Kim Dowling was, he wasn't open. She hadn't taken to him much, didn't like the clipped, efficient way he spoke, the way he didn't answer questions, made no attempt to fill silences. She was sure they weren't getting the full story. She regretted now that she'd not stayed in the room, got more out of him. But she couldn't, not when he started describing the wounds. The different wounds that different bullets made.

Dowling had arrived at about three-thirty and they'd gone into Gil's study. Susan liked the study. It had none of the frugality of the rest of Redington House, the thin grass mats on parquet flooring, the uncurtained windows, the functional furniture – she knew the Aitchisons had hardly two pennies to rub together, everything went into keeping the college going, but a little more colour and comfort wouldn't have gone amiss. The study was quite different. Book-lined walls, Persian rugs, Art Deco desk lamp, mahogany desk, two deep leather armchairs. Susan sat in one of them, Reg in the other.

Dowling sat on Gil's desk chair. He took a brown file from his briefcase and put it on the desk. Stapled to it was a sheet of paper covered in handwritten notes. He couldn't let them see the file, he said, apologising, it was just there for his reference. It was the report on the debrief of a Scout who'd been in the same unit as Colin that day of the firefight.

"African. He was recruited a little over two years ago. Called Siya. I can't tell you his second name. He was one of four Africans in the unit."

He paused to offer them cigarettes and lit one himself.

"You'll know from Scouts HQ about the unit tracking the terrs from the Isakata junction to the Inveraray river, the day after the ambush. Then setting up the OP – er, observation post – on a kopje that night, suspecting that about thirty terrs were holed up by the river and that the locals were probably feeding them. Then, at dawn, the Scouts unit moving down from the kopje, their suspicions being confirmed, and calling in FireForce. Yes?"

She knew all that. They both nodded.

"Three of the unit went to the village nearest Croggan's, to question the villagers. Siya stayed on the kopje, operating the radio. The other three – an African, two Europeans, including Colin – started following the tracks from the village to the river."

There was a tap on the door and Marion came in with tea and biscuits. They thanked her and she closed the door softly behind her when she went out.

Dowling continued. "After calling in FireForce, Siya radio'd all six Scouts to withdraw immediately, clear out before the FireForce drop. Then had a final exchange with the K-car pilot, packed up the OP and headed down to link up with the others away from the drop zone. But on the way he heard screaming – 'a terrible screaming', it says in the file – and ran to where it seemed to be coming from."

Screaming. The same screaming that Billy had talked about?

"A woman screaming?" Susan asked. "Did he say?"

Dowling looked at her. "If it's all right, I'll go through the main points of what happened, from my notes on the debrief. Then I'll fill in the gaps later. Answer any questions I can."

"Of course," said Reg.

"To go back to Siya. The choppers were coming by this time and while he was still running they started dropping the FireForce sticks. He ran on, came to Croggan's Place, didn't see the African Scout there, but the other two were there, with some captured locals. The file mentions 'an incident with an African female resisting arrest'." He paused. "Perhaps she was screaming when she was arrested? I don't know. There's nothing else on any woman."

"Was she carrying a baby?"

"Susan, let Kim…"

Dowling looked at Reg, then at Susan. "Nothing about a baby," he said. "Where was I? Yes. Siya got to Croggan's and saw FireForce, running there from another direction. Shooting." He paused. "White Scouts black up on operation, you'll know that, and all Scouts carry AKs, like the terrs. Siya shouted to the FireForce troops to stop shooting. They were shooting at white Scouts."

He took a deep breath. "But it was too late."

Friendly fire. So-called. For some reason, Susan wasn't surprised. She felt a deep sadness that it had happened. But she wasn't surprised.

"Did he shout, too? Colin? To stop them shooting?" she asked.

"I can't say. It isn't in the file."

Did he *know*, her bush boy in his floppy hat? Before he died, in that helicopter, did he *know* that it was FireForce? That he'd been shot by his own side?

"Siya radio'd for a casevac," Dowling went on. "And stayed with

156

Colin till the chopper came. By that time the firefight had started, down by the Inveraray. Later, after Colin had been airlifted out, after the fight, they carried the bodies up there. To the smokestack at Croggan's."

The photos in the *Gazette* of the bodies around the smokestack. She remembered her shock, seeing them there in the paper, just two days after Colin had been killed.

Reg stood up and went to the window, stared out.

"Surely…" he began. "Why were they still there, Colin, the other Scout? Why hadn't they left the drop zone, as ordered? Surely they…"

Dowling said, "I don't know. It doesn't say."

Jamie's voice. 'He was good with Colin, held him…'

Susan said, "This Siya. Is there… is there any chance we could see him? Talk to him?"

"I'm afraid not. He's dead. Probably."

It came like a gunshot. She hadn't expected that. She'd begun to feel a link to him, this African. She was sure he was the one Jamie had talked about, who'd held Colin, kept him comfortable, carried him into the helicopter. Who'd been kind to Billy too, Jamie had said. As Dowling talked, she began to picture him, the 'good Af' with furrows in his cheeks. There at Croggan's, with her sons, the three of them waiting for the helicopter.

"How sad…"

Reg glanced at her.

Dowling continued. "It's likely that he was killed. Last month. During a raid on a camp in Mozambique."

Reg moved away from the window, sat down again. "The firefight by the river – you're sure that it didn't start till after Colin had been shot? That he wasn't caught up in it, that that's why he was there still, couldn't get away? In which case, he could have been killed by the terrs?"

Dowling shook his head. "I'm sure. As to being killed by terrs, the ballistic evidence says not." He looked down at his notes. "The bullets came from FNs, not AKs. Unless there was a terr there with an FN. Which isn't likely. The difference is…"

That was when Susan had left the study.

Reg had stayed talking to Dowling for another twenty minutes or so, then they both came out of the study and Dowling said goodbye and drove off. Reg said he needed to go to their bedroom for something or other, and after about half an hour came back and sat down next to her on the verandah. He'd hardly said a word since. Except to say that he thought Dowling had been as open as he could be.

At length, Susan said, "That African. The Scout – Siya – he's the one Jamie must have been talking about when he was staying with us. Do you remember? About Billy saying an African looked after Colin while they waited for the helicopter, about him crying, being a good African?"

She waited for Reg's response. And while she waited, she realised that Billy would have known it was friendly fire. He must have. Was that it, then? Was it the friendly fire that they – Billy, Scouts HQ – were keeping from them? Or was there more that she and Reg weren't being told?

"Reg?"

He looked at her.

"Yes?"

"Siya, the African, he's the one Jamie talked about, isn't he?"

"I expect so."

She knew, from the way he said it, that his mind was elsewhere, that he had no idea what question she'd asked.

* * *

Susan picked up the *Saturday Gazette* from the verandah table, scanned it briefly, put it down. It was much thinner than it used to be. You'd think there'd be more to report on these days, not less. The thinness was because of censorship, she supposed. Although there were rumours that the country was running out of paper. It might be that. Where had Reg got to? He said he'd be back by twelve. It was ten past now.

She could see Marion down near the bottom of the garden. You couldn't call it a garden, really, more a mosaic of granite rocks and grass, falling away down the hillside from the verandah. The granite rocks glinted in the sun, it was the mica in them, Reg said. Here and there, some shrubs and small trees, all indigenous, Marion was keen on that. Susan watched her snipping clusters of white flowers from a monkey-bread tree, moving on to the cassia and snipping some more, adding the bright yellow sprays to her basket. Some people had been invited round this evening, for drinks, a buffet supper, and Marion was redoing the vases.

"Ah, there you are."

It was Jamie. He drew up a chair next to her. He'd not been around at all yesterday. There'd been a big firefight up in the eastern mountains, lots of casualties flown to Alexandra hospital, they needed all the hands they could get. And she and Reg had gone to a drinks do in the evening, with friends in the suburbs. So she'd not seen Jamie since Kim Dowling's visit. She asked if things were all right now at the hospital, if they were coping. He nodded.

Then she said, "You knew, Jamie, didn't you?"

"Knew what, Mrs H?"

"That it was friendly fire."

He blinked, bit his lip.

"How long have you known?"

"Since October. When I came to Isakata. I'd picked up some talk. A rumour. I asked Billy. He said you didn't know, you and Uncle Reg, and he didn't want you to know."

"Well, we do now."

"Yes."

"What else did he say about that day? That he didn't want us to know?"

"Nothing really, Mrs H. At one point he seemed about to tell me something else, but then he stopped. Seemed upset. Asked me not to ask questions. Said he couldn't handle any. So I didn't."

"Could that 'something else' have been rape, Jamie?"

He turned sharply, stared at her.

She told him what had happened on the night of the Club's Independence party, the little Billy told Reg the next morning, about a rape at Croggan's, a baby killed. Just that they had happened. No details.

Jamie was shaking his head, slowly.

"Rape... Bloody hell, Mrs H! I don't know. It might have been. There *was* something about a woman, but he started looking tearful, went quiet. Left it there. So did I." He paused. "What about Kim, though, did he say anything?"

"Nothing. Said there was nothing in HQ's report about a rape. Just something about a woman resisting arrest."

"Not surprising. They'd cover that sort of thing up."

"But Dowling did start me thinking that..."

A shadow fell over them and they looked up to see Marion, standing there at the edge of the verandah, smiling, holding up her basket of flowers.

"Can you smell the cassia?" she said. "Isn't it heavenly?"

"Lovely," Susan said.

But she didn't want to talk about flowers, she wanted to talk to Reg. She'd go to her room until he came back. "If you don't mind," she said, "I've a bit of a headache, I think I'll go and lie down for a little while."

"Of course," Marion said. "We'll tell Reg when he comes back. There's some aspirin in the bathroom cabinet, if that would help."

In the bedroom, Susan pulled back the counterpane and adjusted the pillow and lay down. She closed her eyes. She saw Croggan's Place and men in floppy hats and a woman screaming, a baby somewhere, and gradually the thought came to her that if Billy *had* seen a rape there, the rapist could have been one of the Scouts there. She opened her eyes and went through everything Dowling had said. Every detail. And she remembered Reg being puzzled that the two Scouts were still there, at Croggan's, when they shouldn't have been.

She sat up. *That's* why he'd hardly said a word since the meeting with Dowling. Of course! He must have had the same thought too!

He'd been so quiet at the do last night that she'd felt the need to apologise for him, saying he was under great pressure at the mine, and so on. He must be thinking what she was thinking, got there before she had.

Was he back? She got up and went out onto the verandah. They were all standing there, Reg too, and turned when they heard her footsteps. No-one smiled. Something was wrong.

"What is it?" she asked.

Marion came towards her. There'd been a phone call, she said. Baba Sibanda had been killed, that morning.

"Just before dawn," Jamie said.

"Sibanda?"

"At St Anselm, dear. The priest."

"Kim's on his way out there now," Gil said. "He's persuaded Beth to come in and will be bringing her back here on Monday. And the baby. Grace insisted that the baby came in too, apparently. And one of the young nuns, to help Beth with the baby."

Susan asked, "The Coloured baby? They're bringing him here? On Monday?"

Gil nodded. He said that it had been Silas Chipere who'd called. Susan had met Chipere a few times, when she'd taken a patient to Nhika hospital. She thought him a bit bumptious. Gil said that one of the nuns had been knocked about a bit and Chipere had tended to her, might take her back to Nhika, but everyone else was all right. It was just the priest.

"They took him from the red house down to the church," Gil said. "Shot him. In front of the church door."

Marion said she'd get a room ready for them and she went off to ring a friend for a cot. Reg said he'd call the mine and ask someone to drive out to St Anselm, see if there was anything Isakata could do to help. Gil would try to find out more from the police at Mandura, and Jamie volunteered to get the cot. Soon after Jamie had driven down the drive, Chipere phoned again, to tell Gil what he'd learned from Rejoice, the nun who'd been hurt.

As Gil relayed it, Rejoice had gone to the kitchen to help get the fires going. A man in a long coat, African, appeared, asking for Baba. Rejoice said he was sleeping, the man would have to wait till sunrise. He said it was urgent, he couldn't wait, so she went with him to the red house. Baba must have been up already, she said, because he came out as soon as she knocked, saw the man, greeted him. The man said they needed to talk in private and they walked off towards the church. After a while, Rejoice followed. She felt something was not right. Another man appeared, also in a long coat, told her to go back. When she stood there, refusing, he took a gun from inside his coat and raised it and she saw the uniform. He hit her across her shoulders and she fell and he ran off into the darkness. Then there were gun shots and Amai Grace came and they hurried to the church. That's where Baba was, lying on his back, arms outstretched, blood coming from his chest. All around him the ground was soaked with blood, Rejoice said.

The gunshots woke the rest of the community and soon everyone was there, Beth, Agnes, all the other nuns. Beth phoned the police. And Silas. The sun was rising and they all knelt around the body and prayed. The police came at about 6.30, picked up cartridges, asked Rejoice and Grace for their stories. Rejoice said it was army, she'd seen the uniform. The police threatened her for telling lies and showed her some cartridges. One of them said, "These are not from army guns. They are from terrorist guns. In cases like this, we do not need an inquest. You can bury the body."

When they had gone, the nuns washed Baba's body and carried it into the church.

"As I feared," Gil said, "The vanquished letting rip while they still can."

Marion murmured, "Oh dear, I rather wish we weren't having people here later, I don't feel up to it. At all."

Susan wasn't sure what to make of the story Gil had told. She'd never met the priest, had only seen him from afar once or twice, at St Anselm. And he might have been the driver of the old blue station wagon that day at Molly's Store when she saw his wife. With the baby.

"If there's a silver lining to any of this," Gil said, "it's that Beth's coming in at last. Just in time, too."

"In time for what?" Reg asked.

"Kim's flying back to the UK in a few days. At least now he can go knowing Beth's here. Safe."

"Is he? Oh. I wanted another chat with him… It'll have to wait then, till he's back."

Gil looked at Marion, then back at Reg. "I don't think Kim's coming back. Not for some time, anyway."

The phone in the study rang and Gil went to answer it, then called to Marion to come in, it was Silas Chipere again, with Grace. She wanted to talk to them.

Susan thought it odd, Dowling not mentioning anything yesterday about leaving, not coming back. She said as much to Reg. But before he had time to comment, she said it didn't matter. What did matter was that at last everyone had gone and she could talk to him in private. He looked apprehensive and she suggested they go down to the bottom of the garden, to the bench beneath the cassia.

When they had sat down, she said, "You don't have to hide it from me, what you're thinking."

He stared at her.

"Whether or not it was Dowling saying more to you yesterday, after I'd left the study, I don't know. But you got there, and now I've got there."

"Where?"

"That, if there *was* a rape at Croggan's, that day, it must have been one of the two Scouts there. One of the two European Scouts. And you *must* realise, as I do, where that might lead?"

Reg didn't say anything, so she said it for him. "To Colin."

He turned to look at her, nodded slowly. "Yes. I saw that yesterday, when we were with Dowling. Saw the possibility. After you'd gone, I put it to him. Told him what had Billy said."

"And?"

"He said he couldn't comment. Didn't know if there had been

a rape. And if there had, didn't know who might have done it. Any more than we know, Susan." He paused. "Or will ever know, unless Billy says more."

He leaned back, lit two cigarettes, gave one to her.

"Dowling did suggest something else."

"Oh?"

"He suggested that if there was a rape, could Billy be referring to someone in his own stick? Someone who, on realising he'd shot one of his own, went beserk, his bloodlust up, went for the woman?"

They sat there for a moment in silence.

Then Susan said, "I can't see it. The way Billy talked, it sounded as though his stick had run into what was happening. They ran there because of the screaming, because of what was happening."

"The screaming, yes. A woman screaming because her child was being attacked, but then the guys getting there, shooting, killing one of their own by mistake, going beserk?"

This was not the picture that had embedded itself in her mind, the one she felt instinctively was the right one. She shook her head. "No, I don't think Dowling's right. But I *do* think, as I said before, that he's holding something back. Just as HQ is."

She waited for Reg to respond. When he didn't, she said quietly, "I have to *know*, Reg. That's why…" She felt tears coming, blinked them away. "That's why I still want to talk to Beth Lytton. I still think she knows something that could help. Maybe we should stay on. Till she gets here on…"

"No!"

Susan jumped. Shocked by his shout, the anger in it.

"No," he said again, more quietly this time.

He stood up. There was a lot to think about, he said, especially about Billy, telling him what they now knew, hoping it might help him to open up. They could start talking about all that tomorrow, when they got back to Isakata. He'd rather not talk about it anymore till then, till they got home.

The guests started arriving at about 7.30. They milled about on the verandah, their conversations humming and swirling and drifting down the garden. Some of the college students were on hand to keep their glasses topped up, and there was a buffet laid out in the dining room. The talk was about the talks, of course, and Soames' arrival next week, and the likelihood of a ceasefire, if there was one, holding.

Susan picked at the food on the buffet table and wondered if she cared very much. She was tired, she wanted her bed.

There was a shout from somewhere and Jamie came dashing into the room.

"Everyone! Outside! Quickly!"

They all went out and stood there, on the verandah, gazing towards the south-east. Bright white flames were shooting upwards into the night sky, turning it red and orange and yellow. The big oil storage tanks were ablaze. Everyone stared. No-one said anything. The air was filled with billowing black smoke and, as each new explosion ripped through the depot, great white flashes lit up the sky and all the land beneath it, as far as the eye could see.

There was a strange light over the city centre and the pearl on the top of the skyscraper took on a pale reddish hue.

Someone said, "The war has come to the city. Finally."

10

St Anselm mission and the city;

late January – early March 1980

"At least the buses are running again," Grace said.

The army had started clearing landmines on roads in the Reserves and the buses were coming back.

"But the rain, Mukoma, we have had almost nothing. The mealies, ah... there is going to be a big problem with the harvest." She sighed. "And Agnes, I am so worried for her."

Agnes had been unwell again. The police interrogations had taken their toll on her, especially the hot-boxing. They had stopped now, but there was a frailty about Agnes, she moved more slowly these days, and Grace had decided that Rejoice must take over the kitchen duties. Not that those duties were very heavy, with only six nuns left at the mission now. Some had panicked and left after Baba's murder. A few had gone to nurse family members who'd contracted anthrax, there'd been an outbreak of the disease in the Reserve. Grace was still hoping that Shohiwa – the only one of her sons who'd expressed interest in the priesthood – might come home from Canada to fill Baba's shoes, help build up the community again, attract some of the nuns back, but there'd been no word yet.

"We have brought the medication you asked for. We'll get Ambuya back to being well again very soon, you'll see!"

"Ah, Mukoma, you are the medicine that she truly needs. That we all need! We are missing you. And our Munetsi. Very much. Is that not so, Silas?"

Beth smiled at her, took her hand.

They were sitting, the three of them, in the cane chairs on the verandah of the red house. It was the first time Beth had come back to St Anselm since Baba's funeral in mid-December. Silas had driven her back. The Aitchisons had insisted she have a week at home as soon as the ceasefire looked as though it might hold, they would take care of Munetsi while she was away.

Four weeks into the ceasefire now, and so far, so good. Beth was still pinching herself. Everyone was. Finding it hard to believe that peace, so elusive for so long, had come. There *were* incidents, of course, and fear and uncertainty everywhere, but for the most part it did feel like peace.

Silas had been at Redington House on the day that the news of the ceasefire had come through from London. 21st December. It was the same day on which Munetsi had had an echocardiagram at the Alexandra. Silas had arranged that to reassure himself that the hole in Munetsi's heart had closed. All the signs were that it had. Marion had driven Beth and Munetsi to the Alexandra and by late afternoon they'd got the all-clear and headed back to Redington House, singing.

They'd hurried up the steps, to find wine glasses and a bottle of champagne on the verandah table and Gil and Silas standing there, broad smiles on their faces.

Silas said, "So, it's all over!"

"Yes, isn't it marvellous! The hospital rang you?" Marion asked.

Gil looked puzzled, then laughed. "No, no, Silas isn't talking about Munetsi. And yes, the hospital did ring. Confirmed what Silas thought. Very good news. No, what Silas is talking about is that they've signed. The whole lot of them!"

Beth said "Who?" And then, "Oh, you mean at the Lancaster House talks? There's a ceasefire?"

"An agreement on one, yes," Gil said. "It'll start in a week. And a general election at the end of February, early March. Fingers crossed!"

Silas was wide-eyed. "It is a miracle, is it not, Mukoma!"

"But everything looked doomed a week ago," she said. "What turned things around?"

A grin spread across his round face. "Bluffmanship, it seems." And he said that Agnes's brother, Isaiah, who was at the talks, had called and told him that watching Lord Carrington and his advisers at work in that final week had been like having a front seat at a masterclass in bluffmanship.

"Aided and abetted, it appears, by a few last-minute long-distance phone calls," Gil added. "From Maputo, Lusaka, Addis, telling recalcitrant delegates to sign – or else."

Would it hold, the ceasefire, Beth asked? And if it did hold, how soon might the *vakomana* start coming home from the camps? From Mozambique? Silas said the plan was early January apparently, and her heart surged.

Gil looked around at them all. "So, a glass of champagne, everyone?"

"Oh, I think we ought to, don't you?" Beth said. "With so much to celebrate."

Marion lowered a sleeping Munetsi onto a chair and they all drank to the ceasefire. They drank to Munetsi and to the hope that Kundiso had survived the Chizonya raid – estimates were that more than half the people there had – and that she would soon be on her way back home. They drank to peace, at last.

And now, across the borders to the east and to the north, the *vakomana* were coming back from the camps in their thousands. Their orders were to head for the Assembly Points – APs, as they'd become known – that the British were setting up across the country.

"The AP near Nhika, Mukoma, many *vakomana* are there now already," Grace said.

Silas added that a few days ago he'd seen about a hundred *vakomana* marching along the Nhika road towards the AP, chanting and singing, waving their AKs. Beth shuddered. What if it all went terribly wrong? All those *vakomana* in the dozen or so APs that had been set up – sitting ducks for soldiers who'd just lost a war.

Grace said that trucks with white crosses on them were everywhere. British trucks, keeping an eye on the *vakomana* coming home, coming in. And that Rejoice had heard there was now a British flag flying at the AP near Nhika.

"How strange that must be for some of the more ancient souls around here," Beth said. "They must be a little confused about the reappearance of the Union Jack!"

When Beth got back to the rondavel, Agnes was sitting out on the stoep, shining a torch onto the pages of a book on her lap. She looked up and said, "It is very beautiful, Mukoma." Gil had found the book on his last trip to London, had bought it for Agnes and Beth had brought it out from the city to her. An early edition of *Saint Anselm's Book of Meditations and Prayers.*

Agnes looked down at the book. "Here is something, Mukoma. 'Let my soul ever yearn for the glory of Thy Face; let my whole being be…' " She paused, and pointed to a line on the page.

Beth leant down and read, "…my whole being be held in thrall with love of it."

"*Ehe*," Agnes said softly, and closed the book.

Beth stayed there, on the stoep, after Agnes had gone to bed. She sat looking out into in the dark night, listening to the crickets, the distant animal calls. It was joyous, being back.

Torchlight. Someone was coming along the path. Grace.

"*Manheru*, Mukoma. Agnes, she is all right?"

"Yes, Amai Grace, she is sleeping now."

"There was a telephone call, Mukoma. Mrs Haig. The Sister."

"Oh?"

"She was saying that tomorrow she is going to Nhika hospital. She is taking a patient there, a man from the mine compound, he has been in an accident. She said she is coming here to the mission on her way back."

"Why? Did she say?"

"No, Mukoma."

"Does she know Munetsi isn't here?"

"She knows. It will be in the morning. About eleven o'clock, she said."

* * *

"Beth."

Beth turned around. Susan Haig was standing just inside the church door, in her white uniform and her starched cap, next to the basket of red sashes.

"They said I'd find you here."

She was early.

Beth got up, genuflected and made the sign of the cross and walked down the aisle towards her.

"I'm earlier than I thought I'd be," Susan said. "The boy died en route, so nothing much to do except leave the body there and... Good God!"

She was looking towards the altar. She took a step forward, then another, and stared at the white cross above the altar. "Is that a black Christ? On the cross?"

"Yes."

"Good God," she said again, quietly this time, and turned and walked out of the door.

At the rondavel, Beth made tea and arranged some biscuits on a plate and took them out to the stoep. Susan was sitting there smoking and Beth fetched the ashtray.

"I don't know how you do it," Susan said, "living out here, alone. Mind you, one has to admit it *is* rather lovely, your view. The river down there, the Inveraray hills on the horizon. I sometimes think they got all the prettier bits, the Africans in the Reserves, don't you? While we got all the rather dull flat bits. Not that any of that matters now, does it? The minute the new lot get into Government, they'll just start taking whatever bits they want."

Beth poured the tea.

"Is Reg well?" she asked

"He's all right. Not terribly chatty. Tired. With sanctions lifted,

170

it's all systems go again and… well, he's got a lot on his plate. He's in Mozambique for a few days. They're queuing up there now, ships from Britain, America, Sweden, to fill their holds with our chrome!"

Agnes came out onto the stoep with an empty mug in her hand. She greeted Susan and told Beth she was going to take some tea to the driver.

"Oh, the driver…" Susan said. "Can you tell him to bring the box?"

Beth looked at her. "Oh dear, I hadn't realised you had a driver." She turned to Agnes. "Thank you, Ambuya. He's in the van still?"

"*Ehe*, he is there."

The Isakata clinic van was parked beneath the tree between the rondavel and the guest house, a green van with a red cross on it.

Agnes poured tea and milk into the mug, and said, "I can show him our church, Mukoma."

"No, no, there's no need for that," Susan said. "I shan't be long. He doesn't mind waiting. Just tell him to bring the box."

Agnes smiled at Beth, added sugar to the tea, and went off to the van. She came back a few minutes later with the driver, who put a large cardboard box down on the stoep and then he and Agnes went off along the path to the church.

Susan watched them, tight-lipped, then turned to Beth and pointed at the box. "Some bits and pieces for you. Or rather, for the baby. SMA, nappies, some babyfood. We've masses at the clinic, and I thought I'd drop some off here seeing that I was passing." She smiled. "SMA's not always easy to get hold of these days, is it?"

"Well, that's very kind…"

"I'll bring some more, from time to time, if you like. He's well, I take it? The baby?"

Beth said he was, and the Aitchisons were marvellous with him.

"I was wondering, on the way here from Nhika," Susan said, "whether you'd ever heard anything from the mother?"

The question took Beth by surprise. After a moment, she said, "No, not directly."

"Meaning?"

The search for Kundiso had begun as soon as the APs had started going up, after Christmas. Gil, Grace, Silas, they were all doing what they could. Agnes's brother too, Isaiah. "There's a Maseka on the list in an AP up in the north-east, a woman," Gil had said in a recent phone call. "We're following it up."

But it was a dead end, again. None of the APs were yielding any clues as to Kundiso's whereabouts. Silas said it seemed that many women combatants were simply walking out of the APs and melting into the rural population – they didn't arouse suspicion the way the young men would – or had stayed in Mozambique, with thousands of others, waiting there to see how things turned out. So perhaps, here, they'd just have to wait too, until Kundiso turned up.

Beth wasn't sure how to reply to Susan. Was there any point, now, in covering up, the way she had back in August when Reg had asked about the mother? What she'd told him – and anyone else who asked – had been skimpy. Deliberately. Baba and Grace had thought it best that as few people as possible knew the full story, there'd have been too many awkward questions otherwise. So all Beth had told Reg was that a woman had arrived at St Anselm one night, given birth, then disappeared. That was it. Nothing about her being with the *vakomana*. And that was how it had stayed.

But perhaps it needn't stay that way any longer, Beth thought. Everything had changed. And anyway, when Kundiso came back she'd not hide her part in the Struggle.

"She's in Mozambique, Susan. Probably. She came from Mozambique. Had her baby here, in the Sibandas' house. Then went back there, to Mozambique."

"She's Mozambican?"

"No. She's a guerrilla, in one of the camps there."

Susan sat forward. "Bloody hell..."

"We think she's still there, waiting to see how the elections in February go before she comes back."

"You *think*?"

"Kim managed to get a message to her about Munetsi, that he was well. Thriving. And he sent her a photograph. We got a message back that she was fine. Early November. But it's gone a bit quiet since then."

Beth expected a reaction to this. Condemnation about the mission "being in touch with the terrs". Something like that. But Susan said nothing.

Agnes came back along the path from the church, walking slowly, and when she reached the stoep she was out of breath, panting, and Beth told her to sit down, have a rest. Agnes sank into a chair. The driver wanted to stay in the church a bit longer, she said, he liked it very much. It was peaceful and cool.

"A lot cooler than sitting in a hot car!" said Beth. "Thank you, Ambuya."

Susan lit a cigarette.

"Were you there, Beth, at the birth?"

"We both were, Agnes and me. And Amai Grace, of course. They were at the actual birth, I got there a little later."

"The girl, did she say anything about the father?"

"Not really. You wouldn't, would you, if rape was involved. From the little she said, it seems it was a white soldier, blacked up."

Susan stared at her. She stood up and walked from the stoep onto the bare ground in front of it, turned, stood there for a moment, looking at Beth.

"She said that it was rape? You're sure?"

"Yes."

Agnes was shaking her head. "*Eh eh*, such a bad business. Many girls, they had to run away from the villages because of that. It was coming from everywhere. From the *vakomana*, from the settler forces. Now, when they come back, those girls who suffered, it will be a big problem for them. Their families, they will not want them."

Susan walked back to her chair and sat down.

Agnes went on, "But that one, she was tough. The baby, when

he was coming she was not crying. There was no talking, no crying. She was saying nothing."

Susan looked at Beth. "Is she right? That the girl said nothing?"

Beth smiled at Agnes. "If Agnes says the girl said nothing to her, that's what happened. She said nothing to me either."

"Said nothing about the father, about where it happened?"

"No. Just that she was raped."

The driver was walking down the path from the church. He turned to look back up at the bell tower silhouetted against the deep blue sky, stood there a moment, then walked on past the rondavel towards the clinic van.

Beth watched him. "Oh, there *was* something, now that I come to think of it." She turned to Susan. "Something about a chimney. She said, 'There by the *chimini*'. Yes, I think that's what it was. But nothing else. She didn't..."

"Ah, Mukoma! You are sure?"

"You had gone by then, Ambuya. And until now I'd forgotten all about it. Not that it tells us much."

Agnes began shaking her head slowly and muttering, "*Eh, eh, eh.*"

"What is it, Ambuya?"

"The *chimini*. It is the name that some people use for that place called Croggan's."

"Oh? Could that be where she...?"

Susan was staring at Agnes.

She turned, looked at Beth for a moment, then slowly leant down, picked up her handbag, put her cigarette packet and lighter into it and stood up.

"I must be going," she said quietly.

***

On the TV screen, the queues stretched as far as the eye could see. On and on they went, winding their way along streets in the townships, across fields and barren ground in the rural areas, through villages. In every place, there they were, thousands upon thousands of people, standing in lines, awaiting their turn, some breaking the lines now and again to dance or ululate or wave at the TV cameras. It seemed that the whole world had turned out to vote. Exuberantly.

"Extraordinary," Beth said quietly, marvelling at a sight once so unimaginable.

She took a tissue from her pocket and dabbed her eyes. And saw that Gil and Marion, too, were looking a little overwhelmed.

What a long and bloody wait it had been, for this. In recent weeks the waiting had become almost unbearable. To see if the ceasefire would hold, to see if the Governor, Soames, would keep his nerve amidst the loud and incessant cries of 'Foul!' from all parties, to see if despite everything – reports of attempted assassinations, rumours of voter intimidation, of plans to rig the vote or mount a coup – the elections would actually take place.

They had, and now the wait would begin for the outcome. And its aftermath.

Silas had commented that it was not the outcome that was in question – "the war has been one long election campaign, a reality that seems to have escaped most whites, even those who should have known better, the CIU for example" – but the reaction to it. He wasn't optimistic.

"You have to hand it to London," Gil said, "they've organised a damned good show. They've run like clockwork, these elections."

Marion smiled. "For which Kim must take some credit, of course. He must be so pleased, watching all this."

Kim would be watching it in a hotel in the city centre, with members of the Commonwealth election monitoring team. He'd flown out as an adviser to them, his first time back in the country since he'd left rather hurriedly after Baba's funeral.

"Bless him," Beth said.

An elderly man with a walking stick, on reaching a tent-like structure that served as a polling booth, did a little jig for the TV cameras, hopped about on one leg, then the other, the people queuing behind him hooting with laughter, urging him on.

Gil raised his glass. "A toast to you, old man!" He looked at Beth. "And to Kim."

It wasn't until that day in December when Kim had brought her and Munetsi here after Baba's murder that Beth had learned that Kim was not quite who he said he was. He'd not spelled it out, just said it was time for him to go and Gil would explain. Which Gil did, once she and Munetsi had settled in at Redington. Kim was with British Intelligence, he said, had been all along, and he smiled broadly at the relief that spread across her face.

"He was becoming increasingly outraged at what the 'dirty tricks' section at Scouts HQ was getting up to. That's why he let on to me who he was. I wasn't surprised, I must say. He wanted my support in urging the new Thatcher Government to get talks going again to stop it all. Stop the war."

"What were they getting up to?" Beth asked.

"Testing toxic chemicals on captured insurgents. Contaminating wells along the insurgent infiltration routes, knowing they were also the refugee escape routes. Air-dropping anthrax spores over the Reserves. Poisoning clothing and distributing it to the unsuspecting enemy – who'd die a few days later of something that looked like an extreme case of malaria. To name just a few. War is war, but..."

Beth wished she hadn't asked. There'd been rumours, but they'd seemed too extreme to be credible.

"And OM, Kim's boss, where did he fit into all this? Did he know about Kim?"

Gil had smiled and said, "It's complicated." And had left it at that.

When Beth heard that Kim was coming back with the election monitoring team, her initial reaction had been one of fear. Mightn't someone be out to get him? Kim assured her that as long as OM was still in position – which he was – he would be fine.

The TV coverage of the elections came to an end and Gil drained his glass and said he'd turn in. Long day tomorrow, including taking Reg Haig to the airport and bringing Susan back

176

to Redington for lunch. Reg was flying to London, would be there for two weeks for meetings at Head Office. Susan had come into the city with him, wanted to do some shopping, she said. They were staying with friends in the suburbs.

"I'm surprised Susan isn't going to London too," Beth said.

"I'm not really," Gil said. "When I met up with Billy for a drink, last time I was over there, he seemed anxious that Susan *didn't* go over. At least, not yet. He said she's talked a lot about going over, being with him, but he isn't ready. Has been putting her off. I think it's that he's not ready to answer questions yet. Reg knows when to hold back. Susan doesn't."

By the time Gil came back at lunchtime the following day, with Susan, initial assessments of where the elections were heading all pointed to a winner who was not the one the Government or most whites had expected – and hoped – it would be. Nor was it the one that London had predicted.

"I expect the shredders in the Government offices have been working very hard this morning," Gil said.

Beth smiled. Already, the old Government seemed an irrelevance.

Lunch was a quiet affair, Susan seemed preoccupied. Beth felt uncomfortable. She'd not seen Susan since late January at St Anselm, since her rather unpleasant visit there. The Aitchisons made occasional stabs at conversation, but kept away from the elections, the rumours of a landslide.

When Marion brought the coffee, Susan dabbed her lips with her napkin, scrunched it up slowly and put it on the table, and turned to Beth.

"How is the baby, then?"

"Munetsi? Oh, very well."

Marion laughed. "And very plump!"

"Almost normal weight now for a six-month-old," Beth said. "Just under sixteen pounds."

"So being in the city has helped. Proper doctors, facilities. I thought it would." Susan took a sip of her coffee, then pushed her chair back and stood up. "I'll go and take a look." She walked to the door, calling back, "His cot's in your bedroom, Beth? The one we use?"

"Would you mind waiting till later?" Beth asked. "When he's awake?"

Susan swung round.

"I haven't *got* 'later'..." She looked at her watch. "I've got to be at the rendezvous point by two-thirty."

Marion said, "Susan, it's just that his daytime sleeping habits have become a bit hit-and-miss. He wakes at the slightest disturbance."

Susan stood there, her face reddening, lips tight. Then she said, so quietly that Beth wasn't sure if she'd heard correctly, "I've every right."

Gil stared at her. "What *are* you talking about, Susan? *What* right?"

She looked at them, from one to the other. She walked back to her chair, sat down, took a cigarette from her packet and lit it.

"Reg is going to kill me for this," she said. She leaned back in the chair. "He refuses to have anything to do with it, wants us to keep out of it. Completely. But I'm beyond caring what Reg thinks or wants."

She smoked her cigarette and they waited.

When she spoke again, it was in measured tones. "The baby. He could be Colin's. He could be our grandchild."

"Oh, Susan, no! Oh, my goodness. My dear..." Marion said.

"Everything points to it, Marion." Her eyes had filled up with tears. "Everything points to him being the child of a rape by one of two Scouts at Croggan's Place on the day Colin died. Colin was one of those Scouts. Colin could be his father. But Reg won't..."

Gil muttered, "Good Lord!"

Susan's hands were shaking. Beth realised that hers were too.

"I'm convinced he *is* Colin's child," Susan went on. "In my bones, I *know* it. I've taken on board the... circumstances. Understood that these things happen in war. Colin had been to hell and back. A dreadful war for him. Then Hendrick – his best friend – being killed. In the heat of the moment, men sometimes... But Reg won't have it. Has stopped me even talking about it."

Silence.

Gil said, "I don't recall Reg mentioning that there was anything in the report on Colin's death about a rape incident."

"There wasn't. And Dowling knew nothing either. It was Billy. He told us. Or rather, he told Reg. Not that it was Colin. Just that a rape happened. I had to work things out from there. And I have."

Beth saw it now. Susan's visit to St Anselm in January, alone. Her questions, her reaction to being told of the rape, where it had happened. Beth saw now that the visit had not been by chance. Any more than it was by chance that Susan had come here, today.

Susan went on. "The dates fit. Everything fits. There is a final answer somewhere, one Reg can't argue against, and I need to find it. Because if that baby is our grandson, I want him with us." She took a tissue from her handbag, wiped her eyes. "Even if the mother pitches up, although that seems unlikely now, doesn't it? But even if she does, I'll tell her that he'd be far better off with us. Brought up properly. Given a good education, taught the right values."

Oh Lord. "Susan, you can't think..."

"I can't think what, Beth! Don't *you* go telling me what I can and can't think!"

Gil started to say something. Marion leant over, touched Susan's arm.

"Beth's only..."

Susan pushed Marion's hand away, pointed at Beth. "She has no right telling me what to think! No right at all! Here's someone who's been feeding terrs for years. We all know that now, don't we? Someone who put a child's life in danger. Someone who refused to take the child into the city, away from danger. And went on feeding those bloody murderers, inviting more danger. She's got a bloody cheek..."

"That's enough, Susan," Gil said quietly.

179

He got up, went around to her. She leant forward and rested her elbows on the table, her head in her hands. She was shaking again. Gil put an arm around her shoulders. Beth wished that Reg was here, that they could all talk about this calmly with Reg here.

There was a little cry from the bedroom and Beth looked at Marion. It got louder and she saw that Susan had heard it too. Susan looked up at Gil.

"Can I see him? Just a minute or two?" She wiped her eyes again with her tissue. "He's a piece of Colin. All I have left of him... left of my son."

Gil looked at Beth and Marion. They both nodded. "Of course," he said, and helped Susan up and led her out of the dining room, down the corridor to the bedroom.

Later, Beth heard the car going down the drive, Gil taking Susan to the rendezvous point. She felt relieved that she had gone, but fearful about what she'd said, about what she might do next.

When the sun was lower in the sky and the air cooler, Beth spread an old blanket out on the ground in front of the verandah and put a radio there and some cushions and settled Munetsi among the cushions. She sat on the blanket, looking down towards the city centre. Listening to the radio, playing with Munetsi, leaning forward now and again when he toppled a little, this way or that, to set him upright again.

They were saying, on the radio, that victory for the *vakomana* now looked certain. A landslide. As Silas had predicted.

So now began the wait for the aftermath. The wait to see if things would get better tomorrow. Just as everyone had done all these long war-torn years, waited, hoped things would get better. The wind of change might have stopped blowing, but the question was the same. Would things get better tomorrow?

It would all depend, Beth was quite sure, on generosity.

A little generosity. She thought of that long-ago letter in the cloth-covered book, warning what would happen if the white people who were then invading Mashonaland did not bind themselves "with a little generosity" to the black people already living there. She recalled Gil telling her last night about a plea that Governor Soames had made to the British Government, a plea that it keep its promises and act "in a generous manner" towards its old colony. She heard Silas on the telephone this morning, a relieved but sombre Silas, saying that the victors must "extend a generous hand" to **all** the country's tribes, white and black, if they were to avoid tarnishing a country that one African President had called "a jewel in Africa".

But not until tomorrow would they know if a place had been found for generosity – a little generosity – in the new dispensation. Not until tomorrow would they know if the waiting was really over.

Beth looked at Munetsi. **His** tomorrow, too, lay in the balance. Would his mother come back? Was Colin Haig his father? Would Susan get her way? Or would Reg prevail, would he manage to keep them out of it? Beth thought about the stance Reg had taken, what it was based on. An inability to acknowledge that his son might have raped someone? Or the view – rational enough, she thought – that it could just as easily have been the other Scout? Or the conviction that, whoever the father was, it was in Munetsi's best interests to be brought up by his African family?

She offered up a prayer that Reg would prevail, and resolved that she would do all she could to ensure that he did.

11

Isakata mine; mid-April 1980

The room was the same. The metal bed with a thin mattress, the small table by the old yellow cupboard, the chair, the green walls with brown and grey patches where the paint had come off. On the cupboard was a big red vase of flowers.

The woman on the bed sat up and pulled her skirt down and put her takkies on. Nyanye took a packet of sanitary pads from the cupboard and gave it to her. On the woman's card it said that she had given birth to a stillborn child a month earlier. There was still bleeding, but Nyanye could see that it would stop soon.

"Ndatenda, sisi," the woman said, and went out into the hall. She was the last patient to see in this room today.

It was nearly two weeks now that Nyanye had been here, at the clinic, but before today there had not been time to linger in this room, alone. To stand still and look around. The afternoon sunlight was coming in through the window by the table and on the bed she saw her father. Next to the bed, on the chair, there was her mother. Eight years ago. Some men had come running to Maseka village that day, bringing news of a big accident at Isakata mine, and Nyanye had come here with her mother. They said something had gone wrong with the powder for blasting and it had sent rocks high into the sky above the quarry and they had fallen on the workers, the blasters like her father, and others. When Nyanye saw him in this room he was not awake. A truck took him away later to Nhika hospital, and he did not come back from there.

It was being at the clinic that day that had made Nyanye decide that one day she would go to train as a nurse.

"Ah, there you are! Standing about. Come on, hurry up."

"I am coming, Sister."

Nyanye tidied the bed, closed the cupboard and locked the door, and went through the hall to the dispensary.

She heard the phone ringing, heard the Sister saying, "Where the hell is he, then? I told him *yesterday* about the fridge leaking!" She saw the Sister slam the phone down. "Bloody Portuguese!"

Tamuka could do it, he had fixed everything in her house, there had been some things not working when she had moved into it. She was sure he could fix the clinic fridge.

She said, "I know someone, Sister Haig, he might be able to fix it."

The Sister did not reply. She seemed to be angry, this one, much of the time. Today was her last day here, she did not want to do any more nursing here. The other Sister, the new one, she was not a settler like this one, she had come last month from Sweden.

At the interview for the vacancy of nursing assistant, there had been only the new Sister there, not the old one. A doctor from Mandura came too. He was the doctor who visited this clinic once a week. He had lived in America for many years, now he had come back. He and the new Sister asked her many questions, told her about the work of the clinic – the only time she had been here before was on that day of her father's accident – and then the doctor asked her about *n'angas*. What did she think about them, would she refer patients to them sometimes?

Nyanye was not sure how to answer. Was this a trick question? In America he would have learned to use only western medicine, to forget the old ways. Was he testing *her* ways? Or her truthfulness?

Before she answered, he said, "I can tell you that, even with all my western training, since I have come home I have consulted *n'angas*, once for my daughter, sometimes for a patient." He turned to the Sister. "They are the traditional healers. Herbalists, spiritualists. It is to do with religion, communion with the ancestors. Some white people call them 'witchdoctors'."

She smiled. "I have heard about them. We are the same. We also sometimes mix medicine with religion, with prayers. Especially when someone is very ill."

Nyanye liked the way they talked, and when they said later that she had got the job, she was overjoyed. They said they would help her get her nursing certificate, and told her she would be allocated a house in the compound. She moved into her house towards the end of March, a few days before the job started.

In the dispensary there were some files on the desk, and papers, and all the supplies cupboards were open. The new Sister wanted Nyanye to learn about supplies, so that she could take over some of that job from Sister Haig.

"Right. Make some tea, then we'll start," Sister Haig said.

Nyanye put the kettle on and washed her mug and the Sister's cup and saucer with the red roses on them and gold around the edges.

When she handed the Sister her tea, she said, "It is very pretty, Sister, your cup."

"Oh?" She seemed surprised at Nyanye's comment. "Yes. Well. Now, let's get a move on."

For one hour they worked, looking at the supply order forms, how to complete them, studying the stock cards and talking about stock control, checking lists against supplies in the cupboards, talking about storing different medicines and doing equipment checks. It was not a big clinic, this one, but its medicines and instruments and 'supplementaries' – that was the word the Sister used for items like swabs, gloves, bandages, syringes – they made it seem, to Nyanye, as if she had come upon great treasure. Antibiotics, analgesics, anti-malarial treatments, vaccines against many things, diphtheria, polio, TB, against the anthrax that was happening in the area. Everything was here.

She wondered how she had managed over there, in

Mozambique, with so little? Ah, the things she could do now, here, with so much! She smiled, and stood tall, seeing it all in front of her.

When the work was over, they put the files back on the shelves.

"Do you think you have understood everything?"

"Yes, Sister, it is clear."

"Any more questions?"

There was one. But Nyanye had not asked it because there could be trouble. She would ask the new Sister. Or was it better to show the new Sister that she had known to ask the old Sister? It was better.

"I am not sure about the Depo-Provera, Sister. There is a tick in the box for ordering more, but maybe I should not? The stocks here, they are enough for one month. Then, after that, no more? It is what the Government is saying."

The Sister stared at her. She took a cigarette from her packet on the desk and lit it. She got up and walked over to the cupboard where they kept the Depo-Provera boxes. She stood there looking at the boxes, her back to Nyanye, her hands on her hips.

Then she turned around. Her face was red.

"Do you know what? Why don't I just put all these boxes, the whole bloody lot of them, into the car and drive to the Inveraray river and throw them into it? What do you think? Would that be a good idea? Hmm? Would that please your Government?" She stared at Nyanye. "And people wonder why I've decided to stop working here!"

Nyanye was about to say that her idea would not be good, many people drank from the Inveraray river, washed in it, drew water from it for their cooking. But the Sister was talking again.

"Or here's another idea. You simply take no notice of that clown of a health minister of yours. He's already been spouting off about bringing witchdoctors into the health system, for God's sake. Straight back to the Dark Ages. Now he's got a bee in his bonnet about Depo, that it's all about white men interfering with black women's bodies, or some colonialist plan to wipe out the

185

black population, or the cause of every known ailment, from cancer to madness to epilepsy. All utter tosh! What does he know anyway, typical bloody African male?" She was shouting now. "Why don't you ask the women? The women who are fed up with being pregnant every five minutes, who understand that too many babies equals too little food. Maybe *they* still want Depo? The mine office can always get supplies. I bet your minister hasn't asked the women what *they* think!"

She walked to the chair and sat down. Some ash from her cigarette fell onto the floor. Nyanye remained standing. It would have been better to ask the new Sister about the Depo-Provera supplies.

"It's quite obvious what this is all about. It's about trashing everything we Europeans have done for this country. Taught you people about medicine, how to be healthy, slashed your death rates, your disease rates, educated you. But none of this fits, does it, with all the nonsense you've picked up sitting out there in the Reserves? About imperialism, colonialism, this -ism, that -ism."

She inhaled deeply from her cigarette and blew out the smoke. "When I think of all *my* work for you people…"

Nyanye stood there and waited. In the compound the name they had for this Sister was *marujata*. 'The quarrelsome one'. That was why the last assistant had left, they said.

"Well?"

"Sister?"

"Which is it?"

What was she asking? Nyanye had stopped listening. She was surprised at herself, not listening, the way she would have done before, intently. She found some words that she hoped would be right.

"It will be as you say, Sister."

The Sister stubbed her cigarette out in the ashtray and stood up. From a trolley she took the big cardboard box she'd brought with her today, empty, and put it on the desk.

The first time Nyanye had heard the word 'Depo' was at the college where she had gone for nursing training. She asked her mother about it. Had she had Depo? Her mother told her about the mobile family planning unit that used to visit Nhika hospital. She went there for Depo, but after some time she did not feel well, she was vomiting and the bleeding was too much, her breasts were painful, so she stopped going. Later, after the accident at Isakata mine, it was not necessary anyway. But other women in the villages in the Inveraray valley went there, even if they did not feel well from Depo, otherwise they might be refused treatment for their children. There were some, though, they wanted to go because they were tired from having many children.

What would her mother think now, about the things the Sister said, the things the Government was saying? Nyanye would never know that. Her mother did not hear anything anymore, she did not talk.

Nyanye had brought her mother to the compound house, to look after her there. Every day she would sit in the front yard, under the pawpaw tree, smiling at the people passing by. Sometimes she would tend the vegetables in the back yard, or gather grasses and start making mats, but she never finished them. At night she slept well and in the daytime she would smile at Nyanye and Tamuka as they came and went. But no sound came.

That was how she was when Nyanye had found her.

In the camps in Mozambique, when they had got the news about the ceasefire and orders came that comrades should go over the border to the Assembly Points that the British were establishing, the Commanders said non-combatants should go first, and the others should wait, some in the camps, others across the border in the bush. Nyanye was glad to be going, she wanted to find the end of the story of her mother. Whatever that end was.

It was Christmas-time when the trucks took them to the border, dropped them there. They were given old AKs and some supplies and divided into groups of ten or twelve – the Commanders said that if the ceasefire was a trick, it would be easier to escape if they moved in small groups. They walked north, away from trails where the wells had been poisoned. They walked at night. In the day they stayed in caves in the kopjes, slept, went out in pairs to forage, get water. Above them, the settlers' spotter planes were flying around. When they walked they kept away from main roads. They were watchful, every hour, night and day, in case there was a trap.

At dawn on the fourth day they came close to a village and two from the group went there to ask about the Assembly Point. When the villagers heard that they were comrades they came rushing to greet the rest of the group, cheering and shaking their hands. They gave them sadza and tea and told them the Assembly Point was just an hour away. It was called Oscar AP. They said many comrades were going there now, moving in large groups through the bush, along the roads, singing, and Nyanye began to feel less afraid.

"Your name, miss? Your real name?"

The man in the reception tent at Oscar AP smiled. He wore a blue uniform and a tall blue hat with a silver badge on it. He was a British policeman, she knew that from the pictures of men in this uniform in her school textbooks. Someone in her group said all the men wearing this uniform were called Bobby.

He asked to see her AK and wrote down its serial number and gave it back to her. Then he handed her a book, it was like a notebook.

"Your pay-book, miss," he said.

Nyanye had heard that they would be paid when they were in the Assembly Points, but she had not believed it. And a white man calling her 'miss'! If someone had told her *that*, she would not have believed it either.

About two thousand comrades had come to Oscar AP – some were combatants from the camps in Mozambique, but most were non-combatants and there were a lot of *mujibhas*. The *vakomana* still hiding in the bush had given the *mujibhas* old AKs so that they could pretend to be combatants. Soldiers and policemen from many countries were there, but no settler forces, they were not allowed to be there.

There was enough food and sometimes parcels of clothes, shoes, soap, other things, came in trucks or were dropped from the sky by parachutes. There was also food from the many people who came to the perimeter of Oscar AP, looking for brothers or sisters, sons or daughters. If they did not find their relatives, sometimes the food they had brought for them they gave instead to the comrades. An old woman came one day and looked, but it was in vain, and she gave Nyanye the packet she carried.

"They are groundnuts and sweet potatoes," she said. "Take them, eat them. You are the daughter I will not see again." And she walked away.

In Oscar AP there was much fear that the settler forces would come and cause trouble. People were anxious and there were arguments. It was good to have food and money, but Nyanye began to think it was too dangerous to stay there. Then, about ten days after she had arrived, two *vakomana* walked across the perimeter into Oscar AP and pointed their guns at one of the British policemen. These *vakomana* wore uniforms from Russia and on their caps they had red stars, the ones for communism. More policemen came and some soldiers who were from Kenya, and there was loud talking. One of the policemen went to fetch some food for the *vakomana*. When the *vakomana* ate the food, they used their left hands, even though that was unclean, and kept their right hands on their guns, fingers on the triggers, barrels pointing at the policemen and the soldiers. They did not speak to any of the comrades watching. Nyanye was there. When they finished their food, they put the tin plates on the ground and stood up and walked off across the perimeter into the bush.

Nyanye did not want to stay any longer after that. Some said that maybe they were *skuz'apo*. She hid the money she had been paid in her underwear and went to get water beyond the perimeter and left her gun in the bush and did not go back to Oscar AP. She wanted no more of guns. She walked to the main road and caught a bus that was going south, and then another one that was going to Mandura.

All the way along the road she saw thin cattle and empty huts and cut telephone lines and abandoned stores and schools, so when she got to the Inveraray valley she was not surprised to see the same there. Abandonment.

In Maseka village, Nyanye walked from the burnt remains of one hut to another. She felt her mother's presence. Heard her.

"Why do you not go out and play under the white moon anymore?"

Would things have been different, in the end, if she had heeded her mother? She did not think so. Maybe easier, but still there would have been the burnt huts, the broken pots, the scattered livestock, whatever she had done. Only the granary had survived. There was nothing else.

Nyanye walked along the path to Croggan's Place. When she got near, a big bird flew up from the *chimini* and she flinched. It disappeared over the woodland. Some of the old walls had tumbled down a bit more and in some places on the ground there were shell casings.

Then she saw that there were beads, too, on the ground. Blue glass beads. She stared at them. She knelt down. Shungu. Her cousin Shungu. One by one she picked the beads up, held them in her hands. Shungu in her red dress. Shungu with her baby on her back. Nyanye stared at the beads in her hands and saw that day in her head. Saw what she had seen that day, what Kundiso had seen, suffered. Saw all those days since that day. The sickness, death, hunger, weeping, blood. Chizonya...

Nyanye threw her head back and cried out, a long moaning cry that shattered the stillness of the place, and then she crumpled down and bent over and held her stomach, sobbing. She stayed there hunched over, sobbing, for some time. So much pain. Too much pain.

When she was quiet again she sat up slowly and wiped her eyes and her cheeks with her hands and shook herself. She sat there. The bird came back and she heard a twig breaking.

"*Sisi?*"

A boy was there, leaning against the archway.

Nyanye stood up and went to him and asked him where he was from, where his village was. He pointed across the Inveraray river to the other side of the valley. The villages here on this side, he said, had no people, but on the other side some had people and each day more were coming back. She thought that maybe on the other side there would be someone who could tell her the story of her mother.

She followed the boy along the river towards the Inveraray hills to a place where there were many rocks in the river and they could cross if the rain had not been too heavy. She knew the place well, they used to go each day in term-time, she and Kundiso and other children from the villages here, over the river and along the path up the other side of the valley and on to their school near Nhika.

The boy took another path after the crossing place, a path leading away from the hills, and when they came to his village Nyanye asked about her mother, but no one there could tell her anything. She went to some of the other villages and in one of them some elders said they had heard of a woman who had been found wandering in the Inveraray hills, about a year ago. One elder said he thought she had been taken to Mandura hospital. Nyanye went there. Attached to the hospital was a unit for long-term patients who were suffering from mental disturbance, one part for whites, one part for blacks.

That was where she found her mother.

The nurses said that they did not know who she was because she did not talk, did not communicate in any way. She had been brought there with nothing except the dress she wore and a blanket, both like rags.

She was thin and there was a scar across her forehead and her mouth was deformed, some of the top lip was not there, cut off. But when she saw Nyanye she smiled and smiled and the deformity went away, and life came into her eyes, and she reached up from the chair she was sitting in and took Nyanye's hand and held it against her face.

***

"You do know, don't you, that the magical starship that your new leaders have promised you, the one carrying new cars and televisions and washing machines and watches for everyone, is not coming?"

The Sister was putting things into her cardboard box on the desk. There were some books in it, a towel, some files. From the wall by the door she took down her nursing certificate and put it into the box too. Sometimes, when Nyanye had been alone in the dispensary, she had looked at the certificate. It was in a silver frame, behind glass, and there was beautiful handwriting on it and a picture of a badge that was the same as the one that Sister Haig wore pinned on her uniform.

"Why you people fell for all that propaganda, voted for that Marxist terrorist, is beyond me."

She took a big carrier bag from the box, put it next to the box, took the flowers from the red vase and put them in the bin, and washed and wiped the vase and put it into the box.

"Just as it's beyond me why my own people seem to have fallen for all his talk about 'oneness' and 'joining hands' and 'forgetting the grim past' and forgiving everyone. Joining hands with that… murderer! It's as if they've already forgotten that it was him who created that grim bloody past!"

Her cup and saucer were on the desk, next to the old radio. She wrapped them in paper, picked up the radio and pushed its aerial down. She sat down, held the radio on her lap. She stared at it and said quietly, "How *could* they forget? How *can* they forgive?"

Nyanye stood there, watching her. There was nothing to say.

"After everything we've been through, how hard we've fought to save this country from going to the dogs. After all we've… suffered."

192

She took a tissue from her pocket and wiped her eyes and blew her nose. Nyanye saw that there were tears. Of sorrow or anger, she was not sure.

The sound of people talking outside drifted into the dispensary. It was the men passing by, coming home at the end of their day's work at the mine and the office. Some of those who worked in the office had told her and Tamuka, when they first came here, that more whites would be leaving the office soon. Before the Struggle, Tamuka had been a supervisor in the maintenance section of a big hotel in the city. Also, he had two 'A' levels. He was hoping that he could get a job in the mine office. He had been to see one of the clerks there.

The Sister was looking at the dial on the radio, turning it this way and that. She passed a finger along the radio handle, picking up dust. A tear fell on the handle. She passed her finger back again, slowly, wiping the tear away.

"I had two sons." Her voice, it was quiet now. "I have lost them both. One was killed in the war. The other is… not right in the head. Because of the war." She looked up at Nyanye. "You don't know. You wouldn't understand."

Nyanye started to unwrap the cup and saucer.

The Sister said, "What are you…? I didn't tell you…"

Nyanye put the cup on the saucer. She made tea and poured it into the cup and put the cup next to the Sister, on its saucer.

"Too much killing, too much sadness, Sister."

The Sister sat there, looking at the cup.

Nyanye said, "My mother, she too has suffered much with death in this war and it has made her unwell in the head." She paused. "It is the same. For you and for me. For us. The same. My mother, she does not talk now."

She could not stop herself from saying all this. She had to say it, even though it could mean trouble, talking like this. But the Sister said nothing. She put the radio back on the desk and picked up her cup of tea, sipped it, then looked up at Nyanye.

"'Us'?" she said softly.

Outside, the sound of a car engine. The Sister stood up, put the radio in the box, straightened her uniform and wiped her eyes again. She opened one of the cupboards, the one for infants, and took out packets of nappies, jars of babyfood.

"You are taking those, Sister?"

"Yes, just a few things," she said, putting them into the carrier bag. "There's a child at that mission. St Anselm. He was left there. Coloured. He shouldn't be there. I can't do much about it at the moment, him being there, but I *can* take some things there that a baby should have."

She closed the cupboard door. "There, that's my lot, just about." She looked at Nyanye. "All yours now. All over to you."

A woman came through the door. The Sister smiled at her. "Ah, Hentie... Nearly ready."

She finished her tea, washed and dried the cup and saucer, wrapped the paper around them again, and put the package on top of the other things in the box. "I had a call from the mine office. Reg is flying back tonight, got an earlier flight."

The woman said, "That's nice, hey?" She looked at Nyanye. "Is she the new Sister here, Susan?"

"No, Hentie. A Swedish woman is the new Sister. This one is..."

"I am Nyanye Maseka. I am the nursing assistant."

The woman looked surprised when Nyanye spoke.

"Nyanye? I haven't heard that name before," the woman said. "Does it mean something? The names you people have, they always mean something, hey? Like one of my housegirls at the farm, her husband ran away and she was pregnant and when she had the baby she called her... agh, I forget now. Anyway, she said it meant 'help me'."

"The name, it was Batsirai maybe," Nyanye said. "The names women give their babies, it is a way they use sometimes to send a message to their husbands or families."

And it is a word that people shout when they are drowning under gunfire in a fast-running river.

"What does your name mean?" the woman asked.

"My name means 'the second twin'."

"Oh? You're a twin? And your twin's name? Is it a name that means 'the first twin'?" The woman laughed and looked at the Sister.

Nyanye was about to say 'Theresa'. But because of the woman's laughter, she said, "No, it does not mean that."

"What does it mean, then?"

" 'We have conquered'."

The two women looked at each other. The Sister picked up her handbag and the cardboard box, the woman took the carrier bag, and they walked together out to the car. Nyanye followed them and stood at the top of the steps. The Sister put the box and carrier bag on the back seat of the car and got in on the passenger side in the front and the engine started. The car went a little way along the road, then stopped. After a moment, the passenger door opened and the Sister got out. She was holding something. She walked back to the steps.

Nyanye saw that she was holding the cup and saucer wrapped in paper. The Sister held it up to her.

"For your mother," she said. There was a small smile there.

She turned and walked back down the steps, back to the car, and they drove away.

In the dispensary the phone was ringing and Nyanye ran in. She put the Sister's gift on the desk and answered the phone. Tamuka. He was in Mandura today, collecting his demobilisation payment.

"I have called the mine office from here and I have good news – there is a job for me!"

Nyanye shouted with joy and Tamuka laughed and when she put the phone down she could not help singing as she went about closing and locking the cupboards, sweeping the floor, emptying the bins, closing the windows. She put the Sister's gift into her basket. Then she locked the dispensary door and the main door and went down the steps onto the dusty road.

The evening air was cool and the woodsmoke was rising into the air from fires across the compound. Nyanye could smell food cooking. Some children were playing by the side of the road, drawing in the sand. "*Manheru, sisi*," they greeted her as she passed them. "*Manheru*," she said. With the news from Tamuka and the gift for her mother, it was a good evening for sure. What joy there would be on her mother's face when she opened her gift! When Nyanye got back to the house she would make some tea straight away, so that her mother could drink from her cup with red roses.

12

St Anselm mission; late April 1980

Beth stood up and stretched, arched her back and wiped her forehead, and marvelled at how quickly Rejoice worked. Bending down, cutting the roots, pulling the plants up, shaking the soil off them, adding them to the nearest bundle, moving on to the next plant, her long body bending down again. Cutting, pulling, humming. She never seemed to tire.

She called to Beth, "It is nearly done for today, Mukoma, and then you can truly rest!"

Thank the Lord.

Rejoice had said not to expect a good harvest this year, but they had both been pleasantly surprised at how many of the groundnut pods had turned brown, and the seeds in them dull pink, ready.

When they'd filled the back of the old blue station wagon with as many bundles as it could take, they climbed in and Beth drove slowly along the track towards the road to St Anselm, passing fields that, at this time of year, would be showing the first shoots of winter wheat, passing the place where a scarecrow used to stand. But there were no shoots now, and all that was left of the scarecrow was the pole it had been tied to, leaning over, small remnants of the clothes it once wore fluttering in the wind.

"A good neighbour, that one," Rejoice said. "A good white. Even though he was a Boer."

Mr Van Rensburg's land was up for sale, all but the fifty acres he'd leased to St Anselm. Those acres, he'd given to Grace and then he'd gone north across the Zambezi, where many white farmers were going now, or thinking about it, attracted by tempting offers of cheap land and State support. When he'd visited Beth at Redington House in February, to tell her about his plans, about his gift to Grace, he said he thought that one day there might be trouble over land – "because of unresolved matters" – and he did not want to stay for that, it would be better to go now.

"We Boers, the land, the soil, it is part of us, our soul," he'd said. "It is the same for the African people. You English, you do not understand how it is with us, with the Africans, the way we feel about land."

As he spoke, an image came into Beth's head of two great beasts fighting over a piece of land until the soil beneath them was red with their mingled blood and they both collapsed onto it. Exhausted. But perhaps not exhausted enough. Perhaps Mr Van Rensburg was right, and the fight was not quite over yet.

Beth drove through the gates of St Anselm. There was a red car parked outside her rondavel, Reg Haig's car. He was early. Or was she a little late? Grace would be looking after him. Beth parked the station wagon by the kitchen, next to the patch of ground where they'd been stacking the bundles of groundnut plants, to add today's harvest to them. There'd be more to add tomorrow and probably the next day, and then the stacks would stay there in the sun for about six weeks, until the seeds were dry and ripe, ready for shelling. Grace had decided, this year, to turn most of the groundnut yield into peanut butter and sell it in Molly's Store at Isakata, to make up for the poor mealie yield. Beth thought that an excellent idea. So did Mrs Moleiro, Grace said.

Two nuns came to help them unload and Rejoice said, "You go to your visitor, Mukoma, we can manage here."

Beth set off along the path up to the red house. It was four days since Susan's funeral. Nine since she'd died.

Beth had been in the city when she got the news of Susan's death. She'd gone in to watch the Independence celebrations on the TV with the Aitchisons. A night that was still playing over and over again in her mind... Standing out on the verandah at Redington House and watching the fireworks light up the sky above the big soccer stadium on the south side of the city. People gathered in their tens of thousands from across the country, alongside princes and presidents and prime ministers from across the world. Then turning on the TV in the sitting room to watch the ceremony inside the stadium. A hundred soldiers, the guard of honour, marching side by side, some black, some white, but all clad in khaki, presenting arms beneath the blazing floodlights. The crowd, packed on the rising terraces, cheering at the reverberation around the stadium of the booms of a 21-gun salute. Cheering again for the two soldiers walking up to the flagpole, one to lower the old flag, the other to raise the new one. And, on the stroke of midnight, the new flag reaching the top of the pole and the whole stadium erupting!

And Silas, somewhere there on the VIP dais, invited because of his work in getting medicines to the Mozambique border for the camps – sometimes via Baba and his old blue station wagon – telling her later, "The roar of the crowd that went up at midnight was so great, Mukoma, that if there had been a roof on the stadium it would surely have been blown off!"

It still all felt extraordinary. Not only that the handover of power had happened peacefully and with dignity, but that it had happened at all. No coup, no uprising, no bloodshed, no dash to the borders to escape turmoil, no helicopters on the lawn of Government House to whisk the British Governor up and away from danger.

And then, on the morning she was due to go back to St Anselm, someone from Isakata had phoned Gil to tell him that during the night Susan Haig had committed suicide.

Beth looked up and saw Reg and Grace on the verandah, sitting in the old cane chairs. She waved. Reg waved back. She hadn't spoken to him since he'd flown to London last month, apart from a few words at the funeral. She knew that he knew what had happened at Redington the day after he'd flown out, when Susan came to lunch there. Gil had told him. She felt anxious about seeing him, was still shocked by the suddenness of Susan's death.

Grace had given Reg tea and biscuits, and was telling him that they'd just received the news that her son Shohiwa was coming back from Canada, after all, to take up Baba's duties.

"Marvellous, isn't it?" Beth said. "And once he's back, God willing, St Anselm will start attracting novices again, and some of our nuns will return, and the church will fill up again on Sundays with people and song."

Grace smiled. It had brought her contentment, at last, knowing that her son was coming home.

"And now," she said, looking at them both, "I must go to wake our little boy and prepare some food for him."

She stood up, touched Reg on the shoulder. "You would like to see him? Munetsi?"

He smiled at her, shook his head. "No. Not for the moment. Thank you, Grace."

***

They walked along the path to the rondavel, neither saying anything until they reached the stoep, sat down, and Beth told him what she'd been about to tell him nine days ago, but then she'd got the news about Susan's death and had held back.

"We've found Munetsi's aunt, Reg. Or rather, she found us, the day before Susan died."

If Reg had heard anything about this already, from anyone else, he gave no indication of it. Beth told him about the aunt contacting them, what had happened since, the phone calls, the meetings, and that today was the day of the big reunion, at St Anselm. This afternoon.

When she'd finished, he said quietly, "I'm very glad."

He looked up at the church. The bucket-bell glinted in the mid-morning sun. He took a cigarette from his packet and lit it.

"How are you coping, Reg?"

"Early days yet. A lot to take in."

She nodded. He smoked his cigarette.

After a moment, he turned to her. "She never liked Africa, Beth. She never really forgave me, you know, for bringing her out here. And she was finding it hard to forgive Africa – or me – for what happened to our sons."

Beth had guessed some of that. Guessed that some of Susan's anger stemmed from being somewhere she didn't want to be, didn't think she deserved to be, but couldn't do anything about.

"Had it all become too much for her?"

Reg said nothing.

"Colin's death, Billy going away? The possibility that Munetsi might be…"

"…our grandson." He sighed. "Except that she'd stopped seeing it as a possibility. She said she knew, instinctively."

"Yes. We sensed that. And we were surprised, Reg, that she seemed to have accepted what had happened, that Colin could be the father."

"More than accepted it. Wanted it to be so. The child had started to become a sort of substitute for Colin. She'd got into her head that we had to have him."

"And you were trying to stop her going down that road?"

"Can you imagine it, Beth? You know her attitude towards Africans, she made no bones about it. And Coloureds were only slightly higher up the ladder. Can you imagine the child, as a little boy, as a teenager, doing something that upset her, disappointed her, angered her, what she'd do? How she'd react? I couldn't get past the thought that he'd grow up being forever at the wrong end of her mourning for Colin. And that nothing I did would compensate for that. For his sake, I had to stop it. Somehow."

He tapped his cigarette ash into the ashtray, sat there, smoking.

Then he went on. "We'd talk and talk. I'd try to make her see that she didn't know, any more than I did, if Colin was the father. I'd say we should keep out of it, that even if the mother never came back there'd be family somewhere and the mother would want them to take him in, bring him up. Susan would insist that he'd be better off with us than with any African family. I said the choice was his mother's, not ours. Also, that if Munetsi was with us, he'd be a constant reminder of Colin's death, it would be intolerable for her. But the more I talked, the more determined she became to have him."

"Was it the aunt, then?" Beth asked. "Had she just heard about the aunt? Was that too much for her?"

"No, she didn't know about that. Neither did I. No, it was something else."

He stubbed his cigarette out and leaned forward, looked up at the kopje, elbows resting on his knees, hands clasped, and said quietly, "Something else that now I wish to God I'd never told her."

He gazed out. After a moment, Beth asked him if he wanted to tell her what it was. But not if he didn't want to.

He did want to. "Taken me a while to feel strong enough to look at it, head on. This is the first time that I've talked about it, Beth. Out loud. To someone other than Billy." He paused. "And Susan, of course."

He went back to early March, when he'd flown to London. He'd been thinking about contacting Kim during that trip, he said. The discrepancies between what he'd read in the Scouts HQ report, what Billy had said in November the morning after the Club party, what Kim had told them at the meeting at Redington in December, they were still niggling at him. Susan had long said something was being covered up and he thought that perhaps she was right on that point.

"Did you contact Kim?" Beth asked. "I don't remember him mentioning it."

"No. The more I thought about it on the plane going over, the more it seemed to me that it was Billy I needed to talk to. He'd said nothing more since that morning in November."

He stopped, lit another cigarette, blew out the smoke. "We were walking in Kew – Susan's brother's house is there, Billy is staying

202

there. It overlooks the Green. Daffodils everywhere, red camellias. Crocuses. Quite splendid." He paused. "I told Billy about Susan and the baby at St Anselm, that she had become convinced the baby was Colin's. He didn't say anything. Kept walking. I told him I wasn't convinced. I said that I wanted things left as they were. But that his mother was talking of having the child with us..."

Reg turned to her. "It was like turning a tap on, Beth! He yelled 'You can't, pa! She mustn't!' and then it just gushed out, a jumble of words and emotions. All those months saying nothing, not talking – now he couldn't stop... I had to ask him to slow down, start at the beginning."

Billy had talked about his stick being dropped between the Inveraray river and Croggan's Place, with orders to head for the village nearest Croggan's. Talked about hearing, as they ran to the village, high-pitched screaming coming from Croggan's, screaming that went on and on, and so two of the stick had gone there instead. Billy and another guy.

"We knew about that before," Reg said, "about Billy going to Croggan's instead of the village, but not that it was only two of them. We didn't know that."

He paused. "When they were running there..."

'When we were running there, pa, we see these terrs. What we think are terrs. Three of them there, at Croggan's. One runs past us as we get there, right past us. Disappears. The second one is by the woman who is screaming, she has a red dress. Jeez, that screaming! There's a baby on her back. Howling. The terr there, his bayonet is fixed, he's attacking the woman, like he's trying to shut her up. Pulling the baby off, the woman's staggering, then falling. The third terr is by the smokestack, fighting with a woman and she's shouting. He's got her pinned there, against the smokestack. Everything is happening at the same time, pa, and so fast, and there's all this noise with more choppers coming in. Mixed up with the screaming. And then I realise, and my mate does, that what we are seeing – at the smokestack – is rape. We open up. At him and the other terr standing by the baby, his foot on it.

Someone is shouting 'Don't shoot! Don't shoot!' and some other stuff, but I can't hear properly, with the woman by the smokestack shouting and the choppers and all that. Then I see that the one with the fixed bayonet is on the ground, next to the kid, head in his hands. Sitting, lying, I don't know. Messed up, anyway. The other one is slumped down by the smokestack. The woman there, she's gone, vanished. I go there, to the smokestack. Blood everywhere, on him, on the ground around him. Everywhere. I turn his head and there's white on his cheeks, lines, like scratch marks. Scratch marks on his cheeks and all down his neck, and I can see his hair is dyed. Black… It was Colin, pa. I'd shot Colin, pa.'"

Oh dear God.

Her hands gripped the chair and she stared at Reg.

At length, she said, "I am so sorry. So very, very sorry."

Reg stubbed his cigarette out and sat there, twisting his hands.

"So Susan's instinct, that the baby was Colin's, was right," Beth said softly.

"Yes."

"And Billy is sure, is he? That it was his bullet?"

Reg said that, like everyone else, he'd assumed that Billy came late to the scene. And that there were more soldiers there. But Billy didn't. And there weren't. He was at the scene, just him and the other guy. And he was sure it was his bullet. Or, at least, that one of the bullets that killed Colin was his.

"He cried so much, Beth, telling me. Wept and wept. There was a bench on the Green, we sat there. He said that in the helicopter, as Colin lay dying he kept muttering something about the women 'feeding Hendrick's murderers', that he 'couldn't handle it'. First time I'd seen Billy weep over Colin. And when he stopped crying… God, so much anger there! Mixed up in his grief. Asking why Colin was there in the first place? Scouts weren't meant to operate in home territory, what was HQ thinking? Why hadn't someone warned him about Colin being in the contact area? What was Colin playing at, not clearing out when FireForce came?"

Billy had told Reg that in those months afterwards he'd hovered on the edge of suicide. "He was terrified of blurting things out, Beth, things he never wanted us to know. Things we must never know. In the end he found it too hard. Said that when he and I talked that morning after the Club party he'd come so close to blurting it all out that it frightened him. That's mainly why he went to the UK. Where no one would ask him questions anymore, push him for answers."

"Who else knows? Does he worry about that?"

"There's no-one, he says. HQ had done ballistics tests, he knew that, but only to confirm that it was 'friendly fire' that killed Colin, not to name names. Billy and the other soldier made a pact not to report the rape. And the Scout who tried to stop the shooting, who stayed with Colin till the chopper came, he said the same. And anyway he died later, in Mozambique. Kim told us."

Beth realised that it was Siya whom Reg was talking about.

"So, nothing in the records about the rape," Reg went on. "Billy said the Scout attacking the woman in the red dress, and the baby, died not long afterwards. Landmine."

He paused.

"There it is, then. What really happened that day at Croggan's Place. And what I told Susan."

He lit another cigarette. His hands were shaking.

"By the time I came back from London, she had become obsessed with the child, insisting on doing something, hardly talked about anything else. It was overpowering. I was at my wits' end. That night – the night she died – she started again. Said she'd take things into her own hands, soon, if I did nothing. I'd never intended telling her what Billy had told me. Never. The thought of her knowing that Billy... But she went on and on. It was late, but she didn't let up. And it seemed to me, then, that if I *did* tell her, it would make her see, once and for all, why having the child in our lives, with the story he carried with him, would be impossible."

He looked at Beth and said quietly, "And so that's what I did. I told her. And then afterwards, when I'd finished, I said that, if she wanted, we'd leave Africa, go back to London. Be with Billy. Help him in his new life there."

He leaned forward again, looked out.

"When I'd finished talking, Susan said, very softly, 'Billy killed Colin? You're telling me that Billy killed Colin?'"

"I said yes. She was very quiet. Still. Didn't cry, didn't talk. After about five minutes she got up and said, 'I think I'll go to bed now, Reg.'"

He turned to Beth. His eyes had filled with tears.

"Later – it seems likely it was shortly after she heard me going to bed a little after midnight – she left her bedroom, went outside, walked down to the pool."

They sat there, saying nothing, because there was too much to say. After a while, Beth took Reg's hand and held it and said again how sorry she was, that she'd pray for him. And Billy. Reg thanked her. He got up. He ought to be going, he said. He was sorry to have sprung all this on her, but talking about it to her, letting it all out to someone he knew he could entrust it with, had been very helpful. He had hoped it would be. "And now you need to prepare for your visitors."

After Beth had waved goodbye to him, and stood there watching his car go out through the mission gates and down onto the road back to Isakata, she walked to the church and went up the aisle and knelt on the chancel steps. There was no-one else there. She looked up at the black Christ on the white cross and began to pray.

***

At Chizonya II, Tamuka said, outside the kitchen area and not far from the edge of the parade ground where they used to march each morning, there was a big mango tree. They would queue by it to get their meals and sit on the ground beneath it or near it to eat their meals. Sometimes they would sit under it just for shade, there were not many shady trees in the camp. And sometimes there would be no meals, but they would go and wait near the mango tree anyway, just in case. The Commissars, the ones who taught them about politics, used that mango tree, he said, to talk about commitment to the Struggle, about the rewards that would come from that commitment.

When the mango tree yields fruit, they asked, who will be entitled to pick those mangoes? Is it the ones who tended the tree, who watered it, who took away any branches that were weak or diseased? There are some people who will not have carried a single bucket of water to that tree, and yet when the tree bears fruit they will stretch up and try to pick the mangoes. But we will say to them, you did not give the tree any water, you did not look after it at times of scorching heat or heavy wind and rain, you did not battle against the pests that sought to destroy it, so you have no right to take the mangoes from it. We who have watered the tree every day, day in and day out, who have kept it alive, only we have the right to gather the fruit from it.

"It is not how I think now, Mukoma Beth, not anymore, but many comrades they think this way and a new message has to go to them, one that says that the fruits of victory are for everyone. It will not be easy."

What a lot of unpicking there was to be done! Unpicking of myths and attitudes and expectations. When Beth had asked Tamuka how he thought things would turn out, in the short term, she sensed apprehension in his reply and in the allegory he told of the mango tree, but hope too.

"The whites," Tamuka went on, "the fruits are also for them if they come out from behind their high walls and locked gates and see that it is better to sit around the table with us, not at a separate table. It was not against the whites, Mukoma, our Struggle. It was against their system."

Would they, Beth wondered? Would they come out and share what they had, work with their compatriots to give the country what it needed if its children, and their children after them, were to prosper?

As if on cue, squeals of childish delight, accompanied by loud squawking, drifted up from the yard. Rejoice had discovered that few things amused Munetsi more than to put him on her shoulders and chase the chickens. Beth feigned despair and said, "Down goes our egg count!" and Tamuka chuckled. Grace called down that there was tea and cool drinks and biscuits and Rejoice came racing up the verandah steps with Munetsi. Nyanye was not far behind them.

Such an elegant person. When the car had pulled up at the red house, a little after two, and she'd got out and walked towards them waiting there at the bottom of the verandah steps, Beth had seen the likeness straight away. She was taller than Kundiso, slimmer, but there was something about the eyes, the shape of the face, that was the same.

Tamuka was just as Grace had described him. Tall, gangly, with a wide and ready smile. He'd smiled broadly when he'd greeted them. "*Masikati*, Amai Grace! And Mukoma Beth, *masikati!* It is very good to meet you."

Nyanye had clasped Grace's hands and then turned to Beth and reached for her hand, and said, "Ah, Mukoma, we are here at last."

Beth had spoken on the phone to them, but it was Grace who'd driven over to their house in the Isakata compound, to meet them, tell them about Munetsi, check their stories out, make plans for today when they'd see Munetsi for the first time.

When tea was over and the sun was a little lower in the sky, they went down the verandah steps and walked along the path up to the kopje, four of them. Grace stayed behind, she wanted to put together some things for Nyanye and Tamuka to take back to Isakata with them, eggs, *mufuna* oil, some vegetables. And Rejoice walked down to the kitchen to start preparing the community's evening meal.

Tamuka went racing up the kopje, Munetsi on his shoulders, and soon they'd disappeared down the other side beyond the tall acacia tree. Nyanye told Beth that she and Tamuka had just heard, that morning, that they might be allocated a house near the Club. It would be vacant soon. The people living there now, they were going to Australia.

"Near the Club? You mean one of the European houses?"

Nyanye nodded.

"I never thought I'd live to see the day!"

Nyanye laughed.

"And you, Mukoma Beth, you will be staying here at St Anselm? You will not be going back to England?"

"No, I shall stay here."

There was no going back, apart for the occasional visit. She belonged here, in Africa, in this corner of Africa. But only as a guest. The euphoria she'd witnessed among the people in the stadium on Independence night had thrilled her, but it had also reinforced her awareness that, as much as she loved the country and its people, she was a guest here. Always had been and always would be.

When they reached the acacia tree, Nyanye said, "Shall we go to the graves now, Mukoma?"

Beth nodded, and led the way on the path that ran along the crest of the kopje, threading its way between the granite boulders and coming out into a small clearing. In the centre of the clearing was Baba's grave. Simple, with a headstone in the shape of a cross. The headstone was beginning to look a little weathered already and some of it had become encrusted with lichen, ochres and yellows and soft blues, like the boulders that surrounded the clearing. Timeless. Baba would have liked that.

A few metres away was Agnes's grave. Her headstone had gone up only a week ago. A Calvary cross carved on the left side, the epitaph on the right side: 'Agnes Nyambe – b. 1920 † d. 15 March 1980 – Our Beloved Sister – *Ndichati pamusoro paJehovha, Ndiye utiziro hwangu nenhare yangu, Iye Mwari wangu, wandinovimba naye.*'

'I will say of the Lord, He is my refuge and my fortress, my God in whom I trust.'

"It's from a psalm," Beth said. "Her favourite one."

A tear came and she brushed it away.

"I am very sorry we could not thank them, Ambuya Agnes and Baba Alfred, for their kindness to Munetsi. And to my sister."

"They'll know, Nyanye."

Nyanye smiled. "I hope so, Mukoma. And I hope that they know we have found him. Ah, it is such a blessing! If the Sister at the clinic had not talked about the baby that was left here, I would not have phoned here. I had been looking in other places. Kundiso was not meant to operate in this area. Tamuka, he says she must have been in the next sector, and persuaded the comrades to come here. That night. Because she knew about the mission, knew it would be all right for the baby."

"You know about her yellow notebook, Nyanye? That that's how we found Kundiso?"

"I know, Mukoma. And maybe she did not leave it behind by mistake, that notebook."

Beth smiled. She'd wondered about that too.

Nyanye rested her hand on Agnes's headstone for moment, dipped slightly, stood back, looked at the grave, hands clasped in front of her. Then she walked over to Baba's grave and did the same thing.

"Kundiso too is buried close to someone she loved," she said.

They had not talked about it before, the burial place.

"She was Amai Makare. A good woman. Sometimes she sat there by the big mango tree in Chizonya and talked about the Struggle. She had been in the Struggle for many years, she had been to many places. Everyone respected Amai Makare. And she told many many stories. We would sit on the ground by her and listen to them, we never wanted them to end."

Nyanye paused, then went on.

"She died on the same night that my sister died, the night after the big raid. Like my sister, Amai's injuries were too much. Tamuka found her – he was not there when the settler forces came, I did not know that. He was at the stores in Chizonya I, preparing for a crossing. When he came back from there, he found Amai Makare and took her to Chitepo Block, some of it was not burnt down, and cared for her there."

Nyanye looked at Beth. "That is where I found him the next day. When the sun was rising. I went there to find some cloth, for wrapping Kundiso. There were some mats. Together we carried them to the woodland. We dug graves and buried them there. My sister and Amai Makare. It is a good place. Quiet."

She paused. "I like to think of them together there, those two. Not alone."

Later that morning they had carried others to the woodland, for burial. "One, he was Siya," she said.

The crickets had started their evening chirping and a hornbill came and perched high in the tall acacia tree, looking out. Beth and Nyanye walked back along the path that wound its way between the boulders. They could see Tamuka and Munetsi sitting on the bench beneath the acacia tree, and Nyanye called to Tamuka that it was time to go back to the red house.

Munetsi was tired and Nyanye gathered him up in her arms and set off along the path down the kopje. Beth and Tamuka followed along behind them. A sleepy Munetsi became a sleeping Munetsi, and there was no talking, going down. Only the sound of evening crickets, and someone, somewhere, playing an mbira.

9 781779 223838